FALLING FOR THE SOUND OF YOU

ISBN: 978-968366-03-2

BOOKS BY CHLOE RIGGS

Soulmates are Overrated

Sense of Love Series:

Falling for the Sound of You

Reviving From the Touch of You

FALLING FOR THE SOUND OF YOU

CHLOE RIGGS

For those who love with all they have but are afraid to
let someone love them.

FALLING FOR THE SOUND OF YOU

PROLOGUE

"Grave Digger. You kill'em, we bury 'em. How big is the body?" Piper greets into the phone with disinterest as she flips through an outdated edition of First for Women magazine.

A chuckle comes from the other end of the line, halting her flips through the paper. "That's funny. I haven't heard that one before."

"What?" In all of the times she has used this line on telemarketers, none have answered, let alone laughed. From her seated position, she scours the cluttered apartment to search for the hidden cameras.

"Your joke," the refreshing voice continues to mumble in her ear. "It was funny."

Piper pulls the phone from her ear to check the number. "Unknown". Just as suspected. "I'm sorry, who is this?"

"Right. I dialed the wrong number." He clears his throat as a car horn blares. "Was it not a joke? Do you really bury dead bodies? If so, you should consider a more secure phone number. Or at least a less incriminating greeting."

"No, that's not wha—can I help you?" Piper sighs in frustration. She should have hung up. Every instinct in her body told her to do exactly that—there's no point in continuing a conversation as useless as this one—but then the man with the honey-rich voice spoke again and Piper suddenly lost the ability to make her finger push the red button on the screen.

"Right. Like I said, wrong number. I will let you go, *Gravedigger*. Bye." With that, the line dies.

Piper removes the phone from her ear and stares at the blank screen. Surely she just interacted with a psychopath. No normal human being would stay on the phone after someone introduces themselves as an accomplice to murder. Yet, *he* did.

"Who was that?" Hazel inquires as she rounds the corner, her hands wrapped into a bath towel as she scrunch-dries her freshly showered hair.

Piper sighs and tosses the device to the other end of the couch. She resumes her previous flipping through the outdated magazine the previous renters left. "No one important." Even as the words were uttered, an abashed smile fought its way onto her lips.

Graham pockets his phone into his only pair of unstained jeans. After an exciting call like that, the idea of being on the phone with a potential new boss sounds daunting.

"Grave digger," he rolls the words around in his head.

The woman sounded young, around his age. Maybe she is the woman he is getting ready to meet. Maybe it wasn't a wrong number after all.

His boots scuff against the pavement as he opens the door to the newest bar in town. Once inside, he straightens his clothing and shoves his hands in his pockets.

Someone calls out to him, but he makes a mental note to save the phone number in his contacts later.

CHAPTER ONE

PIPER

A YEAR AND A HALF LATER.

There is a war raging around me. From clanking ceramic to whispered voices, it is all far too much to endure. Squeaky shoes on the linoleum floor only add to the chaos and explosive shots of dripping liquid complete the symphony.

Noise is my specialty—my profession—but sometimes it all becomes a little too much and the desire to rip my ears from my head is strong.

A more logical avenue would be booking it through the only exit of this cafe. One that is both visible and accessible from this vantage point. However, doing so would lead to a long, ear-piercing call from my mother.

"Why did you stand him up?" She would demand. "I raised you better than this, Piper. No matter who the person is, you always show them the same respect you would give someone of high authority." This is where we differ. Respect should be earned, not freely given.

I stare out the window beside the table I picked— the only one without visible stains and crumbs— pretending I am not listening to the nearby conversations.

It's one of my favorite pastimes: eavesdropping. A naive individual never suspects the person looking away to be the culprit invading their privacy. Having a personal conversation in a public place is a mistake entirely of their own.

"So?" a hushed female voice mutters from a nearby table. I'm assuming from the one with two teenage girls behind me, one of which speaks most of the time. "What did it say?"

A pause, and then the other girl whisper-yells, "It's two lines. What does that mean? It means it's negative, right? I threw the paper away and I don't remember what it said."

Guilt begins to form in my stomach.

I try to turn my attention to another conversation, but none pique any interest. A tap on my phone tells me it's five minutes until doom. Soon, he will walk through the door.

Normally I find any excuse possible to decline these setups my mother produces. They are usually blind dates that end in me faking an injury or creating a personality scary enough to keep the helpless man from ever contacting me again.

Not only does dating involve pointless interaction between two people, often more awkward than it is pleasant, but it leads to a world of unbearable heartbreak. Something I refuse to put myself through.

This time, though, Mom promised it isn't a date. Supposedly, Mr. Evans is in the city for the first time of his twenty-eight years of life and is the son of Mom's friend.

I assumed my mother and her friend would be joining. Two minutes before I walked into this cafe, Mom called and said they won't be able to make it.

I vaguely remember suggesting rescheduling, to which she quickly shut down.

Without missing a beat, "No. You are already there and he will be there soon too so you might as well meet him without us."

The whoosh of the main door opening sends a gust of wind through my mind. Three minutes.

"Morning, Tia." A deliciously thick voice greets.

I can't help but lift my gaze to the speaker. He's tall and clad in a muddied shirt, jeans, and worn out work boots. From my experience with this cafe—which is limited to this one meeting—he sticks out like a sore thumb, but it's not because of his clothing choice. It's obvious by the way everyone's attention is now glued to him.

I couldn't care less about how attractive the dirty clothes on his tan skin are or how well the combination compliments the dirty blonde hair sculpted on his head. For me, it's his voice.

It's so…*familiar*.

"Graham," Tia, or so he referred to her as, greets back to him. "The usual?"

Only his side profile is visible, but if I squint a little I can see the tilt of a smile. "You know it." My stomach does a weird flip at the sight of the dimple in his cheek.

I'm staring. Quite obviously. It's evident because now his gaze is locked on me and the grin I only saw the edge of is on full display.

Instead of politely smiling back and admitting to our shared acknowledgement like a normal person, my head whips back to the window shamefully. A soft tint of blush rushes to my skin. Why on Earth am I acting like a middle school girl?

The sound of the door whooshing back open draws my attention forward again. I expect to be witnessing Graham—a name I tuck away for no clear reason—exiting the cafe. Yet, my gaze finds him leaning on the edge of the register.

I need to crane my neck a hair to the left to see him more clearly through the line of customers behind him.

He taps a pattern on the counter. I can only see a glimpse of his hand lifting gently as a soft beat makes its way to my ear. Something so quiet I shouldn't be able to hear it, but for some reason…some unexplainable force has made me quite astute to the noises of this strange man.

Graham's eyes must have found their way back to me because his tapping and whistling—an annoying sound I didn't realize was emanating from him until now—halts. Only a slow beat of time of our eyes capturing each other passes before his teeth are on display in a sly grin. Again.

There's a shuffle of his boots, I hear it before I see it, and I wonder if he's getting ready to make his way to me. Maybe introduce himself. Maybe talk my ear off—although with the honey-like voice he has, it may be more of soothing the chaotic party of nerves in my stomach—but someone steps in front of him before he has the chance to even attempt any of those fantastical actions.

"Piper?" A different, less attractive, voice comes from the man now in front of my table. His hair is tied back in a low ponytail and a pair of black glasses are perched on the crook of his nose. His t-shirt is loosely wrapped around a thin bicep, while his pants are tight around his waist. "You are Piper Brooks, right?" He asks again.

He must have been standing there for a while. A quick tap on my phone tells me it's been a solid six minutes since his estimated arrival.

He begins to take a step back from the table with an apologetic expression. "I'm sorry. I must have the wrong—"

"Yes," I quickly blurt out, ignoring the handsome voice trailing from the corner of the room. Oh, how much I would pay to be interacting with him instead. "I'm Piper. You must be Mr. Evans." I stand, offering him my hand.

He accepts my gesture with a polite smile. "Please, call me Steven."

I nod and sit back down. He follows suit. I'm so disoriented from the familiarity of the other man in the room that I have to shake my head, clearing the noise away so I can focus on the man in front of me. A task suddenly more daunting than it was a moment before.

"So you're new to the city?" I find myself asking. I fiddle with the hair tie on my wrist, busying my hands.

"Um, I'm new to this side of the city," he begins, but the rest of his statement is drowned out.

My eyes are fixed on Mr. Evans—Steven, but my ears are focused on the deliciously loud voice bellowing in the cafe.

What is it about him that seems so oddly familiar?

"How's Miranda?" Graham inquires.

"She's good," his buddy responds. "Scared about starting kindergarten. Says it's stupid and why can't she just stay with Hope instead of going to school with a bunch of stinky people."

"Sounds like Miranda," Graham chuckles. It's short and quick, but my heart skips a beat at the sound. I pat my chest absently to soothe the unusual feeling away.

"Well, I guess you could say I'm an entrepreneur in a way," the man in front of me chuckles too. It doesn't induce a swarm of butterflies in my chest. "What about you?"

What about me? I'm not sure what topic he started discussing. He said "entrepreneur", didn't he? With only that to go on, I share my profession. "I'm a foley artist."

He leans his elbows on the table and crinkles his nose. "Really? What does that entail?"

This is something I can focus my attention on. "I basically pretend I'm a caveman that has stumbled into the future." I fake laugh at the end. It is the same statement I give to test every person who asks about my career. From his next reaction, I will be able to tell if he actually cares about what I have to say or is only asking for the sake of being polite.

The hesitant nod of his head and the way his body slumps back against the chair tells me it's the latter.

I hear Graham mutter a "thank you" to the barista and worry—*thank* the heavens he is about to leave. I bring my mug to my lips.

"You know, I gotta say, you're not what I expected when I agreed to this date."

The mug shakes in my hand at Steven's admission. I'm choking on the little tea actually in my mouth as I scoot my chair back from the remainder of the tea pouring down my shirt. The legs of the chair scrape the floor below me like nails on a chalkboard.

Eyes from fellow patrons bore into me.

"Are you okay?" Steven pulls napkins from the dispenser in the center of the table and passes them to me.

"I'm sorry. I thought I heard you say 'date'." I admit with an awkward chuckle because I clearly had to have been imagining things. I start patting the brown stain but the effort is futile. I will have to continue the rest of this meeting and go into work with a stain on one of my favorite blouses. *Perfect.*

"I did."

"I'm sorry?"

"This is a date, right?" Thousands of stares and hushed mockery are scratching my skin. He pulls his phone out, searching for something. I pray it's some dating profile so I can say he sat down at the wrong table and we are not in fact meant to meet each other. When he shows the screen to me, my blood boils. "Your mother said you were single and looking for someone to settle down with." *Of course she did.*

"Did she tell you I am looking to marry?"

"What?"

"Marriage. Did she say I want to get married soon?"

He gives a confused nod of his head.

"Trumpet," I curse under my breath.

Everything around us has become quiet. Even the machines seem to have died down. I should have ran through the door when I still had the chance.

"Look, it's clear you didn't know about…this, but I'm still down to get to know each other."

Nausea settles into the pit of my stomach. I barely ate anything today but the urge to vomit is strong.

God, someone please save me from this interaction.

"Mr. Evans," I begin—better to keep this formal—but someone cuts in before I have a chance to say anything more.

"Babe," a delicious voice rings in my ears, alerting all of my senses. A pair of tan work boots enters Steven's and I's space.

Graham. The man with a voice so sweet I may get a cavity just from listening to it.

"I didn't think I'd be able to see you this morning." He announces it to the room as though this information is not brand new and needs to be reiterated for our audience.

He comes to my side, a lot closer than he should be. I don't realize how frozen to the spot I am until he bends to my ear and whispers. "Relax a little or you'll give it away." My shoulders instantly sink at his command. He's so…*familiar.*

Straightening, he extends a hand to Steven who looks as though someone ran over his foot. "Hi. I'm Graham."

Steven doesn't bother shaking Graham's hand. "Steven." He turns his attention to me. "You're seeing someone? Your mom said you were single. Why would you go on a date if you are—"

Graham's hand hovers over the small of my back. I fight the instinct to shove him away. Maybe this will work in my favor.

I clear my throat and ignore the man beside me. "I'm sorry, Steven. I think you got the wrong idea."

"She is very much taken." Graham dips and interlocks our hands as if it is all the information Steven will need. "Her mom believes that until I propose, she is single." He brings his gaze back to me and his voice is so convincing I'm entranced, waiting to hear the next part of our story. "But that won't be for much longer."

I study his features, searching for something, anything, to give me a clue as to where I know him from. His emerald eyes are just as random to me as my own. The tiny scar under his eye is so unique that my brain latches on to it. Surely, something is hidden amongst his features.

It's only when I hear the whoosh of the main door and the collapse of the chaotic noise resuming around us that I am brought back to the present. Like someone hit play on the remote to my body and common sense is now flooding back in.

I don't need to check to know Steven was the one who opened the door. He's more than likely going to report these happenings to his mother who will then inform mine.

This should be fun.

Figuring out who this stranger is the least important thing right now. Clearly he's not someone I know, which makes it even more suspicious he jumped in and helped me. Although, 'helped' may be the wrong term. He only made things worse.

I drop Graham's hand and grab my purse before booking it out of the cafe. I'm out the door and almost a few feet away when I hear the same voice beside me. "You know, most people say 'thank you' when someone does them a service."

I don't stop walking. I can't. I need to get away from him. His voice is like a curse. As poisonous as Medusa's snakes.

"Or we can work on that. I'm Graham, by the way." He stretches a hand between us without slowing or stopping.

Doesn't he have somewhere to be?

I don't realize I voiced the question aloud until he answers, "I do, in fact. But it seemed like you needed more help than a barely built office building." I have no idea what that means. "Did I do something wrong? I assumed helping you escape the awkward date was a good thing. I also figured it would be okay that *I* was the one who saved you since you were ogling me prior."

I stop. Why did ever find such an annoying voice charming? "I don't ogle. Especially not you." I may have glanced in his direction once or twice, but it was purely because he was in my line of sight and nothing more. Certainly not an invitation for him to intervene in my personal business. "And I didn't need your help."

The explanation to Steven lays on my tongue right as Graham slid in. I would have politely exited the situation, and *without* causing more complications for me to explain later.

"So you would rather I left you to fend for yourself?"

No. "Yes. I was perfectly capable of handling the situation."

"Noted. In that case, I apologize." He waves the coffee cup in his hand. There's no way he's not being sarcastic. Patronizing. Annoying.

I knew he was too good to be true. Better as a fantasy than a reality.

"Thank you." I don't mean to be as condescending as it comes across, but I can't help it. Something about this conversation is making me out to be a bigger jerk than I intend.

He scoffs. "Anytime. Unless, of course, you find yourself in a similar situation. In which case, I will gladly leave you to fend for yourself as you are so adamant about."

"I appreciate it." The words are laced with sarcasm. "Of course."

It's a moment that passes between us with neither of us budging. Then two. Maybe more. I'm not sure. I don't know how we ended up in this stare off, but we did. I feel an itch of unease creeping up my spine, beckoning me to turn away. I fight it.

"I should probably get to those offices," I hear him say. He mentions it like he's being forced to say goodbye. Like a part of him doesn't want to end this pointless conversation.

I shake the thoughts out of my mind. *Completely foolish.*

"Please." My arms cross over my chest.

He does a quick salute with his hand as he slowly backs away. "Until next time."

There won't be a next time. Not when his voice sends emotions through me in a way I can't comprehend enough to stop. There will be no next time. Not with Graham.

No. The man with the beautiful voice.

No. The man who stuck his nose in something that is none of his business. The man who—

My phone buzzes in my back pocket, halting my rambling. I pull it out, swipe the green phone across the screen, and begin my walk towards the studio. It's where I should have been instead of the cafe to begin with.

"Piper Celeste." My mother's stern voice rings in my ears. "You promised you'd be on your best behavior." A lot faster than I anticipated. Mom must have hired more ears around town.

I don't bother acknowledging she didn't apologize for lying or even greet me with a simple "hello". Instead, I sigh and follow her lead. "Mom, *you* promised to stop setting me up."

"If you would actually go through with one these men, I wouldn't have to keep doing this."

To say my relationship with my mother is strained is a bit of a stretch. Do we bicker? Often. Does she tend to manipulate me into situations? Sometimes. But do I love her unconditionally and speak to her on a regular basis? Unfortunately so.

I love my mother and I know she loves me. Sometimes, she just loves me too much and doesn't know how to properly display that.

"I don't understand, Piper. Don't you want to get married?"

The idea of being so hopelessly in love with someone you decide to spend the rest of your life with them—so the contract says—sends a wave of nausea to my stomach.

"Do you *want* to spend the rest of your life single?"

I'm doing pretty fine on my own so far. "Mom, why do I need to be with someone to be happy?"

"That's not what I'm saying Piper. You can be happy without someone. The person shouldn't take up your entire identity, but having someone add to the joy in your life is only a plus." Says the same woman who got divorced only ten short years ago.

A car's horn blaring brings me back to my chaotic surroundings. "Mom, I have to go. I'm late for work."

"Okay, but I expect you to give me a real reason as to why you refuse to put yourself out there. I mean, honestly, Piper. What's the harm in dating? Everyone's doing it. Is that what it is? You want to rebel against the current trends?" She talks so fast it's hard to say there is a break in between.

"I don't think dating can be considered a trend, Mom." I force a lighter tone. I've learned quickly the best way to get through these conversations is by finding the humor. A trait I clearly inherited from my father.

"Piper."

"I have to get to work, Mom. I will call you later." Despite how much I want to say the last statement is a lie, I know that she will be waiting by the phone for my call.

My mother is one of the most patient people when it comes to getting what she wants. "Love you."

"Love you too," her tone is exasperated like she can't believe I'm ending our conversation.

After the line dies, I find the contact saved in my phone as "Potential Psycho". About a year or two ago, he accidentally butt dialed me—or so he claims—but we became phone friends within an instant. Well, after his continuous pleas and lack of getting the hint to stop calling.

I scroll to our messages and press the record button.

ⱼ"Do *all* men have a fantasy to be a hero?"

I hit send and tuck my phone back into my pocket before honing in on the sounds around me. Focusing on the symphony enveloping me helps to soothe the chaos into something more bearable when my head is clouded with countless thoughts.

An occasional squeal from braking vehicles. A curse thrown out the window. Conversations raising and decreasing in volume as I pass the speakers. Heels clicking on the sidewalk. Fabric brushing against other, coarser fabric. Dogs' paws scraping the cement.

These are the sounds that ground me. The sounds I can decipher and understand. A person's tone and words are where it becomes tricky.
Reading people is not my strength. Never has been and never will be.

My interaction with the strange man from before returns to my mind, although I'm not sure it ever truly disappeared. He's so boisterous I'm surprised I haven't seen him before. It's my first—and last—time at Sun's Cafe, but he is so *familiar*. Why else would I have been so dumbfounded while he intervened in my life?

I scoff at the memory of him aiding me in distress. Who in their right mind would pretend to be someone's partner, especially when that person is a stranger? Then again, I let him. I didn't fight him once.

"Trumpet," I blow the curse under my breath for the second time. It's the only word I could get away with when I was little and it has stuck since.

The studio comes into sight. It's a five-story building with rented office spaces on the second floor. The dark green bricks blend into the shadows of the nearby alleyway. The only part of the studio drawing attention is the white sign poking from the veranda with "Lydia's Foley Productions" printed on it.

I take a deep breath, deciding to throw today's events to the wind.

Someone like him—obnoxious and way too friendly—is not the kind of person I should be involved with in any kind of context. That's what leads to lines being blurred and my rules becoming hazy. And that's something I refuse to do regardless of how honey-like his voice may be.

My phone vibrates in my pocket. I pull it out and press play on the message. "I can't say I haven't ever dreamed about being a woman's knight in shining armor. I bet I'd look great with a sword in my hand."

A laugh bubbles out of me. There is only one man I am willing to flirt with. The same man who has no way of destroying me. You can't fall in love with someone you don't know the name of, let alone never met in person.

I send back, "I'm sure your fencing skills would only ruin the moment."

CHAPTER TWO

GRAHAM

"Fischer!" Jeff shouts from behind me.

I plop the bag of cement in my arms onto the piling stack in front of me and pretend not to hear him as I inspect the bags closer. Yep, still cement.

When Jeff seeks me out, it's usually not for good reasons.

"What do you think you are doing?"

"Moving the cement, Sir."

He shakes his head with annoyance. "I meant *here*, Fischer. I thought we agreed you would be cutting back hours."

Technically, it was more of a demand than an agreement.

Jeff came to the bar I bartend at in the evenings and discovered I have more than one job. I work construction from dawn to the afternoon every weekday and bartend in the evenings. I used to have a day job for the weekends too, but after the funeral home changed their hours, I had to drop the cleaning gig they gave me. It wouldn't be a lie to say I don't miss the smell of formaldehyde.

Jeff thinks I am working too hard and need to drop one of the jobs, preferably this one. If there's anything Jeff lives by, it's the horror stories of the job. While I may be younger and more physically equipped than some of the others, it doesn't mean I'm "any less susceptible to danger". At least, that's what Jeff tends to remind me of.

"You are supposed to be home."

I force a smile on my face and cross my arms over my chest. "And miss all of the fun?"

He scoffs. "Yeah. That's what I'd call it." Then, more seriously, "Is it the pay?" I tense at the question. He asked me this the other night too.

I have plenty of money. I received a large inheritance from my grandparents when I turned eighteen. Add it on top of every penny I have saved since I started working at sixteen, and I am definitely higher in my financial standpoint than any of my coworkers.

Technically, I could survive very comfortably for the rest of my life with the amount stashed into my savings.

I don't need this job or the bartending one, but that's not the reason I do them. The idea of sitting back and wasting away someone else's hard-earned money is irresponsible and lazy.

"You mean the number of zeros on my paycheck?" I joke back to Jeff's previous question. "I'm hurt you find me that greedy, Sir."

"No matter what I say, you're not going to listen, are you?"

"Depends on what topic we're referring to." I used to shy away from Jeff when I first started. After a few months in, I quickly realized how laid-back Jeff is; if not already evident by the soot coated clothes he wears as a uniform.

"You know you are the reason I ask for more vacation days, right?"

I can't help my smile, knowing his statement is far from the truth. I'm the reason he requests more vacation days solely because I force him too. He works a heck of a lot harder than I do and deserves as many vacations as he can afford. Especially with the heart condition he was diagnosed with a few months ago.

He doesn't know I overheard his conversation on the phone when he received the news. Just like he has no clue I pull a few twenties from my weekly paycheck and slip them into his locker.

"Sir!" Vince yells across from us. "We need your eyes on this."

Jeff gives me a once over. "I expect you to at least keep your weekends open. You're going to burn yourself out, Fischer."

"Of course, Sir."

He starts to walk away, but I hear him mumble something along the lines of "Liar."

My body resumes its familiar regime of unloading supplies and doing the heavy lifting. I match the beat of the big machines churning around me. After a few hours or so of the work, I glance around the nearby buildings. I'm surprised no one has shouted out their windows at the noise or attempted to complain to the police yet. Why they find the sounds annoying is beyond me.

The loud and chaotic noises have always soothed me. If I could rid the world of anything, it would be silence.

I bartend to hear the clashing of mixed conversations and clanking of glass. I visit friends anytime I am alone to be surrounded by the laughter and chaos, even if that involves a screaming child sprinting by. Those are the ones I love the most.

"You still up for our date on Saturday?" I hear a woman ask her acquaintance as they pass on the street. The question brings me back to this morning's events and the cute, demanding voice I got to start my day with.

I went to the same cafe I do every morning, Sun's Cafe, to order the same coffee I do every morning. The second I walked inside, I knew something felt different.

I greeted Tia, the barista who works every Monday, Wednesday, and Friday to be flexible with her schedule with classes at the nearby community college. She is studying to be a social worker. Something that fits her perfectly.

Once my order was in, I took a glance around the room. It's not something I usually do. I try to avoid staring at all times, no matter what kind of staring it may be interpreted as. I have no problem with starting a new conversation with a stranger, but sometimes it leads to people confusing my actions as being invasive. Some—Jason—say I come off a little too eager.

I had every intention of carrying on like usual when my eyes caught her. It was for a brief second before she quickly turned her attention back to the window, but I swear I could hear her breath hitch even with the space stretched between us.

I fought the instinct to walk over and introduce myself. There were thirty minutes left until I needed to clock in, but something about the way she quietly stared out the window told me she didn't want to be bothered.

So I did what I usually do and kept my attention elsewhere. Miguel came out from the back and told me a story of his daughter, Miranda. She's only five, but she has the personality of a much more mature and annoyed woman.

I was doing exactly what I needed to do by busying myself with the people around me, and certainly not listening to the conversation of the woman roughly fifteen steps from me. I did not hear the slight confusion in her tone as she talked to the man—whom I would have much preferred to have taken the place of—across from her. Her sentences were quick like she feared if she spoke for too long, he would shy away.

I didn't eavesdrop on any of it or pick up on how beautiful she sounded.

Instead, I focused on Miguel and his story. I muttered a quick "thank you" to Tia when she passed me my coffee and I was almost out the door when I heard a chair scrape and a chorus of gasps.

I couldn't possibly leave the cafe when someone could be in danger.

My entire body turned, similar to the other bystanders in the room, and tuned in to the most entrancing voice I had ever heard. She dabbed a cheap napkin at a brown stain on her white blouse. Her acquaintance continued to casually talk as though she didn't just get drenched.

I swear I was going to leave. The conversation was obviously a private one only meant for the two of them. I was going to resume pushing the door to the cafe open and flee the scene…

When her voice became small and irritation licked at her words, I found my feet carrying me to her. Something kickstarted in my gut. There was this strange inkling pulling me towards her.

So I did what any polite man would do. I pretended to be her boyfriend and scared her blind date away. I didn't expect her to jump for joy or praise me, but I couldn't have predicted her picking up her bag and fleeing the cafe.

Me being as diligent as ever, I followed her outside. If I'm being honest, I may have come off a little condescending or rude. Certainly not my best moment, but every part of me itched to hear her voice, and to have it directed at me. There is something about the way her voice frames simple sentences that made me want more.

My phone rings in my pocket. I peel one of my gloves off and pull it out. It's from the girl I have donned as *Trumpet*.

It used to be *Grave Digger* until she let out the word "trumpet" as a curse. Never has a word described a person so well.

I press play on her message. "Please tell me *you* have not tried to save a woman."

"Define 'save'," I send back. We have never met in person, never exchanged names, never video chatted, or sent pictures so I have no clue what she looks like or who she is. Despite this, I can imagine her rolling her eyes and the thought only makes me grin.

"Fischer!" Jeff calls over to me again. I shove the phone in my pocket. "Got a job for you."

"Why does he get the easy jobs?" Vince comments as he bites into an apple with a crunch.

By 'easy' I assume he is referring to the lack of heavy lifting I will be doing. The task I'm assigned, though, seems far more difficult than pouring concrete or carrying supplies across the field.

"Yeah," I tap the pencil in my hand against my thigh. "Why give me the job?"

I don't need to acknowledge Jeff's annoyed look to know exactly why he gave me the job. He's worried about me. It's sweet, really, but it's unnecessary. I know my limits and working night and day is far from my breaking point.

"Never mind." The last thing I want is for the guys to hear about how many jobs I'm working. It only leads to more and more questions. "I will gladly pass these letters out."

There is not a single bone in my body with the desire to knock on every door in the apartment building next to us and hand them a flyer. Not even an ounce.

Jeff lays a folder on the table between me, Vince, Clark, and him. We're all cloistered into the break room or mobile trailer. Originally, it was only Jeff and I, until Clark and Vince came in to "clock out for lunch". They crave gossip almost as much as a group of private school moms.

"I expect each apartment to receive one of these tomorrow morning." He pats the thick folder. "The last thing we need is another group of people outside yelling we are too loud."

My phone vibrates in my pocket. I itch to grab it.

Gravedigger is the first woman I have ever been this slow with. In one of my previous relationships, I would have already proposed and been dumped by this point.

Maybe going this slow is a good thing.

"Fischer."

I snap my gaze up.

"Are we in an agreement?"

"Yes, Sir."

Do I want to spend my time knocking on doors and having filler conversations? Absolutely not. But I am going to do it with the biggest smile on my face. Otherwise, Jeff might use it as a reason to fire me and I know he's waiting for the first chance he can get.

CHAPTER THREE

PIPER

As I make my way up to my apartment, familiar sounds envelope me. A little girl's giggle from the bottom floor apartment. One flight up, an old football tape plays on repeat. A coach is blowing their whistle just as someone reclines their chair back with a snap. Ms. King's parrot calls "open" repeatedly.

Two more flights up, three hounds bark in conversation on the other side of Mark's door. A gentle scrapping of the nails against the wooden door.

One more flight up and the beat of music reverberates through my ears. Hazel's home. The closer I get to the door, the more prominent Hazel's off-key singing is. The shrieking doesn't faze me one bit when I unlock the door to find Hazel using a whisk as a microphone and the kitchen as her dance floor.

She doesn't notice me until I drop my bag, shoes, and keys at the door, make my way to the living room, and faceplant on the couch.

The volume of her music decreases. "Bad day?" Hazel asks.

I grunt in response.

Bad? Not necessarily. More so just a whirlwind of a rollercoaster that I was far from prepared for.

"What happened? Elias grumpy again?"

Elias is one of my colleagues and the only one I find myself most alike. I turn my head to the side so my words aren't muffled. "Elias is always grumpy. It's ingrained into his being."

"True. Was it the blind date?"

"Was it that obvious?" I wince.

"Piper, your mom ditched you two minutes before you walked into the cafe." I regret texting Hazel after Mom cancelled. "I think it's pretty obvious she was setting you up."

"Ugh. I should have known."

"So? What happened?"

I thought of the scene that occurred at the cafe. How naive I was in thinking my mother innocently found someone to help Kyle. How idiotic I probably sounded and appeared as I discovered I was on a blind date in front of an entire room of strangers. How an annoying man cut his way into the conversation. How hearing the word "babe" from such an entrancing voice sent uninvited butterflies through my stomach.

"Well…" I dive into the story and give Hazel a semi-exact rundown of the events. I leave out the strange emotions that filtered through the event and how Graham followed me outside of the cafe.

"He just threw himself in like that?" Hazel inquires as I push myself off the couch and position myself at the opposite end of the island.

I nod and dip my finger in the bowl of icing on the counter. I don't have to ask to know she's been baking for hours. She once baked for twenty-seven hours straight with no break in between. "Dreams don't come true without a little elbow grease" is her reasoning when I ask if she's slept in the past twenty-four hours.

Hazel's tone shifts into something of teasing curiosity. "Is he cute?"

"Hazel." I have no clue if one would consider him attractive or not. His familiar voice distracted me too much to even notice the features gracing his sculpted face and figure.

"You're blushing."

"And you're burning your cake," I deflect.

"Biscuits!" she curses. Hazel and I practically grew up in the same household. I use "trumpet" to let out my emotions and she uses food.

When she turns away from me and towards the oven, I bring a hand to my cheek. I'm not blushing. I'm just a little overheated from the heat emanating off the stove.

"So what did your mom say?" she yells over the sound of her ceramic pan grazing the metal rack. "I'm assuming she called you after that kind of experience. Carol is always the first to know."

One of my favorite things about Hazel, despite how little I talk about my obscenely large family, she remembers and treats them as though each relative of mine is a relative of hers.

"She chastised me for it ending that way and is expecting a phone call on why I refuse to date."

I've tried to explain this "phenomenon" to my mother many times. I don't do romance in any sense of the word.

It leads to inevitable heartbreak.

A generous handful of people just aren't meant to have a soulmate or someone good enough to spend the rest of their life with. Some people weren't built for a romantic life. *I* am one of those people. Why would I waste my time on something temporary?

Trying to explain this to my mother, though, is like trying to convince a bull the color red is not threatening.

"Do you want me to talk to her?" She places a tray of cupcakes a little too golden on the counter. In a suggestive tone, "I can bribe her with my treats."

"Mom thinks sweets are a gateway drug."

"Yes, but has she tried mine?"

"I don't know how I'm going to get out of this, Hazel."

She moves to rearrange her baking tools and creations. "They are going to keep happening until A: you find someone to marry, or B: you convince her to leave you alone by telling her the truth."

By truth, she means laying my soul bare for my mother to inspect and annotate with a red pen. Something I would prefer to avoid with every fiber of being.

She doesn't need to know the real reason I don't want to be in a relationship. I can only imagine her reaction when she finds out she's part of the reason. Her and the man who is probably at a dog park with the Labrador of his second family.

"If you go with option A, I think the guy from the cafe would be a fantastic candidate."

I almost choke on the scoop of icing I snuck moments prior. "You mean the man who rudely eavesdropped and intervened on my personal business?"

After reflecting on the events, I regret not voicing my gratitude to him. He didn't have to step in the way he did. He could have just followed suit with the rest of the patrons and listened to the scene. He could have left the cafe without a care, just like I originally thought he did.

Instead, he helped a stranger who flailed around like a fish out of water. He probably did it out of pity. Either way, I'm grateful and I regret not telling him so.

"What you see as rude, I see as a hero romantically swooping in and saving the day. Besides, he helped you once. Maybe he'd be willing to do one of those contract marriage things like in the movies."

"I'm not faking a marriage, Hazel."

"You didn't even give it any thought."

I wonder what the words "I do" would sound like with his deep voice. I doubt it would sound as enrapturing as Potential Psycho would make it.

As if reading my mind, "What about psycho-man?"

"Potential Psycho." I correct her.

"Right. What about him? I mean, you two might as well say you're dating."

My skin prickles at the thought. "We aren't."

"Please." She points a spatula in my direction. "You talk all day every day and I can hear you laughing and

I see you smiling at your phone. Honestly, I don't see why you two haven't met in person."

"Why go and ruin the magic?"

"So you admit there is something there."

I sigh. "How long are you going to be baking?"

She eyes the mess in front of her. "Maybe another thirty minutes?"

In Hazel's time, that means at least another two hours. "In that case, I'm going to bed. Going to be another long day tomorrow and I need as much sleep as possible to forget today's events."

"Or to dream about phone man."

I scoff.

"What did you say his name was again? Love of your life?"

"Good night, Hazel." I wave a hand over my shoulder as I exit the kitchen and enter my room.

Our apartment is far from spacious. The kitchen and living room are crammed into a shared space. Our bedrooms are at the same end with a tiny bathroom in between. I imagine it is what a college dorm might feel like.

When I'm in my room with the door shut, I exhale a long breath.

Today has been beyond a roller coaster of emotions. I have spent hours rerecording in the studio because Linsey, Elias, and I couldn't get the footsteps to match just right. My lunch break was pushed later in the day because of it so dinner ended up becoming a snack on the walk home. All of this fluctuation in my schedule, but the part sticking out the most is Graham.

"Usually, people say 'thank you'" is what he told me after he followed my dramatic storm out of the cafe. Again, not my best moment.

A normal person does say "thank you", but a normal person also wouldn't sit still while a stranger took her life into his hands. Why he helped me is becoming clearer the more I think about it.

He felt pity. That's the only logical explanation. He saw me struggling to form a sentence, probably felt bad for Mr. Evans too, and swooped in to save the day and end the torture of having to witness such a dramatically stupid scene for everyone else.

I move away from the door and pick up a Rubik's cube from the small desk in the corner. I don't know how to solve it. All my time fiddling with it over the years, I have yet to make the perfect cube of colors. But that's not why I fiddle with it. I do it because the clicking pattern as the tiles fall into place calms my mind. I focus solely on the clicks and push everything else away.

The movements are so hypnotizing, I almost don't feel the buzz of my phone. I quickly rip it out of my pocket and smile at the name on the screen.

"Did you know penguins mate for life?" His message starts. "They pick a person and just like that— boom. There is no such thing as cheating or divorce in their world. Could you imagine what life would be like if we were penguins?"

Animal facts. It's something he spouts constantly. He told me he watches a lot of *Animal Planet* and reads national geographic when he has downtime in between his many jobs.

I've never been one to be interested in random scientific facts. Not much of an animal person either. Although that could just be due to my resistance of having a pet. Too much care involved.

A smile plays on my lips as I record myself saying "I bet it would be a black and white world."

He's quick to respond. It's times like these, when we both have a break and can go back and forth, I enjoy the most. "Was that a pun? I think I've rubbed off on you."

"Please. No one could ever make as many disastrous puns as you."

The end of his laugh is caught in the beginning of his message. I replay it without listening to the rest of it first. After about the fourth replay, "Oh, just admit you love how funny I am."

I do. I really, truly do. Never before did I realize just how much laughter can make a heart swell with warmth.

This information, however, he does not need to know. "Only if you admit just how much *you* love making me laugh."

"Trumpet, your laugh is my favorite sound."

CHAPTER FOUR

GRAHAM

"You're part of that crowd, aren't you?" The older woman asks me with disdain and without taking the letter from my hands.

I've made it as far as the second floor and this one interaction is taking longer than all the conversations combined on the floor prior.

"I—" I begin, but she immediately cuts me off with a pointed finger and her glasses falling a hair down her nose.

"Do you know how upset Nigel gets? All that ruckus makes it impossible for him to get any sleep."

"Ma'am, I'm sorry to be disrupting your…" I look around her short frame, expecting see one of those hairless cats lying on a velvet cushion or something equally ridiculous, but a bird cage comes into view instead. "…bird, but we—"

"You have no idea what it's like trying to calm down a parrot who needs silence in order to sleep properly. It's bad enough with the people upstairs. They might as well be tap dancers with how often they prance around."

She continues for what feels like hours and I start to wonder if Jeff did this on purpose. Quitting doesn't sound so bad all of a sudden.

Somehow, I manage to get past her and up two more flights. It's a miracle really, but I have her granddaughter to thank for showing up and escorting her mom back inside.

Upstairs, I start on the left side at the end of the hall.

After the past apartments, one housing what sounds suspiciously close to a kennel, I consider just sticking the flyer under the door, but Jeff gave me clear instructions and I am set to see them through.

I inhale a deep breath, put on my sweetest smile, and…my attention gets caught on a poster hanging beside the door.

"In need of college tutors," it reads. There is a university down the street so its presence makes sense. Yet, I'm stuck on it with a sour feeling in my gut. If I had gone to college, would I be one of the tutors they are seeking? Would other students have come to me to spell check their work or give them advice on projects?

The door to the apartment whips open, dragging my attention with it. I clear my throat.

"Good morning, Ma'am, I—" the words fall short when a woman with auburn hair and forest green eyes stands in front of me. She's shorter than I remember and has freckles dashed across her nose.

"How do you know where I live?" She accuses me. Then, after pulling her sweater tighter around herself, "are you stalking me?"

I nearly scoff in her face. Stalking? I may come off a little overbearing, but I am not a stalker. "I am not stalking you."

"Says the man who is standing outside of my apartment."

I cross my arms over my chest. "Why are you opening the door for strangers?"

"You're right." She grabs the door and begins to shut it. "Goodbye."

I place a hand on the wooden door. "Wait. At least take this before you slam the door in my face."

She eyes the paper in my hand as if I am offering her poison. "What is it?"

"Just a flyer letting you know what times we'll be working."

"We?"

"The construction crew outside your window." I have no clue if she can see the sight from outside of her window. It's hard to tell if it's from the lack of elevator or exhaustion of small talk, but my sense of direction is long gone.

"You're one of the workers?"

"Is that so hard to believe?" I cross my arms, removing the flyer from the space between us. "I know I'm handsome, but even pretty boys need a job."

"Pretending to date strangers isn't a profession of yours? Must just be a hobby then."

"Going on blind dates a hobby of yours?"

She rolls her eyes, lets go of the door, and mirrors my stance. Something ignites in me at having her full attention. I've never enjoyed irritating a girl, but none of them reacted to me in the way she does.

"Why, exactly, were you there anyway?"

"Excuse me?"

I straighten. "You clearly were not interested in him, so why go?"

"I don't see how that is any of your business."

"Is he unattractive?"

"What?"

"The guy you were with. Steve something?"

"Mr. Evans."

"Right. Is he unattractive?"

She's quiet as she studies me. I wonder if she's rolling his image around in her head, analyzing his every feature. I wonder if she has done the same for me and who ranked higher.

"I'm going to take your silence to mean he *is* unattractive."

Her posture shifts and I can see into her apartment a little clearer. It's a small space with the kitchen and living room combined. I can make out a pale orange couch with an abundance of pillows and blankets littered on top. There are heavy-looking bags right behind her, leaning against a bench with sneakers and flip flops.

"Look, is there a reason you are still standing outside my door?"

I draw my attention back to her face. She's attractive, but her looks aren't what sticks out to me.

There's something else about her. Something familiar I can't quite place.

"Were you forced on the date?" The question is out of my mouth before I can stop it.

It would make sense. I vaguely remember her uttering something about sign language before her chair screeched against the floor.

Exasperated, she sighs. "What makes you think I was forced?"

"You clearly had no intention of being there. Either that or…" I watch her fiddle with the hem of her shirt.

"Or…?"

"Let's just say that if you were with me, there would be no doubt in your mind we were on a date."

She shifts, but I can't tell if it's from surprise or discomfort. Hopefully not the latter. I knew I should have slid the flyer under the door.

"Why are you so interested in my personal life?"

Great question. I shouldn't be. Definitely not this much over a stranger, but she is so intriguing.

"Why is it so important to you to know why I went on this date?"

"Don't know." I shrug. "Call me 'Curious'."

"Well, *Curious*, I'm not the type to let the cat out of the bag." She grabs a paper from my hand and makes to close the door again.

"Wait," I stop her for the second time with a hand on the door. "I'm sorry."

"For?"

"We didn't properly introduce ourselves," I decide to say instead of the answer she so clearly wants. "I'm Graham."

She scrutinizes me like I'm a snake offering her a poisoned apple. I shove my free hand in the pocket of my jeans.

"This is usually the part where you say your name. No pressure though."

She goes to close the door again and I feel all excitement drain from my veins. I deserve a slammed door in my face, I guess. I can be intrusive, and tend to pry into someone's personal life—a habit Jason never lets me forget.

Just when the door is nearly closed and I'm about to move to the next apartment, I hear the smallest voice say "Piper." The door shuts and I'm left alone in the hallway.

Piper—a beautiful name for the woman with quite the set of pipes.

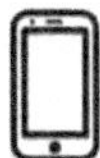

"What's with the long face?" Jason grumbles as I enter our apartment.

I don't bother looking over at him or trying to find him in the room as I kick off my shoes. I know exactly where he's at. Hunched over at the dining table with a stack of textbooks and highlighters. He doesn't even need those books anymore, but I think he just likes to show off how smart he is.

"Nothing," I lie. The last thing I need is for Jason to know about Piper and all the confusing beauty she emanates. I open the fridge, stare at the heaps of food, and close it. "You coming to the bar tonight?"

Jason doesn't drink. It goes against his whole "health regime", but he sometimes goes to help clean tables. He doesn't get paid for it, but Sebastian never complains about the extra hands. "Maybe." His highlighting doesn't falter an inch as he speaks. "I'm being moved to the emergency room tomorrow."

Jason's dream is to be a general surgeon. He doesn't want to be a specialist, for whatever reason is beyond me, so he has studied stitching since before he could properly form sentences.

"Sebastian put you on for more hours?"

I open the fridge, inspect its contents, and close it. "No. He can't afford it." Scavenging the cabinets, I find the box of doughnuts I put in there the day before. There's only one inside. "Are you eating my desserts again?"

"Did you label them?"

"If you want some, get your own." I say through a mouthful. "These were earned through hard work."

"You stole ingredients from Sebastian to get those." He exchanges his highlighter for a pencil.

"It's not stealing if I replace the ingredients with delicious baked goods." It's a trading system I do with Hazel, one of the best bakers I have had the privilege of coming into contact with.

"Sebastian feel that way?"

I ignore him and exit the room

Inside my room, I yank my t-shirt off my back and discard it on the floor. Now is the time to focus on cleaning up and getting ready for my other shift.

My day job lasted longer than I anticipated.

When I yank my phone out of my pocket, a message from Trumpet is listed under a handful of other notifications. I didn't even hear the beep.

I press play as I shuffle through the clothes in my closet. "I started reading that book you recommended. *The Great Gatsby.* Is this your favorite because of the egotistical man at the head of it?"

A small chuckle bubbles out of me. I pick up the phone and press record. "Which man are we referring to?"

The phone has yet to leave my hand before another message comes through. "My point. Remind me why I let you influence my reading decision?"

My eyes find the stack of books peeking out from under my bed. Those along with the few lying on any surface available would total to a three-digit number. Half of them came from my grandmother's library. The other half was paid for with my own money.

I pull *The Great Gatsby* off the pile closest to the head of the bed. Opening the cover, I ignore the outdated college application in the front and flip through the pages. When I find the right annotation, I pick up my phone and tell Gravedigger to keep reading until she gets to this page.

Every book has something special to it. You just got to dig a little deeper.

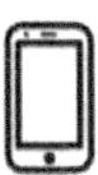

"Hey," I greet as I make my way to Hazel's table outside of the bar.

Her face lights up at the box in my arms. "What you got?"

I lean the cardboard box towards her, showing her the array of ingredients inside. Hazel is an up-and-coming baker. She's been at this corner selling her baked goods for almost a year now. Even in the rain she manages to find a spot with enough coverage to still sell.

Her biggest problem: her lack of funds. So, after trying her treats from heaven for the first time, we made a deal. At the time, I was on my way home from a farmer's market with fresh fruit in hand. She gave me a cinnamon roll in exchange for a bushel of apples.

Now, I bring her ingredients—even if they aren't always from the farmer's market—and she trades me with her delicious creations.

"Ooh, I've been craving strawberries." Her excitement is contagious.

I set the box on her table while she digs in her bags for something. After a moment of rummaging, she resurfaces with a paper bag in hand.

"Here you go, Sir." She feigns professionalism.

I greedily take the bag to find a half-wrapped chocolate croissant inside. I immediately take it out and dive into my first bite. A sigh may have fallen from lips at its heavenly taste. "How do you make these so sweet?"

"A little elbow grease. Anyone could do it."

"No. Not anyone. This is purely Hazel talent."

She waves a hand in dismissal, but her smile grows. "Oh, stop."

"Is it okay if I take a few more? Jason keeps stealing what I bring home."

Her eyes light up with a new emotion as she passes me a few extra. "That depends. When are you finally going to introduce me to him?"

I almost laugh aloud. "Trust me, Jason is far from the dating type."

A ding on her phone from its spot on the table grabs my attention. I glance at the time on the screen and drop the croissant back into the bag. "I have to get to work."

"Same time tomorrow?"

"I'll be here.

CHAPTER FIVE

The house formerly known as the Brooks House used to be considered the loudest one on the block. Not just for the giant, creaking gate at the driveway or the consistently dripping air conditioning unit outside, but also from the habitants inside.

I have been surrounded by noise since the day I came into the world and was carried through the threshold of this very house. There was no easing into it. From the second I entered, stomps were constantly beating against the floor. Household chores—mainly vacuuming—would begin way before the sun woke up. The engine of my mother's and father's car would be revved fifteen minutes prior to anyone's departure.

Quiet is not something the Brooks House knew how to do. But, now that my father is in a condo somewhere south, Sarah is down the street with a noisy family of her own, and Mom has a new job with differing hours, the house no longer lives up to its reputation.

I exit the taxi and make my way up the driveway. It's Tuesday evening and the only time I have available to visit Kyle. He's the youngest of him, Sarah, and I.

When I make it to the porch, I'm greeted by the sound of little feet traipsing around on the other side of the door. The door opens to reveal a smiling Kyle. He instantly wraps his arms around my waist, surprising me. His fingers tap my back, and I don't have to look to know what he's attempting.

When he pulls away, he's wearing a sly grin. I pretend I don't feel the paper clinging to my jacket.

"Where's Mom?" I ask.

Kyle shrugs his shoulders. The back door closes before I hear John yell out to me. "Piper, is that you?"

John is Kyle's father. The first time I met him, he clung to Mom like his life depended on it. Over the years, he has finally reached a point where he strikes up conversations with us kids without Mom present.

John rounds the corner as he wipes his hands on a greasy rag. His entire being is the opposite of my father.

Where Dad is tall, John is closer to the ground. While Dad has a prominent beer gut, John strays away from alcohol like it's the plague. An admiral quality if I'm being honest. My father has the same fiery red hair I inherited whereas John has been balding since long before we met.

"Are you staying for dinner?" He tucks the rag into his pocket.

"Depends on what you're cooking."

He doesn't laugh. His sense of humor is far from my kind. "Your mom is picking up takeout on her way. I can call her and ask to add an order for you…?" An innocent question from the outside.

"I already ate," I suck in my stomach to prevent the growl I feel brewing. Turning my attention to Kyle, "You ready to study?"

Kyle pouts. "Do we have to?"

"Did you finish your homework?" He doesn't answer. "Go ahead up and pull out your books. I'm going to grab some snacks and then I'll be up."

"Can we go out for ice cream?"

Like any normal person, there is an urge to remind him it is November and the wind is blowing, but then I remember who I'm talking to. "Sure."

He throws his hands up in exclamation and shouts "Yay!" before sprinting up the stairs.

"Any fruit?" I throw to John as I pass him on my way to the kitchen.

"Pineapple in the fridge." He follows behind me but stays in the doorway. "Your mom said you had a date today."

My fingers hesitate as I reach for the open container of pineapple chunks. A sinking feeling settles in the pit of my stomach. "You could say that."

"I know she can be overbearing sometimes."

The urge to roll my eyes is strong. I'm twenty-four and John is not my father; Dad never questions me about my dating life. In fact, he applauds my lack of relationships. A part of me misses when John was too afraid to utter a word to me.

"But she just wants you to be happy."

"I know." Fighting is pointless. "Is pineapple all we have?"

His face tells me he wasn't ready to end that conversation. I, however, have been waiting for the finale since the second he opened his mouth. He sighs, pulls the rag back out to wipe his hands again, and makes his way to the back door. "There might be something in the freezer. Your mom loves her smoothies."

A habit of hers that started a year after she met John. The morning vacuuming was replaced by the crush of the blender in the same way the living room furniture has been switched from thrifted couches to a wool sectional.

My parents split unofficially ten years ago. The memory of walking down the stairs with sheet music in hand floods back to me. "What?" Mom's broken voice whispered from the dimly lit kitchen as I sat, frozen, on the steps.

It feels like only yesterday the seven-word sentence fell from my father's lips.

I shake my head and pull out some forks.

The kitchen I'm standing in used to be painted yellow. There used to not be an island in the center. There used to be a very messily spray-painted oval chalkboard on the wall by the fridge. Now the walls are a dark green, there is a giant island in the center, and the chalkboard has been replaced by a pantry door.

My chest constricts and tightens. A stomp from the floor above me reminds me of who is waiting upstairs. I shake my head out of the past, snatch the pineapples and two waters, and make my way to Kyle.

He is spinning in his desk chair when I duck under the space curtain hanging from his door trim.

I set the items down by the door and rip the paper off my back, suddenly remembering it's there. Sneaking towards him, I wait and wait and wait until he starts to slow. Then…I grasp the handles of his chair and bring him to a stop. I stick the paper on his chest, not bothering to read it, and spin him before releasing.

A proud grin forms on my face as he flails his arms and stretches his legs in an effort to stop the chair. As he struggles, I pick up the fruit and pop a chunk into my mouth. Ah, the sweet taste of victory.

When Kyle is settled and I'm in the process of dragging a chair up beside him, he pouts. "Rude."

"Says the…" I glance at the paper taped to his chest. A scoff escapes my lips. "Butt head."

His brows are furrowed as he tears the paper from his t-shirt and tosses it in the trash bin. I point the bowl of fruit in his direction. After a second of his arms crossed in defiance, he gives in and snatches it from me.

I scoot closer to the desk and scan the papers he has laid in front of him. There isn't much work Kyle actually needs to complete. He enjoys doing his math homework, and the school doesn't send him home with anything from science, history, or art.

The issue with Kyle, though, is getting him to put the pen to paper and write. To him, doing English homework is an adult's equivalent of doing taxes. It doesn't help that it only takes all of ten minutes for Mom to leave Kyle to fend for himself or go on his own accord.

I can't say I entirely blame her. It takes a lot of patience to teach Kyle and keep him on track.

I tap the paper in front of him. There's a picture of a boy and a dog with empty blanks below it. "Are you ready?"

"Mom said I don't have to do any more work today."

"Do you have that in writing?"

Cautiously he requests, "Ice cream after?"

"Of course."

He plops the bowl of pineapples between us and beside the waters. It takes a few hours, but we eventually reach a point of success. Minus a few nerf gun breaks (per Kyle's repeated requests). It's not my favorite activity but I always win.

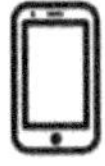

It is ten o'clock by the time I make it back to my apartment. I planned on leaving Mom's house no later than eight, but she pulled into the driveway the second I came down the steps.

"You didn't call me," she tsked as she set her stuff down in the foyer.

I sat on the bottom step. "'How was your day, Piper?'" I mock. "It was great, Mom. Thanks for asking."

"Are you really not going to give him a chance?"

"Considering he ran out the door, I don't think Mr. Evans is a good match." Discussing my lack of enthusiasm and refusal to date would be a torturous cycle. Better to discuss their flaws instead.

"Oh my God. Did you call him 'Mr. Evans' the whole time? No wonder he left."

I rolled my eyes. "He seemed suspicious from the start, Mom."

"Piper, now you're exaggerating." She moved into the kitchen, forcing me to follow behind her. I slid onto the bar stool like a sloth as she set to-go bags on the counter and moved on to pulling out the ingredients for an alcoholic beverage.

"Why did you lie to me, Mom? Why would you set me up like that?"

"Would you have gone if I told you the truth?" I didn't bother answering as she poured strawberry flavoring into a glass. "Exactly. Maybe if you start dating and embrace these men, I might not need to 'trick' you" she puts the word in air quotes and rolls her eyes, "as you like to say so often."

"Mom, you told me he's new to the city."

She eyed me up and down. "I also told you to buy a new wardrobe. Since when did you start listening to what I say?"

"Mom."

She set the glass down hard with a sigh. "Honestly, Piper. Just tell me why you don't want to date. What could possibly be so wrong about putting yourself out there and getting married? Is it the getting married part? I'm fine if you don't get married. As much as I was looking forward to a wedding for my daughter—we both know Sarah is never going to commit enough to walk down the aisle—I will swallow that pill and make do. Maybe we can throw you an elopement somewhere tropical. That would be nice, wouldn't it?"

"I'm not getting married."

"That's fine. As long as you da—"

"I'm not dating either."

"Give me one good reason!"

I was about to lay it all out to her. Explain how those words Dad uttered ten years ago in this very kitchen still haunts me. How I can't even make eye contact with a man without reading every deceiving line in his eyes. How I can't talk to a guy without hearing every broken promise on his tongue.

I'm the kind of person who can predict the ending of a story and tends to skip to the happy bits. But life isn't a movie you can rewind to the good parts.

My lips were itching to get the words out. Maybe then she would finally understand and leave me alone. The blind dates would end, and I would be able to trust my mother again. I wouldn't need to be skeptical of every person she introduces me to.

I swear the admission waited to jump off my tongue, but then the back door opened, and John came into the room. Suddenly, my dating life was yesterday's news, and the new shelf John is building became the talk of the town.

I excused myself when the opportunity finally arose and made it home two hours later than I planned.

I open the door of the apartment, but it quickly slams in my face. "Cleaning!" Hazel shouts from the other side.

She must have had a block in her baking. Anytime she gets stuck on a recipe or has less sales than she wants, she goes on a cleaning tirade. After a moment of sweeps, the door opens back up with the sight of Hazel sweeping towards the kitchen.

"Come on in, Bestie." She does an accent that does not match any existing ones.

"Bad day?" I shut the door behind me and peel my jacket off.

"I got a new strawberry delivery," she motions to the cardboard box on the counter, "but the strawberry shaped donuts aren't turning out correctly."

"It does sound like a strawberry disaster."

"Right?"

I move to the box, inspecting its contents. How one acquires so many strawberries is beyond me.

"So, how was your day?"

"Well, some rude guy banged on our door this morning."

"Mr. Jenkins again?" I ignore Hazel's wiggle of her eyebrows.

"Not this time. Remember the guy I told you about from the cafe?"

"Yeah, why? Oh my—Please tell me he lives in this building. Boy, would I kill to meet him."

"It concerns me the type of men you go after."

She winks.

"He came by to pass out flyers about the building they're putting up next door." I point at the paper on the fridge.

"Wow. Did he recognize you?"

"Sort of."

"Fate is really pushing you two together."

"It was more so a painful coincidence."

"Please, Ms. Dramatic. How painful could it have been?"

"He repeatedly interrogated me like I owe him the secrets to my life."

"He asked about you?"

"Get that happy tone out of your voice. It was more of an invasion than it was genuine curiosity."

His words still haunt my mind. *Let's just say that if you were with me, there would be no doubt in your mind we were on a date.*

A shiver runs down my spine.

"Hmm." Hazel is humming. Something she only does when she is plotting fantasies in her head. Something I refuse to acknowledge.

"Anyway, that's not even the highlight of the day." I move towards her plate of cupcakes on the counter. They are visibly crisp and lack icing, but my stomach is growling. I chomp down on one, ignoring the chunks of carrots.

Hazel scoots the couch with her knees to sweep underneath. "Ooh, do carry on."

"Mom came home before I could leave."

"How dare she show up in her own home!" Her sarcasm almost makes me smile.

"I told her why that guy is not a valid option. She lectured me about marriage. Then John swooped in."

"Ah, one of the many things we thank John for."

I half-laugh, half-scoff. She's right: if there is anything John is good for, it's taking Mom's questioning away, even though it comes with the hard price of taking her attention too.

"So you didn't tell her? I think she might actually understand if you are honest. I mean, she experienced it."

"Trying to connect with Mom on that kind of level is like trying to explain how to work a computer to your grandmother."

"Hey, Grams is a lot smarter than she looks. She just has trouble turning on the computer. And typing. And completing basically any electronic task. Yeah, you might be right."

I bury my face in my arms on the countertop.

"So no more blind dates?" Hazel's tone has softened.

She knows why I don't date. She doesn't understand the pain I experience at the thought of being desperately devoted to someone, but she doesn't judge me and defends me in every situation she can.

Hazel did try to get me to date a couple times by teasing me about potential suitors she thought would be a perfect match, but teasing is as far as it went. Eventually, she stopped asking me about dating and only talks men up to me, before quickly swatting them away the second they try to pursue me.

She is my other half and the only other person I need in this life.

"Until further notice."

"Look on the bright side." My gaze raises from the half-eaten cupcake I sat on the counter, waiting to hear what she has to say. A beat. Then two. "Okay, the bright side is hidden behind some clouds right now, but I'm sure it's there."

"I'm screwed."

"It does appear that way. Or…"

"No. Whatever you are conjuring up in that brain of yours, it is an automatic 'no'."

"You didn't even hear how great of an idea it is." Hazel fake pouts.

"Does it involve a contract and Potential Psycho?"

"You know, sometimes I despise how well you know me."

I laugh and slide my arms off the bar. "Give me a duster." She tosses me a cloth and I get to work with her.

I should be making my way to bed where I can crawl under my sheets, turn on the rain sounds I have saved on Spotify, and drown the rest of the world out. I should be preparing for work tomorrow, but the second I go into my room, the events of the day will come hurdling back. They will be stuck on replay in my mind to the point I will want to tear them out of my skull.

Turning off my brain is a skill I have never acquired. Instead, I am forced to be subjected to the pain of the voices and noise.

Cleaning, as Hazel would agree, helps to remove all of those thoughts. It seems to pick them up, set them in a box, and store them on a shelf for a rainy day. So, I diligently dust every corner of the apartment.

By one in the morning, Hazel and I have the apartment spotless. She showers to freshen herself back up before she dives into another baking frenzy, while I tuck myself away in my room.

When my body is laid on the cheap mattress and the covers are pulled up to my chin, I try to focus on the rain sounds emanating from my phone. I close my eyes and pretend I'm in a rainforest. My imagination, though, sucks.

Suddenly, monkeys climb on the limbs of anxiety trees, with my mom's voice echoing from calls. The rain beats down through the open branches like a cold shower. It's all too much and I nearly chuck a pillow across the room in exasperation.

But then a honey-like voice seems to float its way through the jungle. It climbs the trunks of trees and swings on the hanging vines. It sings through the birds perched on the tree limbs. It uses the rain as its chorus and brings sunlight back into the darkness.

It's asking me if I need a knight in shining armor. It's dulling my mom's voice. It's creating a beautiful symphony in the trees.

I let myself fall asleep with a smile on my face and a handsome voice in my ears.

CHAPTER SIX

GRAHAM

I used to think destiny played a major role in life. I would sprint in circles with a makeshift tinfoil helmet in my parents' living room shouting how it is my destiny to be a pilot.

Then, I aged and suddenly destiny sounded more like a bad omen. When my truck got a flat tire on the road to the farm, I heard "It was destined to happen."

"Destiny is a pain," was repeated to me when my grandfather passed away. They were meant to be consoling words—I'm sure—but destiny became my least favorite word.

Now, I can't help but laugh when someone even mutters the word, which is exactly what I do when a group of women pass me on the street, and I overhear one discussing how some man is her destiny.

I shift the box in my hands, adjusting its weight. It is a cloudy Wednesday morning, and I am dying for a sweet treat; especially with the anticipation of tonight's events. It's Jason's birthday and, as such, his family is throwing an elite party. As his best friend, I am forced to wear a suit and stand beside him. The responsibility of reintroducing Jason to the family members he forgot is one I fulfill.

"Is that what I think it is?" Hazel stands on her tiptoes as I approach her table.

I tuck the box further away. "Depends. What's on the table today?"

She pulls out a container from the stack of tote bags behind her. "Can I interest you in a carrot cupcake?"

I eye the treat inside. It definitely looks and smells appealing, but the idea of "carrots" makes me hesitant.

"Oh, come on. I promise they are good."

"Am I the first to try one?"

"Of course not."

I hesitantly pick one up and take a small bite.

"Well, you are the first one to try *this* batch."

I'm afraid to chew and have my tongue make contact with the dessert, but Hazel's expression is full of hopeful pleading, so I force myself to choke it down.

After swallowing, I inspect the dessert greasing my hands. The white liner is hiding the cake, but the cream, orange icing on top appears safe. "Not as bad as it sounds."

"Right? A lot of people have misconceptions about carrots, but if you prepare them right, they can make the best dessert."

I wouldn't go that far…

"Alright, pass the box over." I carefully set the box down on her table. I continue to eat the cupcake while she inspects the contents of the delivery. "Why do these look different?"

That would be because I actually purchased them from the farmer's market this morning instead of stealing—borrowing from Sebastian. With the anticipation of tonight, I desperately needed a Hazel treat.

"New shipment." Technically not a complete lie.

She nods before moving the box to add to her pile behind her. How she commutes with all of that stuff is beyond me. She must have a car parked nearby somewhere.

"So…" Hazel begins with an anything but innocent tone. "Are you seeing anyone?"

Hazel and I are friends, or at least I'd like to say we are. Hazel on the other hand would probably only consider me a business partner. She's funny about that stuff. The only thing we both agree on is our lack of romantic feelings for one another.

To her, I'm like an annoying older brother. To me, she is the kind of girl who is scarily confident in all areas. We are completely incompatible, and we have come to a silent agreement to ensure it stays that way.

I don't want anything to jeopardize my treats, and she desperately needs the free ingredients. With that being said, she feels it is her moral obligation to find me a girlfriend. "It's bad for your health to stay single," she likes to say.

"No," I answer her earlier question. I've been on a few dates here and there, but none have amounted to anything. The only lasting relationship I've had with a girl is the one I have with Trumpet, but that's more of a friendship than anything romantic. Not by my decision.

"Ooh, can I set you up?"

I steal another cupcake. They may not be my favorite, but they are sweet enough to make me not mind. "With who?"

She ponders this. "Well, I have the perfect woman I think you would hit it off with. She is quiet, funny, stays close to the people she cares about most, and is undeniably sweet." She mentions the last part as her eyes dart between me and the cupcake in hand.

"Who is she?" The words come out jumbled around the bite, but she gets the idea anyway.

"Oh, you can't date her." All the humor and excitement fade from her.

"Didn't you just say…?"

"I said 'she is the perfect woman for you.' Especially because you are both workaholics and don't know how to rest. Maybe pinning two workaholics together would be good for the two of you. Then you would both be forced to take a break."

"I'm not a workaholic."

She raises a brow. "And I'm six foot." I almost laugh at her five-foot-two frame. "But you can't date her."

"Why not?" Curiosity gets the better of me. It's both a gift and a curse.

"She doesn't date. It's not her thing."

I nod, solemnly.

"But you two would be so adorable. Then again, I'm shipping her with someone else. He's more rugged and charming than you so he wins that battle."

I ignore the stab to my chest. "I thought you said she doesn't date."

"She doesn't, but I can still pin her with people in my head. You were number one until he came into the picture. Now you're in second place. I would step it up, if I were you."

Hazel's imagination never ceases to amaze me. "I will work on that." I grab another cupcake, stick it into one of the paper bags Hazel has sitting on the table, and turn to walk away.

"I have another woman I can set you up with," she calls out to my fleeting form.

I wave over my shoulder, but don't turn back. As tempting as it is to be in a relationship with someone—and believe me, it is tempting—I'd rather not be set up by Hazel. Knowing her, if it doesn't work out, I'd never be allowed any more desserts.

That is something I am not willing to give up so easily. Besides, I doubt any of Hazel's friends would interest me any more than the woman whose voice has been ringing in my ears since the first word she spoke to me.

I can still picture the blush on her skin from the frustration I caused. The name Piper fits her almost as well as the fiery red hair atop her head.

"Anymore blind dates on the horizon?" I ask into my phone as I make my way across the construction site.

Gravedigger is on the other side of the phone I have tucked between my ear and shoulder. Her mother consistently sets her up on blind dates and each one ends in the most horrendous disaster.

With tonight's looming event, I could use the laugh.

"Not if I can help it." Her voice is full of exhaustion like the idea of dating itself is dreadful.

"You never know, maybe one of these dates will actually turn out. Who knows, you just might find your prince charming." I used to think I would be him. That dream blew away the more she opened up. She's only interested in being friends.

"Please. I'd rather not be wooed by a man who kisses an unconscious stranger."

I laugh. "Are you saying the most romantic moment in television is creepy?"

"Romantic? Please tell me you have not kissed unconscious women."

"Of course not." Then, after a beat. "I like a woman who can bite back."

I'm grinning, expecting her to laugh, but her side of the call is so quiet. With any other woman, I would be second guessing every word coming out of my mouth. With her, I don't have to.

"Did I lose you, Trumpet?"

"Just praying for the poor woman you end up with."

I open the trailer door, then shut it tight behind me. Someone speaks up in the background of her end. She mutters something inaudible to them.

"Gotta go. Try not to do anything weird."

A smile plays on my lips when I say "No

promises."

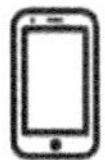

Jason's parents are known for their elaborate parties. They come from old money, which is evident by the mansion they have lived in for generations and the countless "friends" they have acquired. Status is something his parents have always known and Jason will end up inheriting all of it when he's older.

We enter the enormous living room of the Young's house. It is flush with geometric art and modern design. His mother is the director of a hospital and has taken the idea of a clean and pristine environment into all aspects of her life. Even with the room crowded as much as it is, it still feels cold and sterile.

"Jason, dear," A woman in green approaches us. My job at these kinds of gathering: weed through every person approaching.

I know that if it were up to Jason, he would be bent over textbooks right now. It's surprising he hasn't found some shaded corner to hide in and read the dictionary on his phone.

"Mrs. Connahay," I greet her, inadvertently reminding Jason who she is.

She instantly turns her gaze to me. "Graham. I almost didn't see you there." She pulls me to her and delicately kisses the air on each side of my face.

"How's the new cat?" I ask.

"Oh, he's as lazy as Penelope." Penelope is her five-year-old granddaughter. "I see you boys didn't bring any dates again."

Not once have Jason or I brought a plus one to these events. If I brought someone I would be easily distracted, as Jason claims. I dance with a woman one time—leaving him alone to handle the nagging questions about why a man like him has yet to get married—and I never hear the end of it.

"You can't seriously be mad about me dancing with Madison." I whined to him.

He looked like he needed something to punch, and *I* resembled a punching bag. "I'm never giving you a discount again."

At that, I paled. "It will never happen again." He took a swig of his drink. "Promise." I had no problem with pleading about this situation. Healthcare is beyond expensive and having a best friend whose mother directs a hospital is beneficial in many ways.

Since then, I have not brought a plus one or even danced with a guest.

Jason, on the other hand, doesn't know how to talk to women. More so, refuses to.

"Then I wouldn't be able to dance with *you*, Mrs. Connahay." I fake, coming back to the previous conversation.

She pats my arm. "Oh, stop." Someone behind us calls out to her. "Well, it was a pleasure seeing you both again. I expect you each to save me a dance."

I elbow Jason when I hear a whispered curse. "Of course."

When she has disappeared, Jason doesn't hesitate to push through the flush of people with me trailing behind him. He stops at one of the standing tables in the furthest corner from the entrance, ensuring his back is to the wall.

I pick up one of the champagne flutes and take a sip. "Are you going to be this unbearable all night?"

He adjusts his tie. "I'm hoping the night ends fast."

"Your mother planned this event."

"But Jasmine helped."

A little girl with long black hair tied in a braid comes to mind. Jasmine is the girl next door to Jason's parents' house. Since they were young, their parents pushed the two together. Jasmine and Jason, however, couldn't be any more incompatible with each other.

"I'm hoping she convinced Mom to cut back on at least one speaker."

I nod and inspect the crowd. The same snobby people I have been forced to be around since I met Jason.

My family is wealthy too, but we aren't old-money wealthy. My parents don't have local status, let alone international status.

While we all received an inheritance from my grandfather who gained a lot of money in his time, he wasn't a billionaire. He saved about a million over the years, but he kept to himself and lived like a poor man. His main goal was to make sure his children and grandchildren were taken care of.

He worked himself into his grave. Another reason I have yet to even touch the inheritance money I received two years ago. If he was able to work relentlessly and survive, I can do the same.

"Incoming," I announce when I spot Jason's parents. "Do you need me to introduce them too?" "Shut up."

I grin.

"Graham," Mrs. Young nods in my direction for a glimpse of a moment. I smile back. "Jason, how lovely of you to grace us with your presence." She does the same hug ritual Ms. Connahay did to us earlier. If you didn't know their relation, you would have no idea Mrs. Young is his mother.

"It is my birthday, Mother."

"I'm glad you have picked up on it too."

Mr. Young settles beside me, clanking his glass with mine. How Mr. Young is able to handle Mrs. Young is beyond me. He's so calm and laid back compared to her constant state of pristine stress, I'm surprised they have been married for over thirty years.

Mrs. Young watches Jason's expression. "Jasmine is here, you know."

"I heard."

"I'm sure she is dying to see you."

"We saw each other last week, Mother."

"Please, Jason. To a woman, a week is a year. You should go find her. Ask her to dance."

"I don't dance."

"You can't do this one thing for me?"

"How's construction?" Jason's father asks me, pulling my attention away from the mother and son.

"Good. How's the bank?" Mr. Young runs a bank internationally known and used. He offered me a job when I graduated high school, but math is not my area of expertise.

"As good as the stock market. Do you think they would notice if we hightailed it out of here?" he lifts one finger from his glass to point between his wife and Jason.

"I don't think they would notice if a bomb fell in the middle of the event."

He laughs and clinks my glass again before we both swallow the remnants of our drinks.

It takes an hour of greeting people and subtly introducing Jason to the people he should already know— including a few of his cousins.

I yank my phone out of my pocket, open the messages, and press record. "Did you know gorillas hold parties and festivals? I wonder if that's where humans get it from." I hit send and shove the phone back in my pocket.

"You still talk to her?" Jason questions me.

"Who?"

"The woman you said owns a gardening business."

"She doesn't own a gardening business. It was a joke she made."

He shoves his hands into his pants pockets. "Regardless, I'm surprised you still talk to her."

"Why?"

"Usually you've scared them off by now." I hear the slightest hint of humor in his tone. Not enough to ease the tension in my back though.

"She's different." My hands form fists by side. "There is no romantic interest between the two of us. And for your information, I do not scare women away." He scoffs.

A waiter walks by with a tray of champagne. I take one without hesitation and take a big swig of the bubbly beverage.

"Take it easy." Jason comments. "I was just kidding."

The frustration starts to ease from my bones and my shoulder drops at his sudden concern. "I know."

As much as Jason likes to mock me, he is also the only person who has stood by me. He's the only one who hasn't questioned my decision not to go to college. It's a quality I admire.

"I need your eyes sharp to recognize the group of women coming in hot."

The sudden urge to shove him into the group is strong. I should let them have their way with him. Instead, I do what any good friend would do and plaster on a smile before wickedly saying, "Jason, you have to introduce me to such beautiful women."

I don't look in his direction, but I can feel the laser beams he's shooting at me.

When we finally get home from the extremely long event—Jason's hope for fewer speakers was sorely proved wrong—I grab a book from the shelf in my bedroom and start drawing in the words.

Reading is the only thing I can accept in silence. The second my eyes skim the words on the page, a new world is created before me. I'm transported instantly into a place full of characters, parties, and chaos.

My copy of *The Great Gatsby* is battered from the amount of times I have opened the pages. It is full of my scribbled annotations and notes I have made through the multiple reads of this narrative. It's one of the most chaotic novels I have read. Well, minus Wuthering Heights. But it is one of my favorites regardless.

I find the folded application I shoved in the back. I unravel it to read the words I wrote on the page years ago. "English education" is scrawled on a line.

The memory of filling the form out is still fresh in my mind. I can still hear the sound of my heart beating in my chest. The motion of my smile falling into a frown when I reached the next page on financials. Mom's footsteps pounded down the hallway and I shoved the paper into the nearest spot.

Today, what once was a ticket to a life of dreams is now used as a bookmark.

CHAPTER SEVEN

PIPER

The break room lacks snacks but is consistently equipped with coffee. This is generally because Elias has everything labeled with his name on post it notes.

"Good morning, Piper." Jordan greets from behind me.

I smile politely and reach for a second mug in the cabinet to pass to him. "Morning."

Jordan is one of the interns in our studio. We've only had a few interactions, all of which stayed in this room and lasted less than five minutes.

"Here," I pass him the mug with "there might be wine in here" painted on it.

"Thanks."

I busy myself with filling my own mug with water. I already drank three cups of coffee this morning and as much as I need the energy boost, I'd rather not add dehydration to the list of problems.

"So I was wondering if you have any plans this evening?" Jordan pours himself the burnt liquid. The machine has been left on since Elias turned it on a few hours prior.

"Not really," I respond. "Just relaxing."

"That's great." After a beat, he adjusts his cheerful tone. "I mean, would you want to get dinner with me tonight?"

The question surprises me more than it should. An anxious wave brushes my skin as I curl into myself and away from him.

"Why?" I laugh through the question, but it comes out more awkward than anything else.

"Um…I'd like to take you out and get to know you better." He shifts from one foot to the other. "But if you would rather do another night, that's okay too. Can I get your number?"

My heart is beating frantically in my chest. So loud I barely hear his words.

"Actually, I think I lost my phone. Yeah. I left it in the taxi. Sorry." I shrug my shoulders as I feign ignorance.

Glancing around him, I search for any lingering excuses.

Why did he have to stop me on the one floor without an easy escape route?

His gaze falls to the phone grasped tightly in my hand. "Oh…okay."

I tuck the device behind my back.

Giving him my number could give him false hope.

"I'm not looking to date." I admit. Blunt is the best way to go.

"Oh. How about just dinner and—"

"Piper." Elias interrupts as he steps into the room. *Please tell me he did not witness this interaction.* He stops in front of me with a look of annoyance. "You're where I need."

"Oh," I quickly move to the other side of the room and away from the cabinet housing boxes of crackers.

"Anyway," Jordan continues. Somehow, he is closer than before. "I was wondering if—"

"Piper." Elias speaks up again, but he's loitering in the doorway now. "We have work to get done and I am not going to be waiting around all day."

A hopeful feeling fills my chest at the excuse. I turn back to Jordan, "I have to get back to work." With a small, polite smile, I walk past him and exit the room with Elias.

"I'm sorry," I tell Elias when we are far enough away. "I didn't realize I was holding you and Lindsey up."

He sticks a hand into the box of saltines in his hand. "You weren't."

"What?"

"I don't like the looks of that guy. I hear he lives in his mom's basement."

Instantly, the worry fades away. He may be rough on the outside, but Elias is the biggest sweetheart. "Thank you, Elias."

He studies me for the briefest moment before rolling his eyes. "Don't get in your head about it."

We continue to the elevator and past the cubicles of this team. There are three teams in the company—each of which have their own floor with their own studio—but only one has a break room. This forces us to travel two floors down anytime we need a refill or snack.

When the elevator opens to the fourth floor, Elias and I step out. We make a right towards our desks instead of a left into the recording studio.

"How did it go?" Lindsey cheerfully inquires as she stands from her spot. Since the first day I met Lindsey, she has been nothing but sunshine and rainbows. If this were a fantasy, she would probably be a fairy or princess.

I look between the two of them, wondering what exactly she is referring to.

"I told Jordan he should just go for it, but he was so nervous."

My heart stops at the admission. "*You* told Jordan to ask me out?"

"He asked if you were single. So? Are you two going out?"

"I…" I don't know what to say. Now, not only is Mom trying to set me up, but so is my coworker.

Elias grumbles, distracting Lindsey, and I couldn't be more grateful for the diversion. At least I have him.

"What's wrong?"

"We are worker bees meant to follow every demand of the queen," Elias clicks his mouse with purpose.

Lindsey rolls her eyes as she places her lotion-slick hands on my arms. "A few more projects came in to do on the side when you went on break, but everything's okay. I'm starting the outlining and Elias is listening to the current audio. It's nothing too drastic."

"What about the dog animation video?"

"Do you mind taking the lead on that one, Piper? I mean, since it's only the atmospherics left. That way Elias and I can knock out these other projects together."

It's a sitcom about a lawyer who moves to the city to help a bankrupt grocery store. It's not the most exciting project and definitely not how I prefer to spend my time, but it has a deadline for the end of the week. We originally weren't in a rush since it was our only project. Now, I'm going to be working late nights for the rest of the week.

The client is an investor, and they always get top priority. Another reason why it was the only project we were given, but Mrs. Williams must have had a bad day today.

If she's drowned by incoming requests, she pushes them to her best team: us. It should be a compliment and maybe even a good thing, but it only ever feels like a punishment.

"I'll handle it," I assure Lindsey.

"You are the best!"

It's five hours later when we finally resurface from our computers and the studio. The night has shaded our daylight and forced us to turn on the few desk lamps. I stretch my limbs and rub the knot in my thigh.

Lindsey congratulates Elias and I. She spreads positivity like a knife spreads butter on bread. It makes me wonder if she does it to reassure herself more than us. "Let's go out for drinks."

Elias groans. He's not a fan of going out or being around people in general. He's always been grumpy since the first day I met him. Yet, he was the one they assigned to introduce me to the studio.

"You're the one they hired?" is how he greeted me.

"Yes," I responded confidently.

"Follow me. I'm only going to say all of this once, so you better have a notebook and pen."

I pulled the journal out of my bag and scribbled down as much as I possibly could. He showed me the ins and outs. He used to scare me, but over the years I have learned he is only grumpy on the outside.

When I was in the process of getting over a cold and came into work late, a hot cup of tea and some medicine sat on my desk. I initially suspected Lindsey as the culprit, but Lindsey denied it. When I looked at Elias the only thing he said as confirmation was "the last thing we need is for you to spread your germs." Since then, I have loved working with him.

"Oh come on," Lindsey brings me back to the present. "You know you want to."

She beckons Elias to admit he will be going to the bar too. I can tell by the way he is slowly putting everything away that he is waiting until we leave to follow us to the bar. He's not going to let us go alone.

"What about you, Piper? You're in, right?"

"I don't usually drink."

"That's fine. You can have water or a coke or something virgin."

The idea of seeing disappointment on her face or hearing her voice drop, sends a stabbing feeling to my gut. "I don't know…"

Lindsey grabs my purse, turns off my lamp, and pulls me from the chair. "Come on, it will be fun. I promise. Right, Elias?"

She doesn't wait for his response before tugging me out of the office and towards the elevator.

Bars aren't something I frequent. They are loud and full of obnoxious people. Often times, there is a sports game playing in the background as well. The lights are too dim for me to see anything properly and the smell is a mix of sweat and peanuts. All around, a bar is not the place I want to spend my time.

I have drunk in my lifetime, but it's not something I desire or wish to do after a long day. When I do want a drink, I certainly don't go to a bar to get one.

The place Lindsey picks is only a block away from the office. It's as crowded as I had anticipated, but the smell lacks any odors. Instead, there's a delicious apple scent and I wonder if maybe this wasn't such a bad idea.

She finds us a booth in the corner where Lindsey and I take one side and Elias takes the other. Luckily, this booth is located right beside a window. Perfect for the people watching I like to do.

"Piper, do you mind running up to the bar and asking for our drinks? I'm going to run to the restroom." Lindsey tosses her coat in one of the seats.

"Sure."

They give me their orders and I scamper towards the bar. It's hard to weasel through the bodies blocking it, but I somehow manage. Luckily, I manage to wiggle my way to a spot right in front of the bartender.

He has his back turned toward me as his hands fiddle with something on the counter. "Excuse me," I try, but the noise is too loud for him to even hear me. "Hello!" I raise my voice a little louder but the man doesn't even flinch.

"Excuse me," a deep voice shouts beside me.

I look over to see a man in a Hawaiian shirt looking right back at me. He has this devilish smile on his face, one he probably woos women with often. At least, that's what the butterflies in my stomach are telling me.

The bartender must have turned around because now he's asking, "What can I get you?"

I give him our order and turn back to Hawaiian Shirt. "Thank you."

He leans his elbows on the counter, shifting to face the upper half of his body towards me. Another reason I don't like bars—at least this one in particular—you have to wait for your drinks before you can escape back to your table. Meaning, I have to stand next to this man while the bartender—

The space on the other side of the bar is suddenly vacant.

I search the other side of the bar trying to spot the bartender, but the man beside me blocks my view.

"Do you come here often?" His words are as coy as a moment ago but are laced with alcohol induced promises.

Oh, how much I long to be rid of this man as soon as possible. If only I had the confidence to convince Lindsey or Elias to take my spot.

"No." I turn my head to keep his cologne from wafting my way anymore. The scent of pine is repelling.

"That makes sense. I definitely would have remembered you."

Clearly he doesn't realize how his sentence is not the compliment he thinks it is.

"Are you here with anyone?"

"Yes." I'm hoping my one-word answer will give him the hint to move on. "Go!" Is what I want to shout. "I'm not interested."

"That's a shame. Any chance I can steal you away?"

Where is the bartender? Isn't it his job to provide service to customers. *Not* ditch them. "I—Look, you—"

"Sorry for the wait," a familiar voice cuts in. "My colleague had to switch with me." I glance at the speaker, instantly surprised. *Graham.* "What can I get you two?"

I'm quick to shake my head. "Oh, we aren't—"

"A water for her," Hawaiian Shirt interrupts me, "and another beer for me." He waves the empty bottle in his hand as evidence. Graham eyes me for a moment, before getting to work on the drinks. "You did ask for water, right?" Hawaiian Shirt whispers in my ear. I cringe at the proximity.

Focusing on Graham, "Excuse me." I worry he might not hear me like the previous bartender, but Graham immediately lifts his gaze back to mine like he had been waiting for the moment I call to him. "I need to add two more drinks to that list." I give him the detailed names of Elias' and Lindsey's beverages.

Why haven't they come to find me yet? Is it not suspicious to them that I have been gone for a while?

Graham passes us water and beer. He's quick to deposit the man's drink and slow with mine. Then, he gets to work on the others. He's skilled with his hands like he has done this millions of times before.

"I'll help you carry those drinks to your table," Hawaiian shirt offers. I'm so focused on Graham's movements I almost don't hear him.

"Oh, that's okay. I—"

"Please, I insist."

I look to Graham for help. Can't he see how badly I want this guy to leave? He's too focused on his work to notice the daggers I'm staring into his beautiful blonde hair.

"I'm more fun than I look," Hawaiian shirt continues. He winks. Nausea settles into the pit of my stomach.

I silently beg Graham to help me. I would take any form of assistance at this point. In fact, I'll gladly accept him pretending to be my boyfriend again. Now might be the perfect time for it.

"I'll be right back," Hawaiian Shirt winks before departing through the sea of people.

The second he's gone, I turn to Graham. "Thanks for the help." The sarcasm oozes out of me like vomit.

He doesn't bother looking up, but I can imagine the smirk on his lips. "I thought you said before to let you handle these situations on your own."

I knew those words would come back to bite me in the butt.

"Besides, he's clearly into you. Why would I invade on such a happy moment in your life?" There's something in his tone I can't quite make out. Hurt? Anger? Jealousy? Nope. Annoyed.

"Please. Guys like him are the reason I avoid bars."

One of his eyebrows raises in curiosity. "You aren't interested in him? At all?"

"I'd rather rip my ears from my head just so I don't have to hear his stupid pick-up lines again."

He laughs and I can't help the swarm of pride in my chest at the sound of it. His chuckle…it's so *familiar*.

Hawaiian Shirt returns just as Graham sets the drinks on top of the counter in front of me. "I hope you didn't miss me too much," the man sleazily comments.

I try to gather all of the drinks in my hands so I can quickly make my escape, but a hand stops me. I expect it to be Hawaiian Shirt's and am about to come up with some excuse about why he should leave me alone, when I hear Graham's voice instead.

"Sorry. She's taken." I look down to see Graham's hand over mine.

Hawaiian shirt scoffs. "Seriously? Dude, you two look more like strangers than partners."

Graham laughs. It's cynical and I berate myself for the swirls of curiosity in my chest. "Pipes," Graham focuses his attention solely on me and I can't help but feel like we are the only two people in the room.

At some point, I'm not exactly sure when, the rest of the noise falls away and Graham's voice is the only thing my ears have latched onto. "I'll help you take those to the table. I know you're having trouble walking after last night." There's a sinful glint in his eyes.

A blush creeps up my neck and my lips part in surprise. He's taking it too far. The only thing stopping me from smacking him is the man beside me.

Hawaiian shirt scoffs. I focus all of my attention on Graham walking around the bar and straight to me. He picks up the two specialty beverages leaving me with the water. Wrapping an arm around my shoulders, he motions for me to guide him to the table.

I don't realize he has bent down until I feel his breath fanning my ear and a minty smell travels to my nose.

"You're not going to yell at me for helping, are you?"

I elbow him in the side before removing myself from his arm. He mutters a fake "ouch" before following. When I make it to the table, Lindsey is torturing Elias with pictures of her kids. Elias looks at me with irritation. I was gone too long.

I slide in beside Lindsey with my water. Graham stops at the edge of the table and sets the drinks on the table. "Here we are," he announces.

"Thank you." I hope he knows I say it for more than just for carrying the drinks.

"Anytime. Hopefully, we don't keep meeting like this though. If I fake being your boyfriend one more time, I might just have to make us real." He winks horrendously.

I fight the laugh begging to escape. "I think that was worse than Hawaiian Shirt's pick-up lines." He presses a hand to his chest. "Way to wound a man."

Someone clears their throat, reminding me we aren't alone. I duck my head so my hair will hide the blush on my cheeks.

"Hi," Lindsey greets. I don't have to look up to know she's wearing the biggest smile she can muster. "I'm Lindsey and this is Elias. We work with Piper. And you are?"

"Graham. I'm Piper's..." He's at a loss for words.

"Boyfriend?" Unfortunately, I chose this moment to take a sip of my water. I choke on the cold liquid. Lindsey pats my back absently.

"No." Graham is quick, causing something to tighten in my chest. "Not yet."

At that, I whip my head up to find Graham grinning down at me. *What the heck was that?* I silently ask him with a pointed stare, but he either doesn't understand or purposely ignores me.

"Well, I'll let you all enjoy your drinks. If you need anything, you can find me behind the bar." Turning back to me and adjusting his tone, "Piper, always pleasure."

Without another word, Graham saunters away.

"Care to explain, Piper?" Lindsey twirls the thin straw in her glass.

"It's nothing."

"That looked like a lot more than 'nothing'."

"He's just someone I know." Someone that does not deserve their consistent badgering. Elias thankfully shifts the focus of the conversation to something about how horrible the lighting is.

I glance back in the direction of the bar, finding Graham with a smile on his face as he whisks and shakes glasses around like a juggler. A man of many mysteries.

It is weird he spends his mornings doing hard labor only to come here at night and continue working. Why would he do that? Is he in debt? Can he not afford to have one job?

The questions continue to pile one after the other and there's nothing stopping the curiosity from edging its way through my veins.

Exactly *who* is Graham?

CHAPTER EIGHT

GRAHAM

"Rush getting to you?" Sebastian pats my back.

I rewash the same glass that's been in my hands for the past ten minutes. The bar is far from its rush hour. It settled down a few moments ago after the work crowd cleared out. The work crowd and slime balls like the one who hit on Piper.

They were at the end of the bar when I clocked in for my shift. She smiled at him and he leaned a little too close to her and…On a real date, I wouldn't intervene. I shouldn't. Especially after how she reacted last time.

So, I swallowed my pride and pretended they were any other customer at the bar. The man kept flirting, and Piper blushed a flame red.

I nearly shattered the glasses from how tight my grip on them was. "I'm not going to help" is what I chanted repeatedly in my head. "I'm not going to help. I'm not going to help. I'm not going to help. I'm not going—"

I promise I had every intent to stay out of it, but then he disappeared, and Piper pleaded. Not directly, but it was there. She *needed* me. It sent a rush of adrenaline through me.

The second he returned, I did exactly what I craved to the moment I saw them together.

Since then, I have fought the urge to look in Piper's direction.

She's still seated at the booth in the corner with her colleagues. She seems like she would enjoy a quiet evening at home better than a night in a bar.

"I think the dish is clean," Sebastian rips me out of my thoughts. His Italian accent is thick and almost indecipherable in this noise.

"Always better to double check," I joke. Sebastian checks the taps beside me. "Who's the girl?"

"What?"

"The one in the corner you have been staring at for the past hour. I would have to be blind to not notice." I wipe my hands on the towel hanging on the edge of the sink. "Who is she?"

The answer to that question is complicated. Her colleagues asked if I was her boyfriend, and I had the smart idea to say, "Not yet." I wanted to see what it would do to her. The idea of us together. The idea of me being her boyfriend for real. Her only reaction to the sentence was a duck of her head, embarrassed.

We aren't dating and I doubt she would consider us friends. Friends have each other's contact information and don't only interact through coincidental meetings.

"Ah," Sebastian says.

"What 'Ah'?"

"She's special, isn't she?"

She's *different*. "I'm going to take out the trash."

He chuckles and I assume it's to make fun of me. I gather the bags in the back and exit the bar with a handful.

It's only when I'm outside that I realize why he was laughing.

She's here. Leaning against the bricks of the buildings with her hands tucked into the pockets of her jeans. She looks cold. I curse myself for not grabbing my jacket on the way out.

I throw the trash in the bin, gaining her attention. "Getting stuffy in there?" I ask.

"Yeah. Very chaotic."

I cross my arms over my chest. I haven't taken my break yet and right now feels like the perfect time to do so.

"Thanks for earlier, by the way."

"Of course. I will gladly pretend to be your boyfriend as much as needed. In fact, I think I might start a business."

"You would get many clients." *I only want one.*

"You think so?"

"Definitely. Feel free to use me as a reference." She pushes off the wall a little bit to face me an inch more. A little victory I will gladly accept.

"You can't take that back. It's out in the universe now."

She laughs. It's soft and short, but I want another one. I *need* another one.

"You know, I'm surprised you are here. You don't seem much like the bar type."

"I'm not. What about you? Can't sit still?"

"It's both a blessing and a curse. Why are you here if it's not your scene?"

I expect her to shut down. I'm asking personal questions again but talking to her resets my filter every time until I forget social norms.

She sighs. "Because sometimes you have to do the things you don't want to."

"What do you mean?" I lean against the wall beside her.

"I don't like bars, but Lindsey and Elias do." At the eyebrow I raise, "my colleagues. The people I came here with."

"Right. They are…"

"Complete opposites?"

I smile. "I was going to say unique, but yeah."

"They are. But they are also Miss Sunshine and Mr. Grumpy of the office."

A laugh bubbles out of me. "I could see that."

A silence settles between us. I should go back inside. Sebastian is probably swarmed with orders and the last thing I need is to lose this job.

I kick at an invisible rock on the sidewalk. "Can I have your number?"

She scoffs. "Right. First Jordan, now you."

"What?" I smile through the unease in my chest. *Who's Jordan?*

A wary expression, then a slight upturn of the corner of her mouth. "What do you want my number for?"

I'm not sure how to answer that question and her scrutinizing gaze is not helping. "Well, there's this great new way to communicate called texting. You type these messages out on a phone—kind of like letters—and it will instantly send to the person you desire."

"Sounds like a trap."

I lean a shoulder against the wall. "That is an ongoing debate."

She fiddles with the hair tie on her wrist, twisting and tangling it between her fingers. I don't know when, but at some point, we both pushed off the wall and are now facing each other head-on. Except her gaze is bowed to the ground and I am focused intently on the top of her head.

A part of me wonders what it would be like to touch her hair. I immediately shut that part down.

Not cool, Graham.

Her head finally lifts. "Shouldn't you be working?"

"I am. Mingling with customers is part of the job."

"Oh, so you ask all of your customers for their phone numbers?" I freeze. "How do you manage to get anything done?"

Jokingly, "It's hard, but I've always loved a challenge."

Piper eyes me suspiciously but eventually straightens and makes for the door to go back inside.

"Is that a firm 'no'?" I shout after her.

She turns, "Sorry. My phone number is strictly reserved for someone without bad intentions."

"I'm as innocent as they come."

At that, she laughs. "Right. I could tell by the girl's name and phone number written on your arm."

I glance down at the ink. A woman with purple hair and long fingernails comes to mind. The light and fast press of her pen on my skin is still present. It's easier to ignore than to say "no" to such things.

When I raise my head and open my mouth to explain, she's already gone.

The bar is closed and I'm in the process of cleaning up. Piper left hours ago, her and Elias having to balance Lindsey between them. I had to hold the door open to prevent any further accidents.

Over the past few hours, I have had to fight the instinct to call Trumpet. Relationships are something we have never openly discussed. Most of our conversations are random nothings and idle flirting. But she might just know how to get through to someone like Piper.

"I'm going to finish up the back and then I'll lock up," Sebastian notifies me on his way to the back.

With him out of earshot, my urges take over. I pull my phone out of my back pocket and click on her contact.

A quick check at the time and I open our messages. She's usually asleep by now.

"Hi…" I start but instantly delete it. I sound like I'm in middle school again.

I hold the record button again. "Hey, any chance you know how to woo a woman?" Delete. Seriously? That's the best I can come up with?

Wooing women isn't my strong suit. Even though I have done it multiple times, every attempt has either ended with me getting dumped or mocked. I go too fast too soon. I don't want to do that with Piper. I don't want to scare her away.

"I happened to meet this woman the other day. She's caught my eye, but she's a tough nut to crack. Any advice? Oh, and no. She's very much conscious." I add the last part as a joke. Something light.

The bell above the door chimes as Jason enters the bar. I'm so thrown off I don't have time to stop myself before my thumb presses send. "No!"

"Did you lose your game again?" Jason grabs a rag from the bar and starts to wipe down a few tables.

When he gets stuck on something, he comes here to work through the block. Sebastian has no problem with having an employee he doesn't have to pay.

My phone burns a hole in my hand. "She's never going to contact me again," I say aloud, mostly to myself than to Jason.

He straightens from his bent stance and stares into me. "Are you talking about the gardener girl or the one you have been ogling all night?"

"Ogl—how do you know about that?"

"Sebastian called and asked if I could come help. Said his best bartender is too distracted to cater to customers.

My hands tighten around the broom handle. "I was not distracted."

"Okay, then your freak out is about the gardener." I fight the instinct to correct him for the fifth time. She is *not* a gardener. "I wasn't freaking out. I accidentally sent her a message."

"Did you delete it?"

My face pales. "You can do that?"

"Not anymore. There's a two-minute mark." He sighs a long, exaggerated sigh, before discarding the rag on the table and taking the broom from me. "Why don't you ask her out, already?"

"We're just friends." Even though I know it's true and it is all we will ever be, my tongue stings from the words.

CHAPTER NINE

PIPER

"I happened to meet this woman the other day."

It's the fourth time I have replayed his voice message. When my alarm went off, I checked my notifications and instantly went to his message. It's been at least ten minutes and I am sitting up in bed with the blanket loose around my waist.

I rewind the message. "I happened to meet this woman the other day."

I should answer. Maybe send him a voice message back that says "Don't do it". That would be appropriate.

Pressing the record button, I begin with "What do you mean you met a wo—" And delete. My voice doesn't sound nearly as calm as it should

Clearing my throat and straightening my spine, I try again. This time, I barely make through the first sentence before hitting delete. There's no way I'm sending that.

Maybe I shouldn't send a message at all. We have never talked about relationships before, let alone interest in other people. We only ever flirted with each other and I—it was safe.

My body falls back on the bed with my head landing in the pillows with a humph. His voice echoes from the phone I have pressed to my chest. I must have accidentally hit play again.

"I happened to meet this woman the other day. She's caught my eye, but she's a tough nut to crack. Any advice? Oh, and no. She's very much conscious."

I'd much rather the woman be unconscious. Then insanity would be a probable cause for his feelings.

And *advice?* What does he mean by that?

He's asking me—the same woman he has been flirting with for the past year—advice on how to win a woman's attention.

I roll onto my side and pull the blanket over my head.

Once Hazel's bedroom door opens and her slippers scuff across the floor, I finally put my phone down and get out of bed.

"Fresh baked cookies," I shout to passing strangers.

Hazel is beside me, holding the tray on display with a giant showcase smile.

Every other Saturday I stand on the street with her to help with her sales. This Saturday is particularly chilly with the wind blowing at twenty miles an hour. I'm not a meteorologist, but the feel is definitely unbearable.

No one stops or even glances in our direction. Hazel sets the plate down. "I don't understand why no one is fawning over these cookies. Do they not look delicious?" She shoves one in my face.

I instinctively tilt my head back. "They look great, Hazel."

There's a pout on her face when she drops it back down. She's been doing this for almost a year now, waiting for someone to give her a golden ticket. I wish I studied marketing so I could actually be of use.

"Maybe we should package a few and give them away for free. Well, the first one for free. Maybe it will entice people then."

"Great idea! I'll go ahead and pass out the already packaged ones. You want to wrap up a few more?"

"Sure." The word is barely out of my mouth before Hazel disappears in the crowd of rushing strangers.

Even on a weekend, the city doesn't know how to take a break.

I start packaging the few cookies left on one of the trays. We did have a few sales, *and* Hazel and I may have needed a snack break. I run out of paper and turn around to dig in Hazel's bags for more.

"How can someone so clean be so disorganized?" I speak aloud. Her bags are full of recipe books, notebooks, containers of treats, her street survival kit, and many more indecipherable things. I wouldn't be surprised if a bowling ball is buried somewhere in here.

"Selling cookies today?" Someone inquires as the sound of a box being set down follows.

"Yes, chocolate blue—" I turn to find Graham with half a cookie in his mouth. I know when he recognizes me because the raised brow falls and a half-sided smile appears.

"Are you a baker too?" His question is blocked by the food in his mouth and the hand in front of his lips.

"You have to pay for those." I point to the cookies in his hand.

He inspects them like they magically appeared in his grasp. Graham sets the stack on a napkin on the table, bends, and stands with a box in his hands. "I did."

He leans it towards me to show me the contents inside. It's full of fruit and a bag of flour. "I meant with money."

"Do you take checks?"

I'm about to refute his question. The stupid smirk on his lips is making my blood boil. How can someone so insufferable be present at all the worst times?

"Graham!" Hazel appears from behind him. She pats his back before coming to stand beside me. "What did you bring me?" Hazel greedily peeks into the box. "Oh! I've been wanting to make raspberry tarts."

"They were on sale," Graham notes.

"Did you grab some cookies?"

"Yes, but I haven't paid for them yet." His gaze finally goes back to me. There's playful teasing in his tone. I don't like it.

"What are you—" Hazel is half laughing in her sentence, until she follows Graham's gaze to me. "Oh.

Piper, Graham is the one who gives me all of the ingredients I bring home. He brings me food. I give him food; it's a trade we do. You don't have to pay, Graham."

Graham pulls his wallet out, "No, it's no problem. A dollar a piece, right?" He holds out ten dollars. He only grabbed four cookies.

Hazel pushes the money back to him. "No. For you, it's free. The fruit probably cost a fortune."

He nods and puts his wallet away but shoves the ten in a separate pocket with his hand.

"I'm sorry. I didn't realize you two…" They what? Have an agreement? Know each other? Seem particularly too friendly?

Graham focuses back on me. "I didn't realize you and Hazel were friends."

I open my mouth to answer, but Hazel beats me to it. "Do you two know each other?" Her eyes are full of surprise.

"We met at a cafe."

No. No. No. The last thing I need is for Hazel to connect the dots, but by the look on her face and the way she folds her lips into her mouth, she already knows.

"I see." She wiggles her eyebrows at me.

Normally, this is where I would panic, but I hold onto the hope my best friend would never force me on someone.

"Oh, a huge crowd is coming." Hazel grabs a stack of cookies. "I'm going to pass these out. Piper, can you hold down the fort?"

I take it back. I always suspected Hazel would become my enemy.

There's no time to answer before she's gone. I cross my arms and give Graham the most annoyed stare I can muster. "Why would you tell her that?"

"She asked." He picks his stack of treats back up and bites into one.

"Why didn't you lie?"

His eyes narrow and he's biting back a grin. "Are you scared she'll think there's something between us?"

My eyes drift to anywhere but him and his smug face. "There's no reason for her to think that."

"If you say so."

"Why are you here, anyway? Don't you ever sleep?"

He works in construction, at a bar, and apparently grocery shopping for my best friend. When does he ever find the time to do anything else?

"I like to take power naps. It's nice to know you're concerned for me though."

"I wouldn't go that far."

"What are you doing tonight?"

"Excuse me?"

"I have this dinner I have to go to."

"Sounds boring."

A laugh escapes his lips. I'm so surprised that a swarm of something fills my belly. "I thought you might want to keep me company. Be my plus one. Make sure I don't fall asleep during it."

I fiddle with the container in front of me. Open the lid. Close the lid. Open the lid. Close the lid.

"Am I really that unappealing?"

"I would more so describe it as annoying."

A light chuckle. "That's fair."

I don't say anything. Maybe if I stay quiet enough, he'll leave. Maybe his voice along with the squeaky boots he's donning and the obnoxious chewing, will disappear into the chaos.

A paper floats in front of me. "What is this?" I pick it up and read the email scrawled on it.

"You clearly don't trust me with your phone number, or you just don't know how to work your phone. Either way, if you change your mind, email me."

I fight the laugh bubbling in my chest. "You want me to…email you?"

"No, Piper. I want you to talk to me. If emailing is the way, so be it." There's something about the way he says my name. So certain. So firm.

My phone vibrates in my pocket. I don't usually turn on the ringtone. It's too ear-piercing no matter the volume. "I have to take this."

"No worries. I have to go anyway." He makes to leave but hesitates. "I'll keep an eye out for an email. It's at seven o'clock tonight."

When he disappears, I press the phone to my ear. "Hey, M—"

"Piper, where are you right now?" My mother's voice is full of disguised worry.

"I'm out with Hazel. What's wrong?"

"Kyle has locked himself in his room and is refusing to open the door. Your fa—John is trying to find some tool."

Mom carries on her rant. It's not the first time she has slipped and almost called John my father. It's also not the first time Kyle has locked himself in his room. Why Mom and John haven't taken the lock off his door is beyond me.

"Mom," I try to keep my voice calm. "I'm sure he's fine. Did you try using the bobby pin on top of his door trim?"

With the type of door knob my brother has, if you have something thin and strong enough, it will push the lock back into place, which is why we keep a bobby pin on top of the door trim of his door.

"Yes, but it's not working." She's exasperated.

Knowing Mom, she probably tried it once or twice and then gave up. You have to have just the right technique to unlock it.

"I think he's holding his thumb over the doorknob. I don't understand why he does this. I mean, is it that bad to live with us?"

Her question is rhetorical, but I can't stop the answer that appears in my mind and lays on my tongue. "Did you line it up just right with the center?" I look to Hazel who has finally returned to the table with a quirked brow.

"You honestly think I did it wrong?"

"No, Mom. That's not what I—"

"It's about time!" she exclaims, but it's not to me. John's voice is muffled on her end. "Well, hurry up. We don't have all day, John."

After a few beats of silence, I ask "Mom? Did you figure it out?"

"Oh, yes. We got it. Love you." She hangs up before I have a chance to say anything back.

"Everything okay?" Hazel questions.

"Kyle locked himself in his room again."

"Poor kid."

Before I slide my phone back into my pocket, a message catches my attention.

DAD: Hey, honey. Hope
you're having a good day.
Love you.

Ignoring it, I tuck my phone back into my jeans. "What's this?"

I look down to the paper Hazel holds between us, scrutinizing the email address scrawled on it. I take it from her grasp and shove it in my bag.

A knowing smirk is on her lips. "You must be a whole other type of woman to get a guy to give you his email instead of his phone number. I always knew you were the prettier one."

I roll my eyes. "Please, look at you. There is no doubt in my mind who the prettier one is." Hazel's wavy brown hair, flawless skin, and curves lure more men in than she knows how to handle.

"I didn't know you were ready to date. You even asked for his number."

"I didn't ask for his number."

"Sorry. Email. Regardless, I'm proud of you. Finally taking that leap into the world."

"There is nothing to be proud of and there will be no leaping. He gave me his email on his own accord and there is not one ounce in me that has a desire to go to this dinner he invited me to.”

“He invited you to dinner?”

Trumpet. “Is that all of the cookies we have left?” I motion to the stack on the table, but Hazel doesn’t so much as glance in that direction.

“Look, I’m not going to force you to go out with him, but it might be good for you.”

“I don’t date.” I remind her for the hundredth time. “And even if I did, it wouldn’t be with Graham.”

“It wouldn’t be with the psycho mystery man on your phone either.”

My heart seems to drop into the pit of my stomach. Hazel has this theory that I have pushed all of my romantic feelings onto him because he’s safe. Little does she know he is out there swimming in the dating pool.

“I don’t know what you’re talking about.” My voice comes out small.

“Piper, you can’t put all of your energy into some guy you don’t even know is real. Maybe going on a date with Graham—whether it amounts to something or not— will be a good way to get your mind off of psycho-man.”

Going out with Graham would certainly take my mind off things. He infuriates me so much that being in his presence alone clears my mind of anything else. But that would mean leading Graham on into thinking we could be something we will never be.

As annoying as he is, he doesn’t deserve that.

“Maybe.” I finally say. “But Graham is the last person I would go on a date with.”

CHAPTER TEN

PIPER

"Mom has been calling me endlessly," Sarah tells me over the phone.

I press the device closer to my ear with my shoulder as I maneuver the dollar crafts around in front of me. "I don't know what to tell you." I was in the process of making my second wind chime of the evening when my sister decided to call and badger me about these blind dates.

"Tell me you have found someone to go on a date with. Or are going to move to another country. Anything to get Mom off my back."

"Why is she calling *you*?"

"For the same reason she wouldn't stop calling me when you moved out of the house and the same reason she forced me to drop you off at work on your first day."

I remember that day. Mom made Sarah promise to meet my boss and colleagues before driving away. Sarah only dropped me off at the curb outside of the building and gave a wave before departing. Mom, however, thinks

Sarah went inside and has the phone number of every colleague of mine.

"She thinks I'm the only one that can get through to you. Well, me or Hazel, but Hazel always finds a way out of it. She really needs to teach me." The last sentence is quieter, more of a thought to herself.

"Just go on one date. One date and she'll be satisfied."

"That's what she said the last twenty dates."

"I hear Marley's cousin is really cute. And he's in finance. I bet he's got quite the savings…"

I ignore the singsong voice of hers. "Doesn't he also have a cat?"

"Yeah, so?"

"Oh, nothing." I pick up a wooden circle and dab it with a paintbrush. "Just that I am deathly allergic to cats."

"You don't have to date his cat. You only need to date him."

Harmony screams in the background of her end. I latch onto it. "How's Harmony? Is she still learning her alphabet?"

"Nice try." My shoulders sag. "Find a guy. Anyone. He doesn't even have to be interested in you. Just find someone and bring him to dinner on Sunday. Maybe then Mom will get off both of our cases."

She doesn't say anything else or give me the opportunity to speak before she hangs up the phone.

I slump in my seat, pulling the phone from its spot and laying it hard on the table in front of me. It's Tuesday night, which means I have a total of four days to find someone to bring to this dinner. A family dinner.

The urge to fake an illness is strong, but even germs won't keep my mother's persistence away.

I stand and rub the tension away from my thighs. Sitting cross legged is only fun in the beginning of a two-hour period. As I walk down the hallway to the bathroom, I pass Hazel's bedroom. She has some romance movie playing on her laptop and is quoting every word of it. I know because she has her headphones on making her deaf to the actual volume of her voice.

Normally, I ignore it and continue on my way, but something about the confession she echoes on her tongue makes my chest ache.

Romance movies aren't my thing. Romance in general is not my thing. Well, maybe 'not my thing' isn't the right phrase. Do I love the idea of being wooed by someone? Of receiving a bouquet of flowers or cuddling or just being in the moment with someone who gives you butterflies? I only dream about it every night.

The idea of it all quickly turning into something else with the flick of a switch is too detrimental to be worth it to actually act upon those thoughts. I'm much happier alone than with someone who would hold more weight in their hands than they know what to do with.

Instead of going to the bathroom to put on a face mask, I make a beeline for the front door. A bowl of ramen sounds delicious right now.

The grocery store is small, mostly due to the numerous aisles packed closely together. Despite this, I'm able to maneuver through without having to slow my pace or dodge other customers. The best time to go here is when the moon is out.

The styrofoam cup scrapes against my nails as I pick it off the shelf and toss it into my basket. The goal of only grabbing one instant noodles pouch turned into a basket of snacks. Somehow, I ended up with a few packs of chocolate, a case of flavored water, and salt and vinegar chips. Not my healthiest choice, but definitely fit for a Tuesday night.

"These would be perfect for our movie night!" a woman nearby exclaimed as she shoves a box of Swedish Fish towards the man accompanying her. They are both dressed casually, but not as casual as the sweatpants I didn't change out of. I adjust the oversized jacket on my shoulders.

"You don't like them." I stopped looking in their direction, but I hear the amusement in his tone.

"So? Just because I don't like them now, doesn't mean—"

"You won't like them in the future? What is with your obsession of forcing yourself to like food?"

There's a moment of silence before I hear something crash into a cart and an excited "You're the best."

I glance up to find her arms wrapped around his neck and a loving smile on his lips.

A sick feeling settles into the pit of my stomach. I decide to return the can of tuna to the shelf. Probably not the best thing to eat when I'm nauseous.

I turn and make my way towards the front, but something falls from a nearby shelf, dragging my attention with it. I slam into something and cause the basket to tilt in my hand.

"I'm sor—" I start, but when my eyes meet a pair of grass-like ones the apology dies on my tongue. "What are you doing here?"

He bends down to pick up the bag of chips that fell out of my basket and carefully places them back inside. "At the local grocery store? Oh, just taking a stroll. You should try it sometime. The place has quite the artwork." The urge to punch him is strong.

"Having a rough night?" He nods in the direction of my items.

"A woman can't buy herself snacks at nine o'clock at night without being sad?" I'm getting irritated at him for no reason. I know this, and yet…

"Of course not. A woman can totally buy some snacks at nine and be completely elated. But after nine fifteen and with so many salty foods…" I analyze the items I have. The water isn't salty. "It can be a little suspicious."

"I could say the same thing about you with…" I search, looking for any flaw, but the only thing I find is the smallest stain on his t-shirt. "Shouldn't you be working at one of your many jobs?"

I push past him to continue my walk towards the register. He catches up with me.

"I am. We ran out of some things so I ran over here to grab it."

"You ran out of things?"

He shrugs. "Sebastian wanted to try a fall themed night for women. Promote the bar a little with Thanksgiving around the corner. Who knew leaves as garnish would be such a hit?"

I give a short snort. "You came to a grocery store to buy leaves?"

"I told you. This place has quite the artwork." There's a mischievous grin on his face and a glint in his eyes.

We make our way to the only open register. The man working it is slow with the scans of the items for the person in front of me, I assume that is why Graham hasn't left my side.

"So, Pipes, what are *you* doing here? Don't tell me you are throwing a salt themed party."

I almost roll my eyes. "Just wanted something quick to eat that will remind me of the logistics of everything else."

"Ramen is logistical?"

"Nope." I pop the 'p'.

"Well, at least promise me you are going to heat it up first."

"What am I? A psychopath?"

"You certainly do have a uniqueness about you."

We move an inch forward in the line. He doesn't make a motion to leave, only picks up a piece of candy from the shelf beside us and pretends to study it.

"Aren't you supposed to be looking for leaves?"

"I never got an email…" He leaves the statement hanging in the air between us.

He didn't get an email for the same reason Potential Psycho received an 'I don't know' message instead of the advice he wanted. There is not an ounce in my body that desired to fulfill their wishes.

"I just wondered if maybe you typed it in wrong. Or maybe I wrote it down wrong."

"I wouldn't know."

"That stung more than I anticipated."

I begin to set my items on the conveyor belt.

"You know, I've never had this problem before."

"An issue with your email?"

"No. A woman making it impossible to ask her out."

I freeze for a moment, my hand paused above the belt with the pack of ramen in hand, before I regain my composure. "I guess not all girls are eager to fall at the feet of a man who pretended to be their boyfriend."

"Careful, Piper, you almost make it sound like you'd rather it was real."

"How are you all this evening?" The man at the register interrupts our conversation. I wish stores had a way of giving their employees tips. I would give him a very generous one.

"Good. How are you?" I respond. He answers curtly and bags my items.

I'm so distracted in swiping my card and answering the cashier's small talk I don't notice Graham grabbed my bags until I reach for them.

He walks towards the exit and I have to hurry to catch up to him. "What are you doing?"

He glances at me over his shoulder. "I can't possibly let you wallow by yourself with ramen, Piper. What kind of man would I be?"

"The kind that doesn't bother strangers."

When we are outside and the cold air has whisked itself through my hoodie, he stops. "Strangers?" He takes one step forward. There's plenty of space between us. Plenty. But a warmth is emanating off of him and burning my skin. "Well, let this *stranger* at least heat the food up for you."

He doesn't wait for my answer before stalking off towards the bar.

CHAPTER ELEVEN

GRAHAM

"What about the leaves?" Piper questions from beside me. She hasn't tried to snatch the bag out of my hand yet. Then again, I purposely switched it to the opposite hand when she fell into step with me.

"Huh?"

The annoyance in her voice is as clear as day. "The *leaves*? The ones you said you were in the store for." I did say that, didn't I?

In all honesty, I don't even know if the grocery store would sell something like that. Plus, if we used leaves as garnish, we would use the mint leaves we have a continual stock of.

I happened to be taking the trash out when I saw Piper walking into the store. The crowd wasn't large inside the building and Sebastian put two of us on for the night so there's no harm in me taking a quick ten-minute break to wander the aisles of the grocery store adjacent to us. "The event doesn't exist either, does it?" Event?

She must see the hesitation in my eyes because she shoves her hands into her pockets, hard.

I open the door to the bar for her and let her step inside first. She halts barely a foot inside, making her back press against me for the briefest second before she moves out of reach. "Can you give me the bag now?"

Piper holds her hand out but doesn't so much as bother glancing in my direction. Instead, all of her attention is on the tables of customers around us.

"Relax." I whisper in her ear, fighting the laugh bubbling inside me. "I'm not going to make you sit in the center of the bar with your instant noodles. I'm not that cruel."

I press a hand to the small of her back, intending to guide her, but she jumps away from the touch. She shifts, then motions for me to lead. I do so without touching her this time.

I take us to the furthest corner of the bar, the one tucked away in the shadows, and set her bag down on top of it. A part of me hesitates in doing so. What if she runs the second I turn? To be honest, I wouldn't blame her. She probably had an entire evening planned and here I am: ruining it.

Busying myself with other things, I grab a glass and fill it with ice and water. I tell myself it's the safest option because if I turn around and she's no longer there, I can pretend the drink was for me all along. Yet, when I turn, she's plopped on the barstool studying me.

I set the glass in front of her. "Do you always pick up women by hunting them down at the grocery store?"

The corner of my mouth tilts. "Depends. Is it working?"

She rolls her eyes and takes a sip of the cold water. "I guess it's better than an adder hunting their mate by scent."

She gets more and more fascinating by the minute.

At my curious expression. "I have a…friend who knows a lot about animals."

"This friend sounds like someone I'd get along with."

She laughs and the sound is so beautiful I don't care it's at my expense. "Please. You two couldn't be more different."

"Really?" I do a quick glance around the room and when I find there are no customers waiting, I lean my elbows on the bar in front of her. "What is she like?"

"*He.*" The word sends a strike to my gut. "And he's charming, funny, and doesn't stalk people."

"Sounds boring."

Her gaze falls to the motion of her fingers tracing the sweating glass between us. "Perfectly so…" Her voice is barely a whisper.

"Why aren't you dating him, then?"

Piper's head snaps up. "What is your obsession with dating?"

"If he's so perfect, why not date him? What? Does he have a girlfriend?"

"I wouldn't be surprised if he does."

"Ah, I get it."

"What?"

"He's your safety net."

"Safety net?"

"You know? The person you secretly see yourself having a life with, but you would never actually act on it. The safety net."

She looks at me with an expression I can't decipher. If I didn't know any better, I'd say I hit the head on the nail.

I pull a pack of instant noodles out of the bag. "Let me go heat this up."

The break room is right around the corner and the noodles only need two or three minutes, but I intentionally stop at the other end of the bar to check on the few customers sitting there. The other bartender is helping a table in the corner and Sebastian is holed away in his office.

When Piper is staring at her phone and her expression has softened, I make my way back to her.

"Here." I sit the cup in front of her and pass her a fork.

"Thank you." She's quick to shove a bite into her mouth, not even bothering to blow the steam away.

"Can I ask you a question?"

She nods, distracted by the food in front of her.

"You asked me why I'm so obsessed with dating, but why do *you* run from it?"

She stirs the food absently. "I don't run from it."

"Right. Why do you avoid it?"

"You don't know me."

"Not from a lack of trying."

She sighs and slides the cup away from her.

I pushed her too far. The fear is beating against my skull. Why do I always do this? I make a motion to step away, but her next words halt me.

"I'm not a fan of the ending."

I open my mouth to say something, I'm not exactly sure what, but she beats me to it.

"That, however, doesn't seem to matter."

"What do you mean?"

Piper drops her head in her hands with a groan. "My mom is determined to marry me off."

The memory of our first meeting flies back to me. "Hence the blind date."

"Yep." She pops the word and it is so depressing. "No matter what I say, she only grows more stubborn. Now I have to find someone to take to our family dinner just to stop her from more blind dates."

"Take me." I'm so quick to offer that *I* haven't even processed my words completely yet.

She laughs and laughs and laughs. "Right. I'll send you a formal invite tomorrow."

"I mean it."

It takes a minute of scrutinizing me, but eventually she sobers. "You're being serious."

"As serious as the king of the jungle."

"Why?"

"Well, it doesn't exactly seem like the time to crack a joke."

"Why would you do something like that? For a complete stranger."

I almost want to shake her. "I told you. I don't want to be strangers with you, Piper."

"So you want to battle your way through my family dinner?"

I half laugh. "You make it sound like I'm going to war."

"Clearly you know nothing about my family."

"Then allow me to learn."

"You want me to take you to my family's dinner and pretend we are dating?"

"Third time's a charm."

She doesn't say a word, doesn't so much as smile, and I wonder if she's waiting for the punchline. I'm not going to give her one.

I grab her phone from between us and begin to dial my number.

"What are you doing?"

"I'm adding my nu—" I stop dead in my tracks when a name replaces the phone number I type. "Potential Psycho?"

She rips the phone out of my hand and searches for something. Coming up empty, "how do you know his number?"

"His…?" I'm about to ask why she would have someone in her contacts if she considers them a psycho when the realization hits me.

I pull my phone out of my pocket and find Trumpet. I press the call button and hold the phone against my ear, listening to the ring. Piper's phone lights up with an incoming call from "Potential Psycho".

Slowly, I retract my phone from my ear and set it between us so she can read the screen.

"You're…?" The words die on her tongue.

I'm about to say something, anything, to explain, although I'm not entirely sure what I need to explain, but she pauses everything. Without so much as a second thought, she stands from her spot and marches out of the bar.

It's only a few moments later, after I hear the bell from the door closing, I realize what has happened.

"What was that about?" Jason slides onto the barstool where Piper was moments before.

I think I just met the woman I have been falling for over the past year.

Jason opens the bag in front of him. It contains the saltiest foods one could find. "Are you dehydrated?"

"What?" I shake my head and the thousands of thoughts coursing through my mind. "Why are you here?"

He sets a backpack on the stool beside him and pulls stacks of books out of it. "Studying."

"You know? I don't get you sometimes. You don't have any exams."

He shrugs as though it's enough explanation. "Speaking of studying, have you looked into school anymore?"

I wipe a rag over an invisible stain on the counter. "Why would I do that?"

"So we aren't acknowledging your recent search history. Got it."

The idea of delving into my future plans after being abandoned—for lack of a better word—by the same woman I never thought I would meet, is horrendous.

"I have to help the group at the other end." I tell Jason and maneuver to a waiting couple to our left.

I try to press pause on everything else in my head and focus solely on the task at hand, but the chattering and clanking around me seems to only echo my thoughts.

It took every ounce in me to not run after her. I glance at the door in hopes she will appear, but there's not even a shadow left in her wake.

Chapter Twelve

PIPER

"I'm not a fan of chocolate, but if you wait any longer to come grab it, I just might eat your stash." Potential Psycho—Graham's message sounds out in the bathroom of the studio.

It's the twentieth, maybe twenty-first, message he has sent today alone. Last night when he called me and I learned exactly who he is, every logical response fled from my mind. The only thing I could think to do was to run, to find somewhere, anywhere that he does not exist.

Potential Psycho isn't supposed to be real. At least, not physically present in my life. And to make matters worse, he's the same man who infuriates me like no other.

I knew he sounded familiar. I knew all of it was suspiciously easy and I still let myself—

My phone vibrates with another message. I consider shutting my phone off. I press play instead. "Listen, I'm just as surprised as you, but isn't it a good thing that we now know who each other is?"

No. This is the farthest thing from good.

I let myself feel things for the man I didn't know the name of. I let myself envision a life I knew I would never lead. It was my one and only outlet for all of the insecurities and vulnerabilities I tucked away.

Except that man now has a name and a face. He's someone I—someone who has feelings for someone else. It's so clear by the advice he asked for earlier and by the expression he had on his face the moment he realized.

He was supposed to be safe. Potential Psycho was supposed to be a random fluke, a gift the universe granted me, to live out those childish fantasies I will never get to.

I stare at my reflection in the bathroom mirror, noting the dark spots under my eyes. Pinching the skin to life and patting my cheeks, I look for the woman I made. The woman who would never be caught dead standing in a bathroom and second guessing everything over some guy.

When I finally find her, I stand and push myself out of the bathroom.

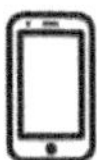

"Wait. I need you to rewind a few sentences." Hazel's fork clatters against her plate of alfredo.

We are seated in the Italian restaurant near my studio. It's the first lunch we have been able to share in the past week. That, and I owe Hazel for the pizza she bought the other day.

"The man you have been talking to for the past year—the same one who has some stalker tendencies and is the only man you have ever shown any interest in—is *Graham*?"

I nod with the mouthful of salad. "Unfortunately so."

Her hands clap together. "This is amazing!"

I nearly choke. "I'm sorry. Did you hear one word I said?"

"I hear what sounds like the perfect opportunity."

"What are you talking about?"

Hazel sits up straighter and clears her throat. "Your mom has been nagging you about dating, right?" I nod hesitantly.

"And you want her to stop bothering you about it, right?"

"Where are you going with this, Hazel?"

"Why not use Graham?"

"You lost me." I take a sip of the sweet tea.

She rolls her eyes. "Stay focused, Piper. You like Graham—" I'm about to refute her claim, when she holds up a hand. "Let me finish. You like Graham—whether you want to admit it or not—and he is now a real human being that you have access to. Why not date him? It would appease your mother and you could finally live out the life of a romance."

"Just when I think your plans couldn't get any crazier."

"What's so wrong with dating Graham?"

"You mean besides the fact that I don't date."

"So? It can be fake."

I laugh. "You want me to fake date Graham?"

"No. I want you to experience the life you have been depriving yourself of for your entire life and if that happens to involve fake dating Graham, then so be it."

Her words catch me so off guard I don't know what to say in response.

Instead, I ignore the vibration from my phone, and shove another bite into my mouth.

"Awe, honey," Lindsey's voice floats to me from the other end of the hallway. She's standing with her husband, a lunch box dangling from her hand. "You are so sweet."

For the tenth time this week alone, I feel nauseous. I dig into my purse for the tums I bought.

"I was thinking," Lindsey's husband starts to talk, "that my parents can take the kids for the evening and you and I can…" I don't get to hear the rest before Lindsey's giggling takes over.

I don't look in their direction. I don't want to find them embraced like I'm sure they are.

My phone vibrates again. I yank it out of my back pocket and press play on Graham's message. "I know this is shocking." His voice is filled with exhaustion. It sends a pang to my chest. "It shocked me too. But…can you please just answer me? Let me know you are at least still alive?" *Trumpet.*

CHAPTER THIRTEEN

GRAHAM

"A gin and tonic," the man across from me requests.

I get to work on making the drink, but it takes me thirty seconds longer than usual to complete it. I'm too distracted by the phantom rings in my pocket to focus long enough.

She hasn't answered one message or phone call. It shocked me too, but I didn't think she'd be that disappointed in me being the one she's been talking to.

Piper is a completely different person over the phone. So much so that it didn't even cross my mind she could be the same person as Trumpet. It explains why I have been so drawn to her, though.

A hand pats me on the back. "Need you at the other end." Sebastian orders me.

I move from my spot towards the other end of the bar where one lone person sits. I don't brother making eye contact with them or even glancing in their directions. I'm still distracted from my thoughts.

"What can I get you?" I ask.

"No cheesy pick-up line?"

My head snaps up to find the one woman I thought I'd never see again. "Piper?"

She's standing. Hasn't even bothered to sit and I wonder…

"You're not going to make another run for it, are you?"

She winces. "I'm sorry. That was a jerk move of me and I—I got in my head about things and I didn't know how to handle it."

"I understand." I soften, letting her see just how affected I am. "It surprised me too, but I think it was a good surprise."

"Please. We lead two completely different lives."

"So it was better when we didn't know who each other was?"

"Yes."

"Ouch." I jokingly place a hand over my heart, but the spot I rub at is sore.

"But it doesn't mean that I should have stormed out like that. I'm sorry."

"You have nothing to apologize for." She looks at me skeptically so I add "I mean it."
She nods. "Okay. Well, that's all I really came to say so I guess…"

Panic seizes me so I do the only logical thing I can think of. "Let me help you."

"What?"

"Take me to your family dinner."

She mumbles something inaudible. Then, "Why would I do that?"

"You need someone, right? And the reason you turned me down before was because we were 'strangers', but now—well, now we are friends."

"Friends?"

"Yes, and friends help friends."

"My family will assume we're dating."

"A side effect I'm willing to endure. We've got plenty of practice in that department."

Her lips twitch and I wonder how often she fights smiling.

"Come on. You know me. What's the worst that could happen?"

A thousand different emotions flash across her face and I can't decipher a single one of them. I can only imagine the list she is conjuring in her head. Do the pros outweigh the cons? Is she going to give me a million reasons why this is a bad idea?

"I promise to be on my best behavior."

"Why are you so willing to help me?"

Because maybe, just maybe, if she sees the good side of me and sees that I'm the same person she has been confiding in, she'll want to take a chance on me. "I want to help you."

After a moment of scrutinizing me, she finally says "Are you sure about this?"

I release a breath I didn't realize I was holding and nod.

"Okay."

CHAPTER FOURTEEN

"You don't think he's attractive?" Mom grills me for the third time. Ever since I walked through the front door—something that took way longer than needed due to Mom's constant interruption—Mom immediately started the interrogation of "who are you bringing to dinner?". Something I have Sarah to thank for.

Mom is chopping up some peppers with me leaning against the wall across from her while Kyle is playing a very loud game of astronauts in the living room.

"Mom." Convincing her to let the subject go is as easy as a tone-deaf person matching one of those perfect high notes: utterly disappointing.

"What? Just tell me, Piper. I'm your mother. You know you can tell me anything. I think he's rather charming. In fact, you two would have some very cute babies."

I showed her one picture—she peeked over my shoulder when Hazel sent me his Facebook profile—and it only fueled her motivation.

Then again, the first picture on his page is of him in an orange vest, guiding a class of children across the street. A part of me wonders who took the picture, but another part is wondering what his intention was in uploading such an adorable picture.

"I am not having his kids." I steal one of the unopened water bottles on the counter and take a sip.

"That's fine. I can get grandchildren through your sister. Speaking of which, have you told her about him?"

"Mom, there's nothing to tell."

She slices into a green pepper with careful precision. "Your sister would love to meet your new boyfriend."

"He's not my boyfriend. He's not even a friend. He's just a boy I happened to run into once or twice."

"That's what I said about your father." The memory of their relationship sends a stabbing pain to my chest and sinks into the pit of my stomach.

She has said a lot of things about my father including how handsome he was and how much of a caring and wonderful person he was and just how much they were made for each other, but the second he uttered that one sentence, her whole world turned on its axle. Suddenly, my father became a dream of a past life for her.

"Listen, all I'm saying is that he is a perfectly acceptable candidate."

"You sound like he's running for president."

She points the knife at me. "Dating one of my daughters is as serious as an election. Not just anyone can marry you."

I scoff and push off the wall. "You set me up with a guy who owns an apartment full of birds."

"He loves animals."

"He ate them."

"And he didn't work out, did he? See my point?" Mom's skill in turning things around to make her sound right has always amazed me. "Graham would be perfect for you."

"You don't even know him."

"I don't have to. The tone of your voice when you talk about him is all that matters."

"What do you mean? This is my voice."

"No," Mom shakes her head. "I know what I'm talking about, Piper."

A handful of guys have been in my life and every single one ran out the door the second I so much as yelled "boo". They quickly learned I am not the quiet type I come off as and I am far from the pushover everyone expects.

Despite how much they seemed invested, they withdrew the second they realized their efforts were futile. All except one, that is, but even he eventually left.

Graham, however, has only imbedded himself more into my life from the second I berated him for his act of kindness.

I'm not interested in him. Not long-term, but maybe a short-term, no strings attached romance wouldn't be so bad.

"What are you smiling at your phone about?" Hazel surprises me as she plops down on the couch opposite of me, ensuring not to crush my outstretched legs.

The couch creaks below us.

I hide the phone in the pocket of my hoodie. "Nothing. Did you just get home?"

"Traffic. Is it Graham?"

Her question throws me so off guard my face turns red. Yes, that's why my face is red. "No."

Hazel wags a finger at me. "Liar. Tell me the truth."

"We're just friends." It's the truth so I beg the tightness in my chest to ease up.

"That's what they all say, Piper."

"He's coming to my family's dinner on Sunday."

Hazel folds her lips in.

"What? Just say it."

Instantly, her expression morphs and she pokes her fingers at me. "You like him."

"In a matter of personality? He's okay."

"Oh, whatever. Can I come with?"

"Where?"

"To the dinner. I want a front row seat to all of this."

I stand, gifting her the blanket I had laying on my lap. Hazel adjusts it to wrap around her shoulders. "Absolutely not."

"Why not?" She whines like she's a toddler and someone stole her favorite toy. "I promise to only take one picture. Scout's honor." She holds her hand up with all fingers pointed to the ceiling.

"As much as I trust your word, there will be no show for you to witness." Upon opening the fridge, I am greeted with bowls of batter, containers of treats, various fruits, and a few containers of Mom's leftovers. I grab the bowl of chili she made a few days ago.

"Heat me some up too, please." I set the bowl on the counter to ration it out and pop it into the microwave. "I won't go, but I fully expect to hear all of the details after."

The microwave hums as it spins with our food inside.

"So Graham told me the bar he is working at is having a trivia night tomorrow…" there's a teasing in her tone and I don't know why.

"No."

"Why?"

"I have to work."

"It will be after."

"I'm not in the mood to drink."

"There's water."

"I don't like trivia."

The couch creaks under Hazel's shifts to face me. "Why don't you want to go? Is there something you haven't told me about Graham?"

He makes me think and feel things I should not be thinking and feeling. He throws my world upside down and makes me forget the rules I carved in stone.

"I have nothing against him," I tell Hazel. "I just don't want to spend my evening out."

"Okay, I'll let it go. For now."

"We are mere acquaintances and that is as far as it goes." I repeat for the tenth time in the past five minutes.

Graham may distract me from the ways of society, but that is a minor inconvenience I intend to avoid for eternity.

CHAPTER FIFTEEN

GRAHAM

"Do you know one of my biggest pet peeves? The silent letters in a word. There is no need for pterodactyl to have a 'p' at the beginning if we aren't going to say it." My thumb releases the record button as I finish my thought. I immediately send it to Piper.

We have been messaging back and forth for the past few hours. If I'm being honest, it started out awkward—mostly on my part—and made me second guess just how old I am. Then, our conversation took a turn when she sent a message back with her laugh mixed in and a strike of electricity struck my chest.

I haven't stopped cracking jokes since. If only to hear her speaking through a laugh again...
I will do whatever I need to make sure she answers my messages.

My phone buzzes on the table. I stop typing on the computer and pick it up.

"How would you even pronounce it with the 'p'?" Piper's voice comes through the phone.

I press record. "Exactly my point." I try to sound out the word using the 'p' and it only proves my argument further. Silent letters are useless.

When the message is sent, my research resumes. I have been reading a university's page on their English program. The poster in Piper's hallway caught my eye and I have nothing better to do at the moment so I researched it.

They have a great course focusing on writing about sensitive subjects like Truman Capote's true crime novel. It's a book I have read five times, but not once did the read get easier. It's a different experience to read something that humanizes murderers. Bone-chilling.

I can only imagine how fascinating the class will be. For actual students that is.

Another buzz from my phone has me pausing my reading.

Laughter pours through the line. "I think this is why they deemed the 'p' silent, so no one has to go through the torture of trying to pronounce it."

I'm quick to respond. "Are you saying my pronunciation is poor? I think I did quite the good job. Should get an award for my pronunciation." I press the delete button and try again. "Or silent letters should just not exist at all. Your turn, Trumpet. Biggest pet peeve."

I set the phone down on the table with a quiet slam. The TV in the living room is playing Animal Planet, a campus video is playing on the laptop, and soft music is floating from the speaker in my bedroom. Yet, the atmosphere is still similar to a suffocating silence.

I don't have time to resume my searching before another message comes through. This one is from Jeff.

JEFF: Are you free
  Sunday?

A notification of a message from Piper pops up at the top of the screen. I'm quick to respond to Jeff.

         ME: I have plans. Do you
           need something?

The second I hit send, I go over to Piper's message. "Biggest pet peeve? It has to be when there are a thousand things going at once. For example, if the TV is on, someone is playing music, and there is another video or talking all at the same time. It's way too chaotic and I don't know how anyone can accomplish anything in such an environment."

A heat creeps up my skin. I grab the remote and mute the TV. The music is still playing, but I feel it's a fair compromise.

"Do you have to work in complete silence?" I ask into the speaker. How anyone is able to do *that* is the real question.

A ping rings out, but I shrink back into my seat when I see "Jeff" as the contact.

JEFF: Don't tell me you
  got another job.

You're going to work
yourself to death, Fischer.

ME: No new job. I have

I stop typing when I get to this part. What do I have? It's not an appointment and it's definitely not a job.

A date? No. In my experience, a date is generally only two people, and I have a feeling there will be at least triple that amount on Sunday.

I don't know how to phrase what Sunday is so I delete the last sentence and hit send.

I check my messages with Piper, but there is still nothing new. Reluctantly, I set the phone down on the table and resume my research.

A key in the lock jiggles, but I stay focused on my task. "What are you doing?" Jason asks as the door shuts and his shoes scuff against the floor.

"Nothing." I slam the face of the computer close.

"Is that my laptop?"

"Yeah."

"Why?" He reaches to grab it so I immediately shove it out of his grasp.

"Because mine is dead and I can't find the charger."

"So you thought you would resort to stealing mine?" I don't bother answering as I continue to protect the stolen—borrowed item. "Why were you even in my room?"

"Relax. I didn't snoop through your things. Interesting box under your bed by the way. I didn't peg you as the kind to hide things in the most obvious spots."

"Shut up. What *exactly* is so important that you resorted to thievery?"

"I'm offended you think so lowly of me." My phone pings between my words and I fight the itch to grab it. "I'm doing some research, if you must know."

"Why?"

"What's with all of the questions?" Jason is never this curious, especially about things involving me. He could care less about how I spend my time or what I do. "Did something happen?" I give up on my fight to protect the device and stand to check the contents of the fridge when Jason scrubs a hand down his face. I pull out a box of leftover pizza.

"Mother set up a date with Jasmine."

Through a bite, "So? Just call it off like you usually do."

"I would, except there will be reporters at the next table documenting whether Jasmine and I show up or not. As much as I despise our parents pinning us together, I can't leave Jasmine to be the headline single in tomorrow's news."

"Then go."

Jason stares at me like I told him to go into the woods and fight off a bear.

"Look, you both are uninterested in each other romantically—which has been made clear on multiple occasions—so what could it hurt to just show up and pretend to satisfy your parents?"

"If I go, Mother will start sending out wedding invitations."

"Can you make sure mine comes to my parents' address? I'm pretty sure Pete from downstairs has been stealing my mail."

Jason groans and snatches his laptop from the table. I'm too pleased with myself to care. That, and the second I hear his bedroom door close, I reach for my phone. There is a message from Piper at the top of the many notifications.

I turn the volume down, click on it, and press it to my ear. "Silence doesn't exist. Even in the quietest moments, you can hear something. Whether it be a cricket or the beating of your own heart or even your breathing, you can hear *something*. So when there's a lot of noises piled on top of that, it makes it hard to focus. I don't work in silence, I just don't like chaos."

Her sentences aren't constructed with perfect grammar or the most astounding vocabulary. What she says isn't even something fundamental or life altering. But the *way* she says it and how her voice bears a truth I wonder if she has ever spoken aloud before, I am dumbstruck.

I turn off the TV and head into my room. The second my bedroom door is shut, I turn the stereo off and sit down. In silence. Except, Piper is right. It's not silent.

If I listen close enough, I can hear a faint hum from someone on the other side of the wall and the breaths escaping my nose. It's not silent at all.

I grew up in a quiet house so I always found a way to fill the void. From blasting music to using surround sound for even one episode of a sitcom to having a thousand appliances going at once or making my own music with these makeshift drums I crafted, I have always filled the silence with something—anything to make it feel like there is something in all the nothing.

I haven't been able to stand silence ever since. Part of the reason I work in construction and at one of the noisiest bars. I'm constantly surrounded by noise and people.

I've grown so accustomed to it that I can't do anything without something in the background.

But with just a few sentences, Piper has changed my entire belief system. There is no silence. Even when I think I am not surrounded by something, I can hear even the faintest noise.

I have never met anyone who could change the way I see the world so quickly. Usually, people (Jason) just berate me for all of the noise and chaos I create. They never told me why they find it annoying or why they can't stand it. Piper, however, has opened my eyes to something entirely new.

The thought makes me wonder what she is doing at this exact moment. Is she also sitting in a silent—*quiet* room listening to everything she can? Or is she somewhere so chaotic that she is dreaming of the second she is alone and free from the noise?

An image of her becoming overwhelmed from everything around her makes my arms crave to wrap around her and hold her tight. For my hands to press gently against her ears and muffle the sounds. For my voice and only *my* voice to be a beacon bringing her out of the confusion.

My entire being itches to do *any* of those things. Or even just be in the same room as her.

This thought jolts my senses.

I know something intrigues me about Piper, but I didn't realize *how* intrigued by her I am.

Every part of me wants to know every part of her. Not just the physicality of it all—although I'm sure I would not be disappointed in that department—but to know the sound of her yawn when she stretches in the morning. Or all of the variations of her laugh and how to produce each one.

I want to know who she is underneath this barrier she continues to put up. I want to know Piper.

I like her. I like her more than the friend I told her I would be. I like her in ways she would probably run and hide from if she knew even a hint of them. I like her and any part she is willing to offer me.

Romance is something I have always been poor at. From the moment I started dating in middle school to my last failed relationship a year ago. Some say I dive in headfirst and scare each one away, but I think I just haven't found someone willing to dive in with me yet.

Piper may just be her.

My thumb holds down the record button on my phone and I bring my lips close to the speaker. I want every word to be picked up perfectly. I want Piper to have no mistake in hearing the words I utter.

"You make it sound like a dream. If only you were with me to show me just how much silence doesn't exist."

I press send and clutch the phone tightly in my hand. My nerves are on fire and every part of me is begging to turn back time.

A minute passes.

I took it too far. Way too far.

Two minutes.

Piper is obviously not the kind of woman to respond to such a thing.

Three minutes.

I got way in over my head and too confident. Why do I do the things I do?

Four minutes.

Way to go, Graham. Messing up just another good thing in my life. Well, it was good while it—

My phone vibrates in my hand and a ping rings out in the silence—quiet.

I'm quick to press play on the message that came through. Her voice is lighthearted, and I wish I could hear it in person.

There is a certain solidarity in reading in the midst of chaos. Leaning against the bar with a book lying on top of the counter and my elbows burning from their strain against the wood, is one of the most peaceful experiences the world has to offer.

The boisterous conversations, party music barely audible from the speakers, and the clinking of glasses sends of a wave of calm through my veins. Some find the atmosphere distracting and far from the perfect place to pop open a book. I find it to be the perfect reading spot.

The book open in front of me is one of my favorites: *The Great Gatsby*. It's the fourth or fifth time I have read the narrative, and I still find myself circling new details or clues I didn't notice the first three or four reads. "How can you read in such chaos?" Sebastian's Italian accent is thick around his words.

He immigrated from Italy to open a bar here in America. He is only a few years older than me, but he treats me like a kid regardless. As long as he is signing the paychecks, it's fine with me.

"Are you pretending?"

I don't bother glancing up from the book or shifting my position. Instead, I circle an interesting word and respond, "It's like inserting myself into the world of Gatsby." With the amount of drinking and chaos in the storyline, it's not entirely a lie.

"Remind me why you work here again?" He has questioned my decisions on multiple occasions of catching me reading during the slow times of the bar. As long as no one is standing or sitting on the other end of the counter, reading is fair game.

"No one is in need of a drink or reassurance." I glance up to double check and am proved right.

"That is not what I meant. Why are you working at a bar and God knows where else when you could so easily be an author of one of those things."

I try not to take offense of him referring to a book as a "thing". "Writing isn't my thing."

"Then something else in the world of literature. I said it before and I will say it again, you would make a great teacher or professor. People flock to you like you are a drug."

I do tend to draw people in, but for entirely different reasons. When I was younger, I thought about pursuing the world of English. I would be doing the two things I love the most: reading and helping others. In order to do that, though, I would have to spend a boatload of money on tuition and would not make nearly enough every year to match the goal I have.

It is a tough price to pay, but money often conquers dreams in the battle of life.

Just when I am about to refute his statement about being a beacon to people, a group of women come up to the bar, calling out to me specifically.

Sebastian laughs and I fight every urge to wipe the stupid grin off his face.

CHAPTER SIXTEEN

PIPER

"Ahh," Lindsey groans as she stretches her arms wide behind her. The borrowed office chair creaks beneath her. "I am ready for a nap."

I feel the urge to remind her it is seven in the evening and not a deemable nap time. I bite my tongue.

"I think it's time to call it a day and enjoy our ever-wonderful lives again."

"Yes," Elias chimes in. "I can't wait to be *alone.*"

A small smile greets my lips. He said the same thing about a week or so ago right before he followed us to the bar.

"Up for drinks?" Lindsey is asking the both of us, but she directs all her attention at me. No point in focusing on Elias. He will deny, deny, deny until we all walk out together.

I check the time for no specific purpose. I should go home and sleep. It's the responsible, Piper thing to do. Plus, I'm not a fan of bars. Never have been. Never will be.

"Which bar?" The question falls out before I have time to stop it.

"The same one we went to last time. *Last Call.*"

The one where Graham works. And I have confirmation he will be there tonight since he called me on his shift not that long ago. Going to the bar would be a bad idea. "I don't know."

"Oh, come on. It's Friday and you never let yourself relax. Just come with us."

"Never said I was going," Elias grumbles but Lindsey only shrugs him off.

Lindsey rests her hands on my shoulders. "It will be fun. I promise. You don't even have to stay the whole time. You can go, get a better picture of the atmosphere, and leave."

I play with the hem of my shirt.

The memory of Graham skillfully concocting beverages with the biggest grin on his face and the friendly words on his lips plays in my mind.

What if Hawaiian Shirt is there again? I can't possibly ask Graham to intervene. Plus, the idea of him stepping in to save me sends a sour punch to the gut. Going to the bar is only going to open up a wave of things I should stay far away from.

"So?" Lindsey eggs on.

The word "no" is dancing on my tongue. I open my mouth to say "not tonight", but the word "sure" falls out instead.

Lindsey claps her hands in excitement before beginning to pack up.

Why on Earth would you do that?

This is a bad idea. Getting closer to Graham is an all-around decision that will lead to the death of me. I know it.

But he is like a magnet and I am a loose screw pulled into his magnetic field.

I'm not going to the bar to see Graham, anyway. I'm going because Lindsey asked and it would be rude to say no. Like I have said before, I strongly despise having to tell people "no". Why would I ruin their fun just to please myself?

The reason I am going out tonight is for Lindsey and Elias and to relax after a long day of work. It has nothing to do with the bartender who just sent me a message.

My fingers itch to press play.

No.

"Are we ready?" Lindsey asks as she stands with her purse over her shoulder and a thermos in each hand. She drinks more beverages in an hour than I do in a day.

"As ready as ever," I say it lightly, but I can't help the weight it seems to lay on my shoulders.

Last Call is one of the busiest bars nearby. Not only because of the inviting atmosphere inside, but also because of the Italian owner. I know many girls who swoon for an accent, not to mention myself. It is the way words are tasted and teased differently on their tongue than what we have heard most of our lives.

It's the idea of new.

Normally, I would be entranced and blushing. I may not date and have sworn off men for eternity, but that doesn't mean I can't admire someone intriguing occasionally.

However, the second I come up to the bar to order our drinks and Sebastian—a name I only know through Graham—greets me with a charming smile and tantalizing voice, a void forms in my chest.

I glance around the bar, searching for the mop of perfectly sculpted blonde hair and chiseled arms. My eyes are sorely disappointed with the results.

"What can I get you?" Sebastian draws my attention back to him. He's smiling politely so I return a small one of my own.

I give him my order, same thing as last time, with a sigh.

I don't even know why disappointment is oozing through me. I didn't come here for Graham. So why am I still listening for the honey-like voice and rich laughter?

"He's on break."

"What?" I blink at the man in front of me. Sebastian—I think his name is—and I have not officially met. The only reason his name and face are notable is because of Graham.

"Graham. He's on a quick break. Drank too much water in the first hour."

How did he—

"If you want, I can pretend to be busy with other customers and leave your order for him."

"Oh, that's not—" I wave my hand in dismissal, ready to tell him I am *not* looking for Graham and he is sorely mistaken in thinking I am. The lie dies on my lips. "If you have other, more pressing customers, I understand."

He chuckles. A blush creeps up my skin, but not from him. He passes me the only beverage he succeeded in making, my water, before sauntering to a different group at the other end.

I slide on to the barstool, waiting. I'm not waiting for him. I am solely waiting for someone to make the drinks I requested. That's it.

I trace a random pattern on the counter, swirling my finger around in a spiral of random lines and curves. There is no meaning to the shapes my finger is dancing.

A pair of men close by, whisper something about the "nice" behind of a woman. One of them mumbles about how she is too crazy to even bother trying to seduce. The urge to dump my water on him is strong.

Glasses are being clinked and set down on surfaces, making the liquid inside slosh around. It is unusually slow for a Friday night in the city, but the voices, glasses, and music are still as consuming as they would be at their busiest.

My gaze raises only to come up empty on what—or who—is on the other end of the bar.
I should just wave Sebastian back over and ask him to finish my order.

The thought of Graham talking about me to others sets my nerves on fire. What exactly did he say? My stomach brews unease.

A light tapping interrupts my thoughts. I lift my gaze, only to be met by a pair of curious green ones.

He smirks. "I thought you weren't much of a bar person."

I clear my throat. "I'm not."

He nods but doesn't say anything more. "What can I get you?"

I repeat the same order I gave him a week or so ago. The days have been blurring together. He starts working on them without another thought but takes his time in each step. I know he can mix drinks faster than that. I've seen him do it.

"Why were you waiting for me?"

"I wasn't." I'm quick to deny.

There's a playfulness in his tone. "Right. I don't know why I would assume you were when Sebastian is far from busy with other customers, and you already have one drink in front of you. Plus, you're sitting. If you were planning on leaving, you would have been standing like you did last time." As if a final thought, "But that's clearly a mere coincidence."

I don't know whether to be flattered or annoyed at how easily he read the situation. The emotions clash within me.

"How could you possibly know all of that when you were on break?"

He doesn't acknowledge my slip up beside a minor chuckle—more like a puff of air—before responding. "You learn to be observant as a bartender. Have to pick up the clues of the people around you so you can serve them better. Everyone likes to be noticed." He passes me one drink, never breaking eye contact.

"Oh yeah? What else did you pick up on?" I'm egging him on when I should be walking away. *Far* away.

What is it about him that makes me lose all sense of myself? It's like being in his presence is equal to a shot of courage.

He halts in his actions, delaying our time more, and studies me. "You're tired. It could be from the long day of work but based on the notes scribbled on your hand in ink," I trace the black scribbles between my thumb and forefinger, "I'm guessing you would much rather be in the office than in bed."

I would. As much as I may despise having more work piled on top of me, I love being busy and I love what I do.

"You also didn't come for your coworkers." He nods in their direction, but I don't bother glancing at the two. I'm sure they are in the middle of another argument. Probably over something as simple as the napkins. "If I was a narcissist, I would say you came for me."

Something flutters in my chest. My fingers skim the sweat around my glass, hoping the cool will transfer to my skin. "A little full of yourself?"

"I said *if* I was a narcissist."

"I'm not here for you." I mean to say it in a way of "don't get any ideas in that pretty little head of yours", but it comes out more as anxious. As though the words are a lie.

"Of course. Can I ask *you* a question now?"

"Sure."

"Why are you still here talking to me when all of your drinks are finished?"

I look down at the trio in front of me. I have no memory of him starting the last drink, let alone setting it in front of me. When did he accomplish that? I have a feeling he did it purposely to mess with me.

He smirks and begins to walk around to my side. "Here, I'll help you take them to the table."

"It's okay. I can do it."

"I believe you, but I *want* to help you."

"You know, you have a tendency of being *too* helpful sometimes."

He shrugs. "I like to put a smile on people's faces." Oh, how I wish I could read people. "Especially such a beautiful one like yours." *Beautiful.*

I've never been called that by a man before. At least, not in the way Graham says it.

Men have called me "pretty", "hot", "a great way to pass the time"—all of which, I rolled my eyes to and ignored—but never *beautiful.*

In fact, I think the only people who have called me that are my father and Hazel.

I have no problem with the way I look. Why fret over something you can't change? Plus, I have always firmly believed that seeking outside validation only leads to lower self-esteem. I may not be as confident as others, but it has nothing to do with the way I look.

When Graham calls me beautiful, though, all I want is to hear the word on his tongue one more time. Then again for good measure.

My heart is beating faster and his close proximity to me is not helping. At some point, the rest of the world drowned out around us. The only focus I have now is on Graham's lips and the words escaping them.

"Are you okay?" His tone is jokingly light.

Are you okay? That is a very loaded question.

He leans down to whisper in my ear, his breath eliciting goosebumps along my skin. Why is he so close? How can he even get any closer? My heart rate beats a tad faster and something swirls in my stomach.

"I think your friends noticed your absence."

At that, the world comes crashing back in. The chaos around us is like a brain freeze. My head hurts all too soon and I'm swept in the chill Graham leaves in his wake as he steps back.

What is wrong with me?

"Piper," Lindsey cuts in. Elias on her heels. "I'm so sorry to do this to you, but we're going to get going. George called and said Jane is puking. George is not so great when it comes to bodily fluids."

The image of having someone to come home to, someone who partners with you so well, sends a stabbing feeling to my gut.

She brings a bag full of containers George packed food in for her for lunch every day at work. Every break she has, she spends it on the phone with him. I can always hear her laughing as I pass her in the hallways.

Her eyes light up every time his name is mentioned. I have only met him in person a few times, but each time, he sticks to her like she is the life source he needs to survive.

Lindsey and George are perfect for one another. When they are together, everyone else in the room pales in comparison.

"Elias is going to drive me back so it's faster." Lindsey drags me out of my thoughts and shoves a wad of cash into my hands. "If you want, we can drop you off too."

Before I have time to respond, she glances at Graham, then back to me as though she realizes something. "Oh, my husband is calling," she feigns and quickly hides the blank screen of her phone. "We should really get going. See you on Monday, Piper."

Lindsey is headed for the door before my mouth so much as opens. I expect Elias to be on her heels, but he's stopped in front of me. He doesn't turn his attention away from Graham, sizing him up, as he asks me "Are you going to be okay alone?"

"Yes," I say it to reassure him, but the sincerity around it surprises me.

He eyes Graham from top to bottom, slowly, with a menacing gaze. If I didn't know the soft side to Elias, I would be worried. Judging by the swallow in Graham's throat, he's nervous.

I bite my lip to keep from smiling.

"My brother is the chief of police."

Graham looks to me for help, but I don't offer a peep. "Sounds like a great hobby." His voice is wobbly.

I can't help the smile breaking out on my lips. Elias finally turns his attention to me, giving me a quick nod and a silent "I'm one phone call away" before departing.

Graham exhales a large breath. "Is he always that…?"

"Sweet?" I fill in.

His eyes are wide as he rubs at his chest. "I was going to say 'intimidating' or 'murderous', but we'll go with what you said."

"He's a big sweetheart. He just shows it differently."

"Yeah. That's definitely the vibe I was getting off of him. 'I like to snuggle and make origami hearts'. It was written all over the daggers he was shooting my way."

I laugh a full-blown laugh I haven't let out in a while. There is a warmth in my chest.

"Origami hearts? Is that what you classify as sweet?"

"What's wrong with origami?" He's smirking. It matches the light in his enrapturing green eyes.

I shake my head with a grin. My fingertips are tracing the rim of my glass.

"Why didn't you go with?"

The question is open to so many secrets. So many underlying meanings I have yet to decipher. I could tell him anything right now, maybe even fib a little.

CHAPTER SEVENTEEN

GRAHAM

Piper is smiling. No, grinning. It is a full-blown grin I have finally earned, and I wish I could glue it in place so it never disappears.

Just a second ago she laughed at a joke I made. She laughed so genuinely and hard that she clutched her stomach a little.

My chest feels lighter than its usual heavy load. I'm dying to hear that laugh again. I would *kill* for that laugh.

I open my mouth to say something, anything, to encourage the atmosphere to stay light, but only one question rests in my mind.

"Why didn't you go with?"

I expect to see the smile fall from her lips. Piper strays from seriousness like silence flees the second a noise is heard, but her lips remain quirked. Her finger does a lazy dance around the rim of her glass, hypnotizing me.

"Hazel's in one of those baking frenzies. Thought I'd hide out for a little while."

Warmth swarms in my chest. "I'm your hideout?"

She nods, hesitantly.

"I think that's the first time you have ever complimented me."

"I don't think you can consider that a compliment." If only she knew how every word from her lips sounds like heaven.

I'm smirking as I lean an elbow on the counter beside her, facing her, close to her. She smells like lemons on a summer day. An image of her in a sundress under the sun on a picnic blanket with me beside her fills my mind.

"Piper," I whisper, "I don't think you realize just how dangerous your words are to me."

Her face reddens. My hand itches to reach out and feel the burn. If anyone were to set me ablaze, it would be Piper. That is a fact I am learning all too quickly.

I half laugh to ease the tension in her shoulders. As much as I love how easily I can unsettle her, I don't want her to make her uncomfortable. Not when I just got her attention.

Backing away and stepping to the other side of the bar I say, "I have to help the group at the end of the bar, but I'll be right back. Will you still be here…?"

Please don't say no. Please don't say no. Please don't say no.

"I'll be here," she says.

As though the universe hates me and refuses to let me have any happiness in my life, the bar suddenly hit its rush five seconds into my leaving Piper.

I have tried my best to stay on her side of the bar—nothing wrong with having customers come to *me*—but the new employee Sebastian hired is slow, leaving me with more orders to take and more people to please.

I'm releasing a rough exhale by the time I am able to rest my elbows in front of Piper and lay my head down.

"Tonight seems busy." She notes. "Maybe I should go."

At that, my head jerks up and a new jolt rushes through me. "No." I rub at the back of my neck. "I mean, it's slowing down. In fact, I get off my shift soon."

There's a daring smile on her lips. "Really? You aren't going to be working through the night?"

I lean closer to her, not knowing how to stay away. It's like she's the positive charge to my negative. I'm constantly pulled to her. "As much as I love staying busy, I love your company more, *Trumpet.*" Never has a word fit someone so perfectly before.

It takes a moment for the name to register across her face. The blush on her cheeks has me biting back a grin. Oh, how I love to tease. No. How I love to tease her.

She is staring me down. A head-to-head I hope to never cease. I will gladly lose to her so long as I get to have her full attention for longer than forever.

Whoops and hollers sound out as a breeze makes it way to us through the crowd. "Please tell me a group did not just walk in." My eyes are shut, willing them away.

Piper laughs lightly. "Depends. What's your definition of a group?"

"I think you enjoy tormenting me."

"It is becoming a fun hobby of mine." The admission sends a spark to my chest.

God, do I wish the rest of the world would disappear so it could just be me and the woman with the tantalizing voice.

"Hey," someone shouts at me.

The urge to throw a few choice words in his direction to teach him a lesson about interrupting is strong. I would only be doing the world a favor.

Piper's light, calming voice settles my nerves. "You should go."

If only I weren't an adult with responsibilities and obligations. I regret ever applying for this job and filling up my evenings.

No. I need this job, even though the idea of putting in my two weeks is suddenly becoming the best plan I have ever come up with.

"I will be right back," I promise her. "Please don't leave."

She smiles reassuringly before waving me away. "I'm not going anywhere."

I'm surprised she has stayed this long. I half expected her to disappear when I was busy with everyone earlier, but she stayed sitting at the same stool, barely touching the water in front of her.

Whipping up the drinks of the newcomers is the fastest I have ever done. If there were awards for fastest bartender, I surely would have won the medal in that moment.

The crowd is dying down and a quick check to the clock tells me I am off in ten minutes. I usually stay until closing hours, but Sebastian hired a few people and with the other job I'm working, it would be rude of me to steal hours from them. They have more debt and need the pay more than I do.

I make my way to the woman at the other end of the bar. The woman waiting for *me*.

"I am officially back."

"I'm surprised you made it in one piece with how those girls were leeching onto you."

She *watched* me. The instinct to fist bump the air is strong. "If I didn't know you any better, I would say you're jealous."

"At least they're conscious."

She's never going to let me live that down. You make one joke….

"I get off work in a couple of minutes." I say it to fill the space. I say it because I have no idea what comes next. I have no idea what would be pushing it and what would be accepted. "If you want, I can give you a ride home?"

"Actually," her words are hesitant. She's contemplating, weighing each thing as she says it. "I was wondering if I could show you something instead."

"*You* want to show *me* something?"

Immediately, she shrinks. "Well, we don't have to. It was just an idea. I have a few things to warn you about before Sunday. With all of the chaos around, I just thought—we don't have to, if you don't want to."

"Trumpet." I will her eyes to meet mine again. "I would love to."

She nods reluctantly.

"Although, I can't say I'm not a little worried you might be luring me away to kill me." Sarcasm is my best wingman tonight.

"I believe you are the one who offered to drive me home. You could have very well led me to my own death."

I lean closer, taking the hitch in her breath as encouragement. "Oh, Piper," I sound every syllable out intentionally. I want her full attention. I lower my voice so she knows my words are only for her. "I would fall at your feet with so much as one of those laughs of yours."

Her face reddens and her mouth parts. The urge to lean in closer, taste the surprise on her lips, reassure her that every word I say is true, is strong. There is not one ounce of falsity in my statement. I'm *fighting* every animal instinct in my body.

She undoes me in ways I don't know how to come back from.

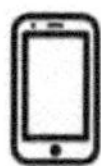

Piper wraps her coat closer around her. I tried to wrap my own around her shoulders multiple times—once including an attempt at distracting her to lay the fabric on her arms—but each time she swatted the gesture away.

"I'm gradually coming to the conclusion this is how I die."

She scoffs and shoves her hands into the pockets of her coat. She has been leading me down the street for fifteen minutes now. If it weren't for her stubbornness, I would say she enjoys the idea of frostbite.

"Just a little longer," there's excitement in her voice. She wants me to want to be here.

If only she knew the electric current she sends through my veins.

"It's right around the corner." She points with her finger still in her pocket.

I can't help the smile on my lips. "Are you sure you don't want my jacket?"

"No. There is no point in you freezing just to give me a little extra warmth." She's perfect.

"Here we are."

We stop outside of a building with the name "Theresa's Foley Productions" lit up above the door. All of the lights are off inside and not a sound can be heard from the looming building.

If Piper hadn't pulled out a set of keys, I would have wondered if she planned on breaking into the place. With a click of the lock and some numbers dialed into a security system, she pulls the door open and heads inside.

I don't hesitate to follow. As suspicious as this all is, my curiosity is a curse etched into every fiber of my being.

"How do you know this place?" I glance around the dark surroundings. Lights flick on as we walk, illuminating our steps as we walk down the hall. The floor is equipped with fake plants and a sleek front desk. The computers behind it shine a white light on the wall. A few chairs are perfectly positioned in a passing room.

"I work here."

"Do you often break into your company after hours?" I mean it as a joke and for her to roll her eyes or maybe even laugh.

Instead, "I spend some late nights or early mornings finishing side projects."

"I'm starting to wonder who the real work acholic is between us."

At that, she rolls her eyes.

I follow her through the door to the stairs. The stairwell slowly lights up with the sense of our movements. I watch the lights flicker above us, hearing the click and buzz of the electricity.

I am not out of shape; I work out every morning and spend my days at a construction site, but this staircase is never ending. My breaths come out ragged.

Piper breathes normally ahead of me. Not a lick of sweat coats her visible skin.

"How many stairs are you planning on climbing, exactly?"

She turns to me. "Out of shape?" She mocks, but the smile makes every embarrassing feeling worth it.

"Only semi."

A light chuckle escapes her. "It's just one more flight."

"Are you trying to wear me out so I'm easier to kill?"

"I would never do that." A pause. "I like a fair fight."

There's a grin on my face and I'm glad she's in front of me so she can't see just how messed up I am. Who knew how appealing threats could be?

We finally reach the top where she shoves a door open, releasing the cold air to wrap around our frames once more. The wind dances across the sweat on my skin.

I follow Piper onto the roof, expecting to go to the edge and peer down from the railing, she stops in the center instead. She pauses for a moment, sucking in a breath and slowly exhaling before turning to me.

"Do you trust me?"

With my life. "This is more and more suspicious by the seconds."

"Didn't you say humans are the mammals who most crave danger?"

"Remind me why I share this information with you?"

I slowly make my way to her, my steps increasing in speed with each inch of her smile widening. She has yet to look away from my gaze and I feel like the luckiest man on Earth to be the center of her attention. "Close your eyes." I raise a brow.

"Trust me."

One sentence. Two words. Three syllables.

I close my eyes.

"Tell me what you hear."

"Wha—" My eyes start to open, before my vision is darkened by her hand on my eyes. Her other hand is resting on my arm, balancing herself. Her skin is warm against mine.

Everywhere she touches is tingling.

Words are stuck in my throat at the contact.

"Just close your eyes and tell me what you hear."

I close my eyes, but her hand doesn't fall from its spot. I listen to our surroundings and take everything in.

There is no clue as to why she wants me to do this. No inkling. But it's clearly something important to her. A piece of her she is sharing with me. A piece I am dying to memorize.

"There are cars below us. A few are honking. The central air unit to the building is humming." I list sound after sound and eventually her hand falls from my eyes.

"See?" She smiles innocently at me when I find her in the darkness. "No murdering."

Little does she know my will and strength are dwindling by the seconds with all of her strikes.

"Why bring me up here?" The question falls out without a second thought.

"You mentioned once that you aren't a fan of silence. I thought I'd show you how to find the noise around you."

"Ah, so you were trying to prove your point?"

She exhales a sigh, turning away from me. "I like to come up here to escape the chaos. I get overwhelmed, too overstimulated, when there are a lot of clashing noises. So I come up here to escape it all. Listening to the little things helps ground me."

I'm enraptured by her admission.

"I thought it might help you for the opposite reason."

"In the silence." I'm drawn back to our conversation the other day.

"Exactly. You thrive in noise. I've seen it with the bar. So I can only imagine what it is like when you don't have chaos around you."

She brought me to a spot–no, *her* spot—to show me that even when I think I'm alone, I'm not.

She thought of me. She waited at the bar for hours just to bring me here. Just to show me how wrong I was. I have never loved losing more.

"Plus," she speaks again. "I want you to be well aware of what you're getting yourself into at this dinner."

"Does your family eat in awkward silence?"

"My family wouldn't know silence if it screamed in their ear. They can be a little…overwhelming. Sometimes I need a quick break from it so I will excuse myself to the bathroom or somewhere else. I just want to give you a heads up so you don't think I ditched you or left you to fend for yourself." Quietly and without meeting my gaze, "And I want to give you an opportunity to get out of it. It's not too late to say 'no'."

"We're friends, Piper. I said I will be there so I will be. There's no getting rid of me."

"You think we're friends?"

"Well, yeah. I think we surpassed the phase of strangers and acquaintances when we found out who we've been talking to for the past year and a half."

She nods her head, almost absently. "Right. Of course."

CHAPTER EIGHTEEN

GRAHAM

There is rap music playing from the speaker in my room and beads of water dripping from my torso. I showered. Twice. Put on some lotion instead of cologne—I noticed Piper's nose curl when Hawaiian Shirt's (as Piper called him) cologne wafted her way. I don't have the same scent, but I don't want to risk it.

Besides, I find lotion stays on longer than cologne and one has to get close enough to smell it.

The image of Piper leaning in to sniff the smell of spice on my skin sends goosebumps across my arms.

I run a hand through my wet hair and pace the small space in front of my closet. I got out of the shower a few minutes ago. I have been pulling at shirts ever since.

This dinner at Piper's house will be casual. I know that much. It doesn't make sense to wear a suit, but the thought of throwing on the same clothes I wear daily causes my chest to tighten.

How am I supposed to capture her attention if I am wearing the same thing she has seen me in multiple times? How am I supposed to impress her family if I am in a t-shirt and jeans?

I stalk out of my room with the towel still wrapped around my waist. I don't bother knocking on Jason's door when I barrel inside his room and straight to his closet.

"Thanks for knocking," he grumbles, but doesn't move from his spot at his desk as he pours over an open textbook in front of him.

"Anytime. I need an outfit that says 'casual, but dang do I look good', but also says 'please see me as a qualified candidate in the dating pool for your daughter'. Got anything like that?" I flip through his shirts, but most are scrubs and suits.

"Sure. Check the section titled 'get out'."

"Nope. Nothing in there."

"Why are you trying so hard anyway? I thought you were only going over for dinner."

"Don't you know anything about romance? I'm trying to get on Piper's good side."

"You're going to have to try a lot harder than clothes."

He stands and bypasses me with a sigh before digging through his outfits. After a moment of sorting, he gives me a nice flannel—an article of clothing I didn't know he owned—and pushes me out the door. "Try not to embarrass yourself."

"Me? I would never. People love me."

"Whatever helps you sleep at night, Graham." His door slams in my face. It opens in the next instant with a comb in an outstretched hand. "Fix your hair."

I take the comb and he shuts the door once again. "Thank you!"

When I make it back to my room, having to hold the towel around my waist tighter, my phone pings from its spot on the bed.

I press play on the message. "Last chance to back out," Piper comments. "I can come up with an excuse for you. Do you want sick with the flu or moved to a different state?"

I smile like the fool I am and press record. "Thanks for the options, but there are no cancellations in my future. I will be there."

I put my truck in park and lean against the seat for a moment, taking in the house.

It's a brick house, painted a fading white. The front yard is small, especially for the amount of people in Piper's family. No decorations or lights are strung on the banisters or littered in the garden. The only thing signifying life are the lights peeking through the windows and the few cars poorly parked in the driveway.

I have to walk in there. Being around people and making conversation has never been a problem for me. It's one of my biggest strengths.

For some reason, though, I have been sweating despite the cold air and I had to turn off the radio five minutes into the drive because each song or station sounded like static in my ears.

I suck in a breath, release it, and exit the truck.

"You're here."

Piper is wearing a white sweater and skinny jeans. The white does wonders in matching the red of her hair and green of her eyes. She's so damn beautiful. But why is she out here with no coat on?

"Do you need help?" She motions to my form half inside the truck and I realize I've been staring.

I clear my throat and step the rest of the way down. "No. Thanks."

She nods. There is this quiet beat between us and I wonder who will be the first to break it. I'm taking her in. All of her. I know she didn't dress like this for me, but I can't help but feel like God sent her to me. Like he knew I needed this gift.

When my eyes travel back to her face, I notice hers are cast down, studying me. My skin burns under her gaze. She doesn't like my outfit. I knew I should have worn a suit. I can impress her in dress pants.

"You aren't wearing work boots," she comments.

I look down at the nicer shoes on my feet. "No, they would dirty up the house."

She smiles. "Trust me, there's nothing that could do more damage than Harmony."

I open my mouth to ask who 'Harmony' is when a little girl screams and runs towards us. The little girl's braids whip around her face as she runs. Her dark arms wrap around Piper's legs.

Piper is grinning. "You ran away." the little girl pouts. She can't be any older than four or five.

"I didn't run away. I just took a short break."

"Mommy said its bad to lie."

"Harm—"

"You're cute." Harmony's gaze is now on me, but she is still gripping Piper's leg.

I bend to be at eye level with Harmony. "You're cuter." I note.

She giggles. "Are you Aunt Pie's boyfriend?"

Piper tugs her closer. "Harmony." Her voice carries a warning.

"Mommy said you have a boyfriend. She said you keep him in a closet."

I try my best to fight the laugh creeping up my throat, but it produces a smile on my lips and an annoyed scowl from Piper.

"Harmony," Piper's tone is soft and the image of her as a mother flashes in my mind. "Why don't we play a game?"

"Really?" Her little body is beaming with excitement.

"Yeah. Go pick one from Kyle's room and start setting it up. I'll be in in a minute, okay?"

"Promise?"

"Promise."

"Can he play too?" She points at me as I stand up.

Piper eyes me like I'm a puzzle she's trying to piece together. "Maybe."

Harmony runs back inside but leaves the front door agape behind her. Piper rubs her hands down her arms.

"You keep me in a closet?" I joke.

"You're eating this up, aren't you?"

"Just a little."

She shakes her head but I can see the faintest smile. Wind gusts our way and I adjust where I'm standing to block it from hitting her frame.

"Thank you for not telling them I'm sick or moved to another state."

"Oh, I did. But my sister said she'll believe it when she sees it."

I release a low laugh. "Funny. So am I supposed to pretend to be your boyfriend in here too?"

A blush grazes her skin. I long to feel it. "No. You are merely here as a male friend."

"Hey, major upgrade from a nosy man." I think back to the first time we met.

She winces. "I was a bit of a jerk, wasn't I?"

"You didn't say anything that wasn't true."

We are quiet for a moment. There is a foot between us, but it's not close enough. I can feel the heat radiating from her skin. The warmth I wish I could wrap myself around. That would be crossing a line, though. One I promised I wouldn't cross. Not yet.

"I'm surprised you let me come." I admit.

"Graham, if you are having second thoughts or even third ones, I completely u—"

"What are you two doing standing in the cold?" A woman shouts behind me.

I don't turn around, too irritated at us being interrupted. Piper glances over my shoulder, standing on her tiptoes for a half second to see over me, and shouts back at the woman. "Be in in a minute, Mom. Just grabbing some stuff."

That must have satisfied her because Piper eventually settles back into her stance and sighs. "We should go in."

"Yeah," I agree, but neither of us make a move.

I want to tell her I like her and that I want to date her. That I'm happy to be her friend as long as I am the friend that gets to make her laugh so hard her stomach hurts. The friend who can make her smile when the rest of the world is trying to push her lips into a frown. The friend who can listen to her endless rants.

I want to tell her that I want an upgrade from just friend. I want *her*. I want to tell her and I want to tell her now.

But an admission like that isn't one you give in the driveway of her parents' house so I settle for grabbing the bouquet of poppies from the seat and passing them to her.

"How did you know I like poppies?"

I slam the door shut and use it as an excuse to step closer. Piper leans into the flowers, smelling their scent. "You told me many times."

She only told me once. We were on the phone about six or seven months ago. I happened to be visiting the farm of a family friend, to which I admitted over the phone, and we somehow got on the topic of flowers. She mentioned poppies are her favorite because they continue to grow regardless of how much of their kind is trampled and killed. I remember arguing that all flowers are like that, but she refuted my claim by saying, "No. Only poppies."

I still don't understand, but I don't need the logistics to want to put the content smile on her face.

CHAPTER NINETEEN

PIPER

To say I threw Graham into chaos is an understatement. The second we walked inside he was swarmed with compliments from my mother, the intense death glare of my sister, John's ignorance, Harmony's hugs, Kyle's questions, and the clashing sounds of everything around us.

The timer to the oven has been beeping since he arrived, and the TV is paused on a Disney movie. All the signs of them watching us from the windows. Not that there was anything for them to witness in the first place.

I have had to remind myself of this fact multiple times. Graham is a friend. A friend. A friend. *A friend.* I made that very clear to him and everyone else. So why is it my heart has yet to get the memo?

Why is it that I wanted him to step closer when we were outside? Why did I want him to offer me his coat again just so I could smell the scent of spice the wind blew towards me?

To top it all off, he brought me flowers. Poppies. My favorite.

"I'm sorry," I whisper to Graham as Harmony places a plastic crown on his head. He has been swept away by Harmony to play some version of a princess alien tea party. It's a game she invented a few months ago after watching an alien cartoon.

She asked Sarah and I, "Why do aliens not get tea parties? Aren't they princesses too?"

Graham grins up at me from his spot on the couch. "Please, this is the most fun I've had in ages."

"You mean you've never had a princess tea party with an alien before?"

"I can't say it has made my list of pastimes, no."

"Hey! You were supposed to pour the tea." Harmony pouts at Graham.

"Of course. My apologies." He is faking a horrible British accent, which Harmony giggles to. I'm fighting the giggle bubbling inside me, myself.

"You two are awfully cozy," my sister mumbles in my ear.

I roll my eyes and quickly move away from Graham to make sure Sarah can't say anything else that would make him raise his brow at me the way he does.

"We are not." I plop in one of the chairs at the kitchen table.

She sits down opposite me, folding a baby blanket on the table.

Sarah got pregnant a month after she graduated high school. The father being the man she has been on and off with for almost six years now. Considering he is not here tonight, I think it is safe to assume they are in their off stage.

Honestly, it's surprising he has yet to be brought up in conversation or to hear his name followed by a bout of curses.

"Please. I saw you two shooting heart eyes at one another." Sarah scrutinizes me.

"I don't think that's a thing."

"He was practically undressing you."

"Okay, and we are done with this conversation."

"Have you guys not fooled around yet?"

"Sarah!" My cheeks are reddening, but it's not from embarrassment. My tongue is begging me to release some profanities at her.

Sarah has always been anything but subtle.

"What are we talking about?" Mom plops down in a chair beside me and across from Sarah.

"Piper is denying her relationship with Graham." Sarah lies.

You can't deny something that doesn't exist.

"Piper isn't the kind of woman to settle down easily, Sarah." I silently thank Mom for coming to my rescue. "But when the time comes," she eyes me, "make sure he has enough saved up. I want a big wedding with all of your cousins. Oh! Somewhere exotic would be nice."

"Can we please talk about something else?" My voice is strained with annoyance.

"Fine. Tell us about Graham."

"Where's Kyle?" If we don't stop talking about Graham, I may just say something I don't mean.

Mom waves a hand in the air. "Oh, he's outside with John. Something about painting bird houses."

"Have you guys found a tutor for him yet?" Sarah stops folding the blanket in front of her and idly plays with a discarded paper towel instead.

"No. Your sister's been searching though."

"I'm happy to help here and there. I can always come over and tutor him."

She means the best, but her offer is empty. When it comes to Sarah and her schedule, one minor inconvenience can throw her entire week into disarray. She will offer to help now and may even give a day or time she can do it, but when the time rolls around, she will cancel and we will never hear about it again.

I can't say I blame her. She has a four-year old and is working during the day while Harmony is in daycare. There are obstacles.

I shake my head. "Don't worry about it. I stop by once a week to keep up with his schoolwork and Mom is usually helping him daily." Sort of.

We fall in and out of various conversations. Even though they mention Graham every once in a while, I'm thankful no one asks anymore inappropriate questions.

When the timer to the oven goes off once again, a faint smell of honey wafting through the air, and John comes back inside, I realize I haven't checked on Graham in a while.

He may be buried under piles of dresses or hiding somewhere waiting to be found. I'm terrible at this girlfriend facade.

I round the corner to the living room, expecting to see disaster and Graham's pleading eyes when I'm met with the opposite.

Graham is bent to be eye level with Kyle as Kyle shuffles a deck of cards in his hands. One card is raised between them to which Graham falls back on his knees and exclaims "how did you do that?". Kyle smiles wide with a cackle.

I'm entranced, watching the two of them like a thriller movie I just can't look away from. Of course Graham is great with kids. He is great with kids and people, and there is something about having him here in my home surrounded by my family that settles me.

If he weren't here, I would be the one entertaining Kyle and Harmony. All the while having to yell back and forth with Mom and Sarah when they randomly call out to me.

It didn't even occur to me that sitting at the table with Mom and Sarah just a few minutes prior was the first time I have been able to do that in a long time. Probably since Kyle was born.

All thanks to Graham.

Kyle runs away with the cards in hand. Graham is watching him leave with a goofy look. When his eyes land on my form leaning against a wall with my arms crossed, his smile changes into something...lovelier. A smile I hope is reserved for me.

"Were you watching us?" He stands and rubs at the back of his neck.

"I didn't realize your charm works on kids too."

"Are you saying I'm charming?"

"Pass me the blanket." I motion to the fallen pile on the floor. He tosses me one end of the blanket but keeps the other side in his hands. Together, we fold the fabric.

He tilts his head. "This is nice."

"Folding a blanket?"

"Your family. They're nice."

"They have their moments."

The blanket shrinks in size as we fold it over and over. He rounds the couch to stand two feet from me. My gaze never strays from his face though. Even when I have to inch my head up to see him properly.

Graham folds the blanket towards me. He grabs the fabric from my hands, but not before letting his fingers linger a hair too long on mine. Long enough for an electric current to pass through and send a shock to my core.

"Where do you want it?"

"On the couch." My voice is hoarse.

He sets the blanket on the back of the couch, then takes one step closer. His grin is wolfish, taking up his entire face as though I'm the funniest thing he has ever witnessed. "How am I doing?"

"What do you mean?"

Leaning down to my ear, "With being your boyfriend. Is it working?"

The room grows quiet. The beeping timer is distant with the mumbled voices from the kitchen. Someone's steps grow softer. All of the noise disappears until the only thing I can hear is Graham's breathing. So close to mine.

When did he get so close?

I can see the green flecks in his eyes and I imagine a field as green as them would be endless. One that would be freeing to run through.

I have never studied a man's face before. Not so closely and not so willingly. Yet, Graham's face is an image I want to memorize every line of.

"You're blushing, Trumpet."

"Why do you call me that?" Our conversation at the bar comes back to me.

"What?"

"Trumpet."

"Would you rather I call you something else?"

"Is there something wrong with my actual name? You know, the one given to me at birth." I fight the instinct to wipe the smirk off his face.

"Yes."

"Yes?"

"Well, maybe not something *wrong* with it exactly. More like it's not a name only I can call you."

"Why do you need a name only you can call me?"

"I thought I was the curious one."

I shrug, feigning nonchalance. "You're rubbing off on me."

"Does that mean my affection has rubbed off on you too?"

I shift on my feet and cross my arms. "You didn't answer my question."

He hesitates. "It's my favorite word."

My heart is pounding in my chest. It's so loud I worry he can hear it. Surely, he can hear the blood rushing through my veins too. He's so close, so close and yet not close enough for me to hear his heart beating too. Is his heart beating as wildly as mine? Or is he doing all of this on purpose?

"That…" his fingers ghost across the skin of my cheek. A cold touch to the burn. "And I love seeing you turn red."

He inches one step closer and I almost step back.

I almost shove him away. I almost end the entire thing with a laugh and a shrug.

But, for once, my heart takes over instead. I let my feet stay rooted to their spot. I let the blush creep up my skin. Forcing my eyes to stay locked on his, I pray he doesn't see the hesitation.

"Piper. Graham." Mom's voice calls out to us and we both immediately step away from one another. "It's time to eat."

I rush away from him, not caring if he doesn't know the way to the kitchen. I fall into the crowd and away from the sweltering room.

After dinner, I'm sure he will bring up the tension between us. I don't doubt it. I know I shouldn't have stayed there. I should have put out every fire he ignited in my bones. That's the responsible, Piper thing to do.

When we are seated at the table, I sneak a glance at him. He's laughing at something Mom or Sarah said. He's filling the room with a warmth I haven't felt in who knows how long.

"So Graham," John starts from his spot. He's not usually the talkative one, especially with newcomers. "Where do you work?"

Graham sets his fork down. "I work in construction throughout the week and at a bar in the evenings."

"A working man," Mom notes. I ignore the "Ah ha" tone.

"That's definitely a lot of work for someone as young as you."

Graham smiles politely, something I didn't know I could recognize, but I feel him tense beside me. "I like to stay busy." It's the same thing he told me, but something is different about it. As I get to know him more and see him at work, I've realized it's only a part of the truth.

"Of course."

"What made you drawn to Piper?" Sarah asks so blatantly I almost choke on my food.

Graham lightly taps my back. His stare burns a hole into the side of my face. I refuse to look at him.

"Do you want the whole story?"

"Yes. Call me curious."

"A lot of people are curious tonight," Graham mumbles so only I can hear it.

I want this dinner to be over. I'm about to speak up and change the subject, shut the whole thing down, but Graham beats me to it.

"Piper and I have been friends for over a year now. I never thought it was going to go anywhere until…"

"Until?" Sarah asks with enthusiasm.

There's a pause and I feel a strong pull to turn my attention to him. He's waiting for me. His gaze finds mine and there's something laced in them. Something soft and cozy. I instantly feel comforted.

His voice is softer now. "Until I had a *wonderful* conversation with her in the same cafe I go to every morning. Ever since then, no one else's company measures up to hers."

We are locked onto each other. By gaze, by erratic beats of my heart. I feel something brush my hand and I realize one of us has reached for the other. It was a quick brush of a finger across knuckles and I'm not sure who initiated it.

I scoot my chair a hair closer to the table and farther from him. "Can someone pass me the salt?"

CHAPTER TWENTY

PIPER

The dinner is over in a blur. After Graham's admission, my family settled in their own dynamic. Eventually Sarah packed her and Harmony up and hit the road. She has an early shift at the real estate office in the morning and Harmony was well on her way to passing out from the laps her and Kyle ran in the living room.

I gave Kyle a quick hug and tickle before he ran back up the steps. He fist bumped Graham too. I'm not sure how they were able to get so close so soon, but my heart melted at the sight.

"Are you leaving?" Mom asks.

I tried to fight Graham on taking me home. I had absolutely no problem with taking a cab. He's already done so much that I don't want to burden him even more.

He shut me down with "Your family gave me food and a place to spend my Sunday evening. Let me take you home."

"Yes." I answer Mom and return the side hug she gives me. She moves to Graham. John is standing in her place, but neither of us move to hug.

Mom shakes Graham's hand—an unusual action, even for her. "Thank you for coming today, Graham."

Graham shoves his hands in his pockets when Mom releases her hold on him and steps back. "Thank you for the invite."

"Of course. You should come more often. Even if Piper isn't here, you are always welcome."

"Mom!" I whisper-yell to her.

"If you are making those stuffed peppers again, I'm not sure I have a strong enough will to say 'no'." He earns a small laugh and wave from Mom. "It was nice meeting the two of you." Graham turns to me, "I'm going to go start the truck. Get it warmed up. See you out there?" I nod.

When he's gone, Mom shoves a fifty-dollar bill in my hand. "Slip it into his glove department or something when he's not looking."

"Mom."

"Don't argue with me. He obviously needs the money."

"What's that supposed to mean?" I cross my arms, feeling my blood begin to boil.

"Honestly, Piper, I thought you would have better taste."

"What's wrong with Graham?" She seemed perfectly fine with him a moment before.

"He clearly is hurting financially."

"You don't know him. Besides, so what if he's not super rich?"

"He doesn't have to be rich, honey, but he has to be able to take care of you. A man like him...let me set you up with my friend's son. You remember Susan, right? Her son—"

"Mom, I'm not going on a date. I thought you liked Graham. Isn't that why you invited him over again?"

"That's called being polite, Piper."

My skin is burning from the irritation building in my chest. I ache to scream. To yell. For once, why can't I be heard?

She sighs like I'm impossible. "He's working two jobs, Piper. Neither of which pay well."

"Dad worked three when you two were married. And four before that."

"That was different."

"Different, how?"

"Your father and I were struggling and so he picked up a few jobs and—"

"Not seeing the difference, Mom."

"Listen, I just want what's best for you. Graham is sweet and kind and he certainly is a family man, but will he be able to support you financially?"

"I have my own job, Mom. I don't need someone to take care of me."

Her voice starts to rise and her entire persona shifts. Like a fire has thawed the ice in her veins only for the wind to blow the flames in my direction. "Piper Celeste Brook. I don't understand why you have to be so independent all the time? What is so wrong with having a man in your life? Don't you see how well John is with me?"

I bite my tongue. Dad used to be good with her too. He was a lot better than John. I remember he would bring Mom, Sarah, and I flowers on random days just because he saw them and thought of us.

From a money standpoint, Dad had that covered too. He built each of us a savings account from the second we were born. It is accumulating quite the wealth as we age. We can only access it when we are thirty—our expected age to have a family of our own. Dad didn't want us to worry about anything, but he also wanted to teach us the value of working.

Dad had the funds and the sweet side, but none of that stopped him from ruining everything all those years ago. A time Mom has never acknowledged. When our family was falling apart, they both shrugged and walked away and that's something I will never understand.

"Your mother just wants the best for you," John pipes in as he places his hands on her shoulders.

Vile burns in my throat. I need to escape before I say something I don't mean. Or worse—something I do.

I take a deep breath. "I know. I promise I am being careful, Mom. You don't have to worry about me. I should get going."

"Okay. Be careful, Piper."

Graham's headlights are illuminating the driveway. He's not inside the truck like I expected him to be. Instead, he's standing beside it watching me.

I keep my head ducked and make a beeline to the passenger side. He beats me to it, opening the door for me. "M'lady," he jokes.

If I weren't still fuming from the conversation with Mom, I might have laughed.

His eyebrows pull down as he studies me. I wrap my arms tightly around my waist, partly because of the cold and partly because of his intense stare. He's eyeing me as if he's checking for injuries.

A part of me wonders if my bleeding heart is visible.

Finally, he shuts the door and rounds to his side of the truck. When he's in the driver's seat, he puts the car in reverse and peels away from my mom's house.

My family's home. The house I grew up in. Half of my life in it was full of happy memories. I didn't grow up with the fanciest things or even have a phone until I was in high school, unlike the other kids I went to school with.

None of that bothered me, though. There were times I envied the students who got to go on trips during our holiday breaks or the girls who bought the most expensive necklaces. In the end, though, I didn't care. Because Dad never made us feel like we were lacking.

We couldn't get dessert every time we went out to eat. Once a month was our allowance, but Dad made sure those singular times felt like a celebration. I didn't care about not being able to have cheesecake each time because I looked forward to the big celebration.

In the winter, we would use the fireplace and mini space heaters and in the summer we would use fans. I never minded because Dad always took care of it.

What we lacked in finances and things, Dad made up for in warmth and love, which is why it hurt so much more when he uttered those seven words to my mom. From that moment forward, our family seemed to evaporate and all that is left are a few particles bouncing around aimlessly.

Mom got a new job and she used things to fill the nook and crannies of the house. A part of me wonders if it is the only way she knew to keep us warm. Dad handled the fire. He was the only one who knew how to light it and keep it going.

Now, the house is equipped with central air conditioning and heating. The fireplace has become a shelf for decor. Another accessory to our broken home.

I stare out the window as we pass building after building. I don't realize how long we had been in the car, quiet, until Graham makes a right and we are only a few streets away from my apartment.

When I glance in his direction, I find he's the most still I have ever seen him. His fingers aren't tapping and his jaw is set. He didn't make a motion to turn on the radio. He is solely focused on getting me home.

I'm such a jerk.

"I'm sorry," The words are a low whisper in the quiet hum of the truck. His engine is soft.

He sneaks a quick glance. "For?"

"You've been so great this whole evening and I…" The words die on my lips. "I'm sorry."

"Piper," My full name. It sounds different in his voice. He makes my name sound so sacred, so special. I ignore the flutter in my chest.

"Thank you for the ride." He pulls up to the curb outside of my apartment complex.

I should get out now, leave him alone—he's probably tired and wants to be alone—but my hand is too tired, too resistant, to grab the handle. I fiddle with the hem of my shirt.

He doesn't make a move or turn off the truck. I shift closer to the heat still blowing on my frame from the vents.

"Do you want to talk about it?" His voice is soft.

"Do you think money is important?" It's not the question I want to ask or even the sentence I intended to utter, but it's the only thing I have enough courage to say.

He clears his throat. "In the sense of surviving? Yes."

I nod, absently.

"In the sense of living?" He angles his head to find my gaze. When our eyes latch, he smiles softly. "No. I don't think you need money to be happy."

"Why do you work so much?"

"That's…complicated. Yes, the money is a big part of it, but I technically don't need to work."

"What do you mean?"

"My grandfather left me an inheritance and that, plus all of the money I saved through high school—let's just say I don't need to worry about money."

"But you do." I voice the thing he left between the lines. The sentence I could hear dying on his lips.

"I don't like the idea of using money I didn't work for. Not when someone else worked so hard to give it to me."

My chest is blossoming with warmth. Graham is perfect. He's so utterly perfect that I fear one more word from my mouth may shatter just how special he is.

"What about you?"

"Hmm?"

"Do you care about money?" He asks it like he's expecting me to say yes. Like he's expecting me to say yes, but is hoping with every fiber of his being I say no.

"In the sense of survival? Yes," I mimic. "In the sense of living? No. I *know* you can be happy without a lot of money. Even though it may be hard sometimes."

We are watching one another. Not studying faces or expressions. Not waiting for someone to say something next. We are just enjoying the sight of each other. Admiring each other without the pressure of being caught or interrupted.

I never would have thought I would love looking at a guy so much. He's beautiful. Inside and out. He's so handsome and all of his attention is on me.

He clears his throat and rubs at the back of his neck. "Can I ask you something?"

I nod. He could ask me just about anything right now and I would answer—a worry that might not be as dangerous as I previously thought.

"Would you…would you want to…." He is hesitant, trying to find the right words. Then, in one quick breath, "Do you want to go on a date?"

I'm frozen and the heat from the vent isn't strong enough to thaw me. Of all things I expected him to ask…

Surely, he must be joking. He is interested in someone else. He told me so. That, and he made it a point to remind me tonight was only pretend. He did it as a friend. A *friend*. But what friend is cruel enough to ask such a question?

As if sensing the tension, Graham continues. "I mean, we don't have to if you don't want to. I know you said you don't date and this is probably too soon and I have a tendency of coming on too strong, but…"

A passing car's headlights shine on his face. His eyes are wide, full of panic. He clearly didn't mean a real date. If he had, he wouldn't be so panicked about the possibility of me saying 'yes'.

He clears his throat and turns so he is facing me head on. "Forget everything I just said. Will you go on a date with me? Just the two of us."
I fiddle with the hem of my coat. Folding and unfolding the fabric. Swallowing the lump in my throat, "Graham, you don't have to keep the act up. You did a good job and I appreciate it, but the audience is gone."

"I'm not acting, Piper."

Not Trumpet, but Piper.

The seat creaks beneath him as he turns to face me. "I mean it. Can I take you on a date?"

"Really?" The shock is clear in my tone.

I imagine he's smiling because the word comes out playful when he says "Yes."

"This isn't some kind of joke?"

"No." Then, softer, hopeful, "Can I please take you on a date, Trumpet?" *Trumpet.*

My chest swells with a warmth and I am biting my lip to keep the grin at bay.

I should say no. I promised myself I would never date. Never put myself through the torture. Graham may like me now, but somewhere down the line, he'll get bored. They all do. That's how it works.

The promise I made myself is one I kept despite the advances of various men. Turning them down is the easy part. At least, it used to be.

Graham though…

My previous conversation with mom floats back to me. Why do I always have to be the responsible, reasonable one?

It's just one date. Not a relationship and certainly not marriage.

For once, I let my heart decide for me. "Okay."

CHAPTER TWENTY-ONE

PIPER

I am going on a date with Graham. I am going on a date with Graham. I am going on a date with Graham. *I am going on a date with Graham.* I am going on a date with *Graham.* I am going on a date with Graham. *I am going on a date with Graham.*

I. Am. Going. On. A. Date. With. Graham. What did I do?

My entire chest is filled with a raging war between vicious butterflies and the guards blocking my heart. I feel as sick as the time I ate too many skittles at the zoo when I was ten. The candy still causes me to gag at the sight of it.

"Hazel." I knock on her bedroom door. She isn't in the kitchen and I'm praying she isn't out somewhere frolicking in the streets.

Please be home. Please be awake.

Her bedroom door flings open. Instantly, her smile falls. "What happened?"

I push past her to pace her room. I've never been one to pace before. I never understood the need for it. It's

194

much easier to sit down and write one's thoughts out than to walk them away, but the thoughts in my head are bursting at the seams.

"Piper, what's going on? You're scaring me." She moves and sits on the edge of her bed. The mattress creaks beneath her.

"I made a mistake. I made a horrible mistake and there is no way of reversing it. I promised myself I wouldn't do this, but I did it anyway. I did it anyway and the regret is instant. I—"

"Piper, slow down."

I stop in the center of the room and face her. My body is frozen, but everything inside me is running a thousand miles a minute. Even my blood is at the pace of a rushing stream.

"Take a deep breath," she motions with her hands. "That's it. In and out. When you have calmed down, start from the beginning."

The beginning? I don't even know where that is anymore. I decide to start at the disaster. "Graham asked me out."

She tries to hide a grin, but it's poking out between her teeth. So much for being my best friend. "So? Did he not take your rejection well?"

"That's the thing…I may not have rejected him…exactly."

"What do you mean?"

Why can't she just read between the lines? Why do I have to spell it out for her? *Trumpet.* "He asked me out."

"Yeah."

"And I said yes because I thought it was a good idea at the time. I also thought he might have been joking. I mean, he likes someone else and this all fake so why would he ask me out on a real date?"

"Okay."

"And then he clarified and said it would be an actual date and by actual date I mean a real date with just two people: him and me." Graham and Piper. Piper and Graham. I ignore the way it sounds like music to my ears.

"And you said 'no', right?"

"See, that's where it gets tricky." I fiddle with the hem of my shirt.

"Gets tricky how? What exactly did you say?"

"I said 'okay', which doesn't necessarily mean yes, but he took it as a yes and I didn't correct him."

She's frozen. So frozen I wonder if I should grab a hairdryer or something to thaw her.

"This is the part where you say something. Maybe that this is all one big—"

Hazel raises her hand and closes her eyes. "Processing."

I nod even though she can't see me.

"Let me get this straight. He asked you out, on a real date, and you said 'yes'?"

I don't correct her on me saying "okay", not "yes" because the two words seem vaguely similar right now.

She eyes me up and down. "Who are you and what have you done with my best friend?"

"Hazel!" My voice is a whispered plea as I plop down on the bed beside her. Maybe if I sit closer to her, then she can see the agony. "What do I do?"

"It sounds like we need to go shopping for the perfect date outfit for you."

"How do I reject him after already accepting his proposal?"

"First off, not a proposal. Although, if you call it that in front of him, you may just scare him away. Second, why do you want to reject him? Clearly you like him and want to go out with him," she pokes my arm playfully, "if you're instinct was to tell him 'yes'."

"I can't go out with him, Hazel."

"Why not?"

"You know my rule. You know how I feel abo—"

"You're right. I know you swore off dating and romance for the eternity of your life. In fact, I watched it happen many times. First with Paxton when we were in middle school. Then again with Paxton when we were in high school. You know, he really had quite the thing for you."

Paxton is a boy we went to school with. He was quiet among our peers and became friends with Hazel and I. More so me than Hazel. We fell into this comfortable quiet between each other and I thought I finally had someone who understood me in ways others didn't. Of course I had Hazel, but Paxton was different.

Then, one day, when we were sitting in the cafeteria for lunch, he said he liked me. I quickly shut him down and said I promised myself not to date. I think he thought of it as a phase I would grow out of because he nodded his head and stayed my friend.

On our graduation day, he asked me out. Again. Right after he swept me up in this big bear hug and congratulated me on a graduation he was a part of too. I remember laughing hard as he crushed my form to him, only for the laughter to be sucked out of me the second he opened his mouth.

I would be lying if I didn't say a part of me wondered what life with Paxton would be like. He used to be a great friend and even better bodyguard when people would pick on us at school. I knew he would always protect me and never judge the quirky things about me. But I made a promise to myself, and no boy was ever going to change my mind.

At least, that's what I thought until I sat in Graham's truck and he asked the one question I had been dying to hear from his lips.

"Man, I wonder where he is now. He's probably some hot CEO." Hazel drags my attention back to her and her ramblings of Paxton. Not the topic I need her to be focused on.

"What am I going to do?"

She sighs. "Do you like Graham?"

"Hazel—"

"Do you like him? It's a simple yes or no question."

"Yes," I admit out loud. I do. I really, really do like him.

"Then go on the date."

"But—"

"No buts. The worst thing that could happen is you realize you don't like him. Then, you can end it and never have to speak to him again."

That's not what I'm worried about. What I'm worried about is what comes next if he only proves me right in how much I like him. What if he shows me just how amazing a guy he is and my heart lets down another wall in his presence?

I don't know if that's something I can handle.

"What if…what if I don't want to end things with him after?" I can't make myself meet her gaze. I don't want to see the pity laced inside them.

"Then you don't." There's a pause. "If this date goes well and you really like him, then continue to date him."

"But I don't date, Hazel."

"I know and you've told me before why that is and I completely understand. I would be scared to put myself out there too. But what if Graham is different?"

Impossible.

"What if he is the perfect guy for you and you're just letting him slip right through your fingers? You don't have to put a label on anything, Piper, or even go on a second date with him."

I finally meet her gaze.

"But at least grant yourself with this one thing. Let yourself have one day, one night, of romance before you swear it off for the rest of your life."

Maybe she's right. It's just one date and I don't have to agree to a relationship because of it. Plus, Graham would be understanding. I know he would. I know he would because he's different.

"And if after this date you decide that it was a horrible mistake and you never want to even look at another guy for all of eternity, then I will block your view of every man on Earth."

I smile. "Why do I feel like you'd be doing yourself more of a favor than me?"

"Maybe. I can't say I will deny a man *all this*." She waves a hand down her frame, and I can't help the laugh that bubbles out of me. "Seriously," she says when the worry has floated away and my shoulders are a little lighter. "Just try it out and if you decide it's not for you and you were right, then I will be right beside you. Okay?"

I nod and she pulls me into a hug. I return her embrace and wonder what it would be like if it was Graham I was hugging instead of Hazel.

If I dated him, would he be the one I run to talk to about all of this stressful stuff? Would he be the one to calm me down in the wake of worry?

Hazel pats my back and whispers more jokes in my ear.

No. Even if Graham and I start dating, Hazel will always be the one I run to. That thought sends a comforting wave through my bones.

It's when I am alone in my bedroom and replaying my messages with Graham that I allow myself to be giddy and excited. It took a while—and a lot of banana pudding—to settle my nerves, but I eventually managed. Now, I'm lying in a puddle of goo listening to Graham's voice.

A recording is nowhere near the same as in person, but I'm not comfortable enough to call him yet. Not when we have a date tomorrow evening.

He said he would pick me up after work. When I asked about his bartending shift, he said he had been cutting back on some hours and happens to be available. It's almost as though the universe is refusing to let me cancel this date.

As I am in the middle of listening to one of Graham's messages, a text from Mom pops onto the screen.

MOM: You're still okay to watch Kyle tomorrow night?

Trumpet.

Chapter Twenty-Two

GRAHAM

It has been less than twenty-four hours since I last talked to Piper. I didn't want to risk changing her mind by bothering her with calls or texts, so I shut my phone off and set it across the room last night. During the day, I tucked it into my pocket on silent. I can't afford screwing this up.

I fought every itch to reach for it and contact her. *I will see her tonight,* is what I kept reminding myself because tonight we are going on a date.

I fully expected her to sigh and remind me about how she doesn't date. Instead, she said yes. She said yes and I am waiting for her to cancel. To say all of this is one big misunderstanding and she isn't actually interested in me.

Another reason I fought the instinct to grab my phone.

I push off the wall outside of her office building when I see her exiting. She hasn't noticed me yet so I take advantage of this moment.

She's wearing a casual sweater with black pants and boots, with a coat perched over her arm. She's searching for something in her bag, causing her hair to cascade across her face as she ducks her head.

Would it be too forward if I brush it away and tuck it behind her ear?

"Don't be weird," Jason's words float back to me.

Would pushing her hair back be *weird* or helpful?

I move toward her with my hand outstretched when I'm within inches. Before I have a chance to make contact, her gaze swings up and she tucks her hair behind her ear. My hand drops back into my pocket.

"Hey," I say.

"Hi," She returns my smile, but it seems forced like the last thing she wants to do right now is smile, at *me*.

"Everything okay?"

"Great."

I pause for a moment.

There's something she's not telling me, but I fear it would be too rude to ask. *Don't be invasive. Don't be invasive.*

I rock on my heels. "So…ready to go?"

She ducks her head. "About that."

My heart sinks. This is it. I didn't get any calls or texts because Piper isn't the kind of woman to turn you down over calls or texts. She's the kind who waits to do it in person just so you get the hint.

She's not cruel, she's determined. "Is there any way I can pick where we go?"

What?

"I know you meant for this evening to be just the two of us, especially because you made it a point to say 'just the two of us', which is completely understandable since it is a date. Although, I'm still trying to wrap my head around the date part. Anyway, my mom texted me last night to remind me about Kyle today so now I have to babysit Kyle this evening."

She rambles on and on and I do nothing to stop her. Instead, I fight the grin trying to break free. I could listen to her talk for days and never get bored.

"I completely forgot about it. I promise. When I told you 'yes', I did not realize I was already booked. Anyway, I was thinking we could go somewhere kid-friendly for Kyle, even though that's not very date-like and Kyle is not a fan of going out. He gets teased a lot and it makes him shy and nervous around others. But if that's not something you want to do, I completely understand. I don't blame you for not wanting to spend your evening with a seven-year-old. Especially when you probably had a completely different idea of tonight in mind."

I did. I planned on swinging by the cafe we first met so I could learn—buy her favorite hot beverage and then we could walk around the park and she can teach me how to know the source of every sound around us.

After that, I would buy her food. A big, five course meal.

When I think about it, though, it is extra cold out tonight and being alone inside a house with Piper sounds like a sacrifice I'm willing to make.

She finally looks up at me. "I will not blame you if you want to cancel the date altogether. In fact, I'll even let you blame me instead. I just—sorry. I'm rambling."

I take one step closer. I tell myself it's to block the wind from reaching her, but my eyes are locked on the gentle red waves falling from her head.

"I would love to spend the evening with you and Kyle."

"What? Graham, you don't have to do that. You are allowed to say no."

"I know, but I don't want to."

"You don't have any better plans?"

"*You* are my plans, Trumpet. I came to pick you up for an evening of fun and if that evening involves your little brother, then that's the evening we will have."

She looks at me like she's waiting for the other shoe to drop.

"Besides, I would love to test out my childcare skills."

A smile breaks free on her lips and I can't help but feel as though it is a trophy I won. I wish I had a camera to take a snapshot of it.

"And we don't need to go anywhere. We can stay in and do something. I wouldn't want to make Kyle uncomfortable."

"It is astonishing how amazing you are."

My heart beats faster and heat creeps up my skin. I rub a hand across the back of my neck. I don't think she realizes just what her compliments do to me.

"Are you sure about this? My brother can be a lot sometimes and you are always so busy that I'm sure you have other, more important things you could be doing right now."

"Trust me when I say this: there is nothing I want to do more right now than to spend time with you."

Piper's home is similar to the one I grew up in. Except, mine is full of outdoor plants turned into house plants. It often reminds me of walking through a jungle without shears to slice the vines out of the way.

Piper's house though, is littered with picture frames instead of leaves. There are frames propped onto every surface and canvases hung on the walls. Some type of invisible picture holder is present in the hallway up the steps. It is a painted tree with a portrait of different persons hanging from each branch.

It's so beautifully delicate, I want to run my fingers across just to see if it's a figment of my imagination.

My parents have pictures around their house too, but only one is actually visible and it's a lonely portrait of us three above the fireplace. Somehow, the big portrait seems small in comparison to the thousands of smiling faces surrounding me.

"There are snacks in the kitchen if you're hungry," Piper meets me at the landing.

"Thanks, but I'm alright for now." I follow Piper into the living. She passes me a bottle of water and sits down in one of the faded recliners: the furthest chair from me.

She's uncomfortable in her own home and it's because of me. I need to do something, anything to erase the look of unease etched into her features.

"Where did your brother go?" is the only question I can think to distract her with.

"Changing into his pjs."

"He goes to bed this early?"

"No," she scoffs the word like it's such a ridiculous notion. "But he falls asleep really easily and I do not—and will not change him into pjs when he falls asleep."

"So he changes early?"

"Yeah. Plus, then I don't feel so guilty about not carrying him up to his room if he falls asleep on the floor down here or on the kitchen table." She tries to untwist the cap to her water bottle but eventually gives up.

"The kitchen table?"

"He has this sleep gene. I think he gets it from John, the snorer. He can fall asleep anywhere at any time. It's almost concerning."
"I can see why that is."

I untwist the cap from my water bottle and pass it to her, trading hers for mine. She's hesitant at first, but then switches, muttering a quick "thanks."

"What about you?"

"What about me?"

"Can you fall asleep anywhere and anytime?"

"No. I need it to be as quiet as possible and with no light."

"Sounds lonely." I don't realize I said the sentence out loud until she whispers, "It is."

I open my mouth to respond, maybe offer to be the body that fills the space but running footsteps on the stairs drag our attention away.

Kyle finds us in the living room with space pajamas on. He runs to Piper and pats her leg. "Can I have ice cream?"

"No. You can't have ice cream until after dinner."

"But Mom always lets me have ice cream."

"I'm surprised Mom even buys ice cream anymore."

"Dad buys it and hides it in the garage."

"We'll steal his stash, then." His face lights up with excitement, but Piper's next statement diminishes all joy from his features. "After dinner."

His shoulders shrink from annoyance, and he turns, finding me on his parent's couch. Instantly his mood changes.

"Will you play Legos with me?" he asks, but he's already making his way back up the steps.

"Sure," I yell after him. I have no clue if I'm supposed to follow him or not so I decide to stay where I am in hopes he will return.

"You don't have to," Piper tells me. She's sitting on the edge of her seat like she's waiting for me to stand up and ditch.

"I want to."

Kyle comes traipsing back into the room with a Ziploc baggie of Legos in hand. He dumps them on the coffee table and drags me to the floor beside him.

I hear Piper's soft giggle when my butt slams against the hardwood floor.

"I'm going to start dinner. Don't terrorize Graham."

He sticks his tongue out at her, and she ruffles his hair. When she glances my way, she mouths a silent "thank you" and heads into the kitchen.

"That's cheating," I hear myself say as Kyle places a yellow four on top of a skip card.

"Nope. It's called winning." A silent giggle escapes Piper.

I sigh. "You know, I'm not a fan of losing."

"I had no idea," Piper's sarcasm may just be the death of me.

After a few more rounds, Piper forces Kyle to head upstairs to go to bed. I wait in the living room as she does so and study the thousands of pictures decorating the room.

There are a few frames propped up on stands and end tables. They are more recent photos with Piper and her siblings standing in the photo. One in particular catches my eye. Her siblings and her are dressed up, maybe for Halloween. Hazel is in it too and the little girl is Harmony, I think.

Standing in the center with Harmony in her arms and Kyle at her feet, is Piper. She's clad in a ballgown that looks very similar to something of a Disney princess. I wonder if that was her intention. I feel bad for the Disney franchise. If they saw how incredibly breathtaking Piper looked in the green gown, all of their princesses would be out of commission.

"You're nosy in all aspects, I see." Piper steps into the living room, making her way to me. Her hair is back in the bun she frequently has it in, putting her features on full display for me to study. Just as memorizing as I guessed. "Curious, Trumpet. Not nosy."

She glances over my shoulder to the picture frame in my hand.

"I didn't know you were such a fan of princesses."

"I'm not. I couldn't make it to their Halloween shopping that year, so they picked something out for me. More so, Harmony picked it, but still."

I set the frame back down. "Well, it definitely suits you."

When I turn, she has her face directed in a different direction, but I still see the blush on her cheeks. My heart leaps with joy.

"What time will your parents be back?"

Piper sits on the couch this time. I follow, making sure I'm not too close to her, but also not far away. "They will probably be back in an hour or two. If you want to go ahead and leave, you can. I appreciate you being here for this long. I'm sure it was boring and definitely not what you had in mind. If I could give you something in return, I would."

"You would give me a reward?" A soft grin plays on my lips.

She fiddles with the hem of her shirt. My eyes are glued to it. I'm not sure what I want to do more: grab her hand to stop the anxiety from eating away at her or remove the shirt altogether. I do neither.

Her voice is barely above a whisper when she finally speaks. "What kind of reward are you wanting?"

I scoot a hair closer. "What kind are you willing to offer?"

Our gazes are locked, minus the few breaks I take to stare at her lips. They are definitely kissable, definitely calling my name.

There's an electric current pulsing between us. Someone plugged jumper cables into each of our hearts and started our engines, bringing us back to life.

Our faces are only inches apart. I could lean in and kiss her. I could lean in and finally touch her, finally let my fingers trace the contours of her face. One glance down though and I see her hands are gripping the hem of her shirt tighter than before and her face has lost all its color.

I reach for one of the candies littering the stand behind her before pulling away. Shoving the candy in my mouth, I say, "this will do," and show her the wrapper.

She takes a deep breath in before exhaling and sitting up straighter. "Take as many as you want. No one eats them."

"Then why buy them?"

"It's the cheapest kind and sometimes you just need a bite of chocolate. Even if it is the most disgusting kind you can find."

"Sometimes, you are a puzzle I just never know if I will truly figure out."

She studies me. "Same here."

She hasn't broken eye contact since I sat down. Even when I invaded her personal space and was clearly making her uncomfortable, she kept her eyes on mine. Almost like she was forcing herself to not look away and to be in the moment.

My chest suddenly feels hollow. If Piper and I are going to be on a date, then I want her to be comfortable the whole time. I want her to *want* to be there.

"Why did you say yes?" The question falls from my mouth before I have a chance to catch it.

"No one eats them. It's really no big deal."

"Not the candy. Why did you say 'yes' to going out with me?"

She's quiet for a beat, then two. "The truth or a lie?"

"Which version makes me sound better?" She half scoffs, half chuckles.

"The truth, Trumpet. Always the truth." Although, I have a feeling if her voice was wrapped around a lie, I would believe it anyway.

"I don't know."

I want to pry. What does she not know? She doesn't know why she said 'yes' or she did know but now it's not so clear? I want to ask a thousand questions, but I force myself to stay quiet. I've pried enough and the last thing I want is for her to shut me out, both literally and figuratively.

She settles back against the arm of the couch and turns to face me. "My turn. Why bartending and construction?"

"You already asked me this. I like to—"

"Stay busy. I know." She waves her hand in dismissal. "I believe you, but I also believe there's more to it than that."

"What do you mean?"

"You're smart Graham. And ridiculously nice. There has to be something you want to do."

I sober at that. Sebastian has called me out on it many times. "You would make a great teacher," he has told me and it's what I used to dream about doing.

I would love to teach and guide kids in the right direction. It is an honor to be their outlet to confess their dreams and be their guide in achieving them. But how am I supposed to do that when *I* don't believe every dream is within reach? Some people just aren't meant to have the life they desire.

"I'm not trying to pry," Piper adds sincerely. "I just want to learn more about you. I want to know the real you."

"Are you suggesting I'm a figment of your imagination?"

She rolls her eyes. "You're insufferable. I take back what I said about you always being nice."

I'm grinning, but then it fades. When the quiet settles back between us and her unanswered question resurfaces in my mind. "It wasn't what I planned." She waits for me to continue. "If you had asked me when I was in the sixth grade, or even in seventh, I would have told you that I plan on being a teacher"

Actually, a writer. It used to be my passion until I quickly learned how horrible and boring it is to write. I would much rather read the works of others and share them with the world.

"My grandmother used to teach. She would invite me into her classes just so I could sit in the back and listen to the lectures on the books her class was reading at the time. She taught eleventh grade English."

"You would sit in a high school class as a middle schooler?"

I let a small laugh release as though it were an exhale of breath. "Yeah. Grandma used to call me an old soul. I was constantly stealing books out of her home library and classroom. Even when I couldn't understand half the words on the page, I wanted to devour every sentence like it was my last meal."

She used to find me sitting in the corner of her library with a flashlight in hand and a book propped open on my bent legs. She would scoot down beside me and hold open a dictionary for me to glance at any time my "eyebrows furrowed, and I looked ready to throw the book." That's what she would tell me.

Then, my grandfather would come home from work, covered in grease and dirt, but wearing the biggest smile on his face because his family was able to enjoy the little things like reading on a carpeted floor. All because he worked his butt off to give us that life.

Which is why I decided not to teach. I had the cushiony life when I was younger, now it is time for me to take a walk in my grandfather's shoes.

"This explains your reading obsession." Piper's voice brings me back to the present.

"Did *Gatsby* ruin you that much?"

"No. I never understood why people enjoy it."

"Maybe you just haven't found the right genre or author for yourself."

"Trust me, I've tried. A friend of mine from school used to bring me different books all the time, begging me to read them. I couldn't get past the first page. There's just something about all of the words that scramble my head. I don't know how people are able to envision other worlds from a pile of words."

"It is magical." I admit and I realize it's the truth. Reading has always transported me into a safer, fuller existence. I didn't grow up as an only child because all I had to do was crack open a book and I became instantly surrounded by siblings; friends.

"You certainly make it sound that way."

"One day, Trumpet, I will convince you."

"Sure. So why not teach?" Her question brings me back to the hollowness in my chest.

"It's not in the cards for me."

"Hmm," she hums, lulling over something in her head. What I would give to crack it open and hear all of her thoughts, especially the ones pertaining to me. "You are only…I just realized that I don't actually know your age."

"Twenty-six." I lean back against the couch.

"Twenty-six. Anyway, you are only twenty-six. There's plenty of time to reshuffle."

I consider that and wonder if she's right. There are lots of people who change their careers halfway into their life or move to another area. I'm sure that works and is even thrilling for some, but I'm just not sure it's for me.

"What about you?"

"What about me?" She takes a sip from the water bottle she picked up to fiddle with a few moments prior.

"Any chance you are going to reshuffle soon and have me in your hand?"

She nearly chokes on the water, and I fight the urge to belt out my laugher. She pats her chest with her face a beaming red.

I let her take a moment to recenter, but I don't take back my question. I wait patiently, egging her on. Even if it was a tease, I still want to know the answer. I want to know if she is considering the possibility.

"I don't know," she finally says. "I never thought about switching things up. I have always wanted to be a foley artist and I am lucky to have everything and everyone in my life."

I'm on the edge of my seat, waiting. She is lucky. I can tell by the way she lights up at the people she loves and with how enthusiastic she is about her work. She's happy and she's living the dream she's always wanted. That much is obvious and I couldn't be happier for her. If one of us gets to have their dream, I'm glad it's her.

"So there's no reshuffling in your future?" I'm not sure how we started with this card metaphor, but I stick to it. It seems to make the topic easier to digest and I want her to be as comfortable as she made me.

She shakes her head. "No." My heart sinks to the pit of my stomach. "But I think I found a card hidden between a few others."

CHAPTER TWENTY-THREE

PIPER

"Piper," Lindsey pokes her head up from the desk beside me. "Did you see the email that just came through?"

I open my email account and find the one from our boss sent not even a full minute ago. I don't have time to skim through the instructions and comments inside before Elias grumbles and Lindsey summarizes it aloud.

"Clients loved the animation—great job, by the way—but we have a few more projects to add to the list." Her emotions are a constant roller coaster her words ride on.

"It's Friday." The sentence falls out of my mouth as an exasperation. I have never minded working late, but my entire body aches from exhaustion.

"Well, they aren't due for a couple of weeks so we can make a plan before we leave, maybe do some outlining, and then knock it out on Monday."

"The workday is over," Elias adds with a groan.

Technically, we still have another fifteen minutes until clocking out is a viable option. With this email, though, Lindsey is right. If we put it off until Monday, we will all come in dreading the day and stressed out of our minds.

The last thing I planned for today was another late night. I scoot closer to the desk regardless.

"I will start prepping the first one," I suggest, "If you two want to move on from there."

"Sounds like a plan!" We could be working for days on end and Lindsey would still be as cheery as ever.

My screen loads in bringing up our database as a buzz from my phone jolts my attention away.

I don't have to pick it up to know who it is. It's the same person I have been messaging long before I clocked in for the day.

About a half an hour ago, when my cup of tea had a quarter of the liquid gone, I stood to grab another and responded to his message on the way. My tea is barely sipped from, and my desk is still piled with the snacks I grabbed on trips prior to that.

Every nerve ending is begging me to pick up the phone and listen to Graham's message. I shift in my seat and pull up a new tab on the screen.

Another buzz from the device. "I have to run to the bathroom," I announce to my team members. Lindsey waves me off absently and Elias doesn't so much as look up from his computer.

Scampering off, I wait until I am far enough away from any prying ears. I double check by listening for any approaching footsteps or hushed conversations.

My breathing is so harsh, it is hard to listen to anything else.

Calm down, Piper. Why am I so on edge?

When I am confident I'm alone, I press play on Graham's message.

"Hawaiian Shirt is here again." His words are the front line of other voices and clanking glasses in the background. He must be at the bar. "The man who tried hitting on you the other night. Anyway, he purposely avoided me when he came up to the bar and went straight to my coworker instead. It's probably for the best. I may have ended up spitting in his drink or putting a moldy lemon in it."

There's a pause and then his next words are rushed and full of regret. "Not that we carry moldy lemons. All of our fruit is fresh and even if they did have mold, we certainly wouldn't serve them."

A beat or two passes and I wonder if that's the end of his message. I pull the phone from my ear and inspect it. There are still thirty seconds left.

He whispers. "Sorry, a woman overheard me and I'm pretty sure she will no longer be a paying customer." The message ends.

My face hurts from how wide my smile is. Suddenly, having to work a few more hours does not seem as bad as it did just moments ago.

I press record and bring my mouth close to the speaker. "It is probably for the best that Hawaiian Shirt is catered to by someone else. Your mold argument was pretty convincing. I'm sure she'll come back." It's a lie. If I were her, I would have left the second he said "mold". I wouldn't have even hung around long enough for him to notice my hesitation or appalled expression.

I'm tucking my phone back into my pocket when I feel it ping again. I still have a few minutes before it becomes suspicious. I pull it back out to press play but am surprised to see the screen lit up with "Potential Psycho". I haven't had it in me to change the name.

A wave of anxiety shoots through my veins and straight to my stomach. My chest tightens a little more than before.

Graham and I have called each other before—lots of times, in fact—but we haven't since before we found out who each other is. Messaging him is already a difficult task—one Graham took the initiative in—let alone calling him.

Calling someone, especially if that someone is a friend you have gone on a date with, is normal, but he hasn't done it once. Not even attempted. Why now?

I should let it go to voicemail. I am technically still at work and he is clearly working too.

Or, what if he butt-dialed me? What if he isn't actually waiting for me to pick up and has no idea his phone is even dialing me?

The phone is buzzing incessantly in my hand with Graham's nickname clearly written on the screen. I feel like I am holding a ticking time bomb that will go off at any moment.

Relax, Piper, I tell myself. We are just friends. Friends wouldn't get nervous over a phone call. I take a deep breath and swipe the green phone across the screen, pressing the device to my ear.

It's eerily quiet on his end. Maybe he did butt dial me.

"You picked up." His tone is full of disbelief.

"Was I not supposed to?" I play with the hem of my shirt. Fold, unfold, twist.

"No, I just—I'm pleasantly surprised is all."

"Oh." I don't know what else to say. What am I supposed to say at this moment? How do you respond to a guy calling you out of the blue?

Thankfully, Graham fills the space for me. "Are you done working?"

"No. Going to be at least another hour. Are you? It sounds quiet on your end."

"Taking the trash out."

"Isn't that a thirty second job?"

"Don't tell Sebastian."

His statement is a joke. My taut stomach seems to release its tight twist a little at the joke.

"What are your plans after work?"

Sleep and more sleep. "Why?"

Please don't ask me out. Please don't ask me out. Please don't ask me out.

It hasn't been a full week since our date. I haven't had enough time to process everything yet. There hasn't even been enough time to ponder everything with Hazel.

"I was just curious on whether or not you and your colleagues were going to swing by for a drink again." *Me* and *my colleagues.*

There's a strange feeling in my chest. Disappointment? Definitely not.

"I'm assuming that's a no, though?"

"No." The word sounds like a claim of defeat. "I mean, yeah, it's a no. At least on my end. For all I know, they could go to the bar after we clock out. I have no control over what they do. In fact, when I walked away to answer your message, I think I heard them starting their fifth argument of the day."

"You walked away?"

Out of that entire spiel, that's what he picks up on? "Yeah."

"I didn't know our conversations were so private." His suggestive tone sends a blush to my cheeks.

"*You* ran outside to talk to me," I deflect.

"That's because I don't want to miss what the voice messages don't pick up."

"What?"

"Your laugh and the hitch in your breath when I surprise you. Those are the things I want to hear."

I fan my shirt against my skin. When did it get so hot in here?

"As much as I love how I can replay your messages, I miss the raw and fresh emotions in your voice."

"Stop." The word comes out before I have time to process it.

"What?" There's a half-laugh around it and I wonder if he thinks I said it only because of the way his words make me feel.

"No flirting. Friends don't flirt."

"Friends don't go on dates, either."

I close my eyes and try to take a deep breath. I can't do this. I knew it was a bad idea to answer his phone call, but I did it anyway because I got lost in the moment. I got lost in him.

The one thing I promised myself I would never do. "Graham, I…"

I what? Don't know what to say? Don't know how to tell him that he is this amazing, handsome, funny man who gets me in ways I never knew would be possible, but I can't ever pursue him in a serious way because of every blockade between us?

Because no matter how charming he might be or how he makes me feel on fire, I can't stop this nagging vision of what is at the end of our road. That's exactly it: our road is a dead end.

"You still there?" Graham cuts through my thoughts, but it doesn't settle the storm in my heart.

My body sighs and leans into the wall at my back. He was merely joking. Or trying to be nice, at least, and I let my emotions get the better of me.

"I'm sorry. I should get back to work. I'm sorry."

"Trumpet." One word—seven letters—and my entire brain stops at the beautiful command. "You don't have to apologize." It's not the first time I have heard those words, but it feels different. If only he knew what I was truly apologizing for. "A crowd just walked in and I'm sure that any moment now, Sebastian will be out to drag me inside."

"That's a sight I'd love to see." I joke.

"I'm glad my torture amuses you."

"It's only fair with how much you tease me."

"If I didn't know any better, I'd say you enjoy the teasing. I bet you love hearing me talk."

I do. "Do you hear that? It sounds like your ego is inflating."

"Funny."

I'm grinning like a fool.

"I'll call you later, Trumpet." I'm about to open my mouth when he speaks again. "Oh! I almost forgot. I called to ask if you wanted to get lunch tomorrow afternoon."

"Lunch?" I'm hoping the word has a different definition than one I know of. That he means it in a very literal sense. Lunch and no romantic obligations. To ensure this, "I usually get lunch with Hazel…"

"Oh, she can come too. In fact, it can be a friend thing. I'll bring Jason."

Jason. Graham has mentioned him a few times and I have heard Jason's voice in the background of our calls. From what I can make out, the two are complete opposites.

"That is, if you are okay with that. I don't want to make you uncomfortable."

I'm butter and Graham is the hot pan melting me down. "Yes. A lunch with friends sounds nice."

"Great! I'll set it up and send you the details later. Good night, Trumpet."

"Good night."

When the line dies and the phone is away from my ear, I allow myself thirty seconds. Thirty seconds to smile at the screen like the fool I am. Thirty seconds to allow the giddy feeling in my chest. Once thirty seconds are over, I slide my phone in my back pocket, wipe the grin off my face, and make my way back to my desk.

I don't plan on dating Graham. We went on a date and it felt nice, but that is as far as it will ever go.

I have no doubt in my mind he will make the perfect partner for some lucky girl, but it's not me. Graham is way too good for the heart I have boarded up with a barrier even a cannonball couldn't break through.

Graham is a great friend and I do not plan on ruining that.

Maybe he can pursue the woman he asked me about before.

My father is the kind of man who gladly puts his needs below everyone else's in his life. This included his wife and his two polar opposite daughters.

Dad always picked up before the first ring made its way through completely. Even at three in the morning, he would always answer with a smile in his voice. At least, that's what my sister told me when she called him about a flat tire while she drove home from her boyfriend's house—a place she wasn't supposed to be at.

Without another word, my father got out of bed, threw on some clothes and shoes, and walked out the door. He didn't wake my mother up but left a note in case she rolled over to find his spot empty.

He knew how hard it was for her to sleep some nights and didn't want anything to disturb her. I used to wonder if he would keep the same attitude during an apocalypse or the end of the world.

Considering how he took a week off of work to give her a bedroom with soundproof walls, I have no doubt in my mind he would have.

My father made it his mission to care for everyone around him without expecting anything in return. That is, until the night he came home from work a few minutes later than normal and my mother's cheeriness instantly dropped by thirty degrees.

Since then, our family has never been the same.

Dad doesn't always pick up on the first ring and his voice has lost its color. He puts "Do not disturb" on at night.

Instead of surprising us with notes on our bedroom door, he sends my sister and me a generic text every few days.

He never stopped loving us. He has always loved us in every way he can because he *has* to. He's our father. I witnessed him pulling away from someone he doesn't have to love. In an instant, his entire persona changed.

I constantly wonder what life would be like if fathers didn't have to love their children. If it wasn't an addendum in the blood contract they sign at birth, what would happen then?

All of this is running through my mind as I glance down at the group chat between my father, sister, and myself.

DAD: How are things
  going for my two favorite daughters?

SIS: We are your only daughters, Dad

DAD: Still applies. I saw this meme today. Have you guys seen the one about the frog and the tadpoles. Reminded me of you.

There is a picture that appears below his message. I skim it before hearting it and sending him a separate "love you" message.

CHAPTER TWENTY-FOUR

PIPER

It has been less than one day. Eighteen hours since I agreed to go out—hang out with Graham, Hazel, and Jason. It has been one agonizing day of me fighting myself on crafting excuses to get out of it.

I could, realistically, say I have to work overtime, and they would be none the wiser, but the idea of lying to Graham, denying him the one thing friends are supposed to be able to do, sends a sour feeling to my stomach.

Friends are allowed to see each other and have gatherings.

When he asked me, I thought for sure he was asking me out on a date. I mean, doesn't the phrase "have lunch" mean "date me"? Without so much as a beat between us, he quickly added there would be two more party guests to the event. It wouldn't be just me and him. It would be the four of us.

One of which I have yet to meet.

Graham has mentioned Jason once or twice, but no more details than how particular and moody he can be. That, and I have heard his voice in the background. He sounds like the type who is easily bothered and overstimulated. Almost like he has one track, one path, and any obstacles in his way are bound to be moved.

I think I will like him. I *hope* he will like me.

"Hey, Hot-tea," Hazel pushes off the wall of the studio as I exit it.

"Hot-tea" is a nickname she came up with for me towards our last years in high school. While everyone drank their lives away, I opted for the soothing, warm beverage of tea. That's what the intended name was meant to describe.

However, she pins the words together to be one each time she says it—which is generally in public—and it sounds an awful like "hottie" instead.

My cheeks instantly redden at the name. "I don't know you," I mumble.

She loops an arm with mine before guiding us down the street. "Oh, please. You love me."

Hazel and I agreed to travel to the restaurant together. The idea of showing up alone and having to either wait miserably for them to arrive or be late and have to wander on my own scares me. It's times like this that I appreciate Hazel the most.

"Are you ready for this?" Her question is loaded in more ways than one and I'm not entirely sure how she wants me to answer.

Am I ready to eat? Absolutely. The half of a muffin I had for breakfast only went so far. My stomach and its party of nerves refused to keep the food down long enough to be considered substantial.

Am I ready to willingly and knowingly meet up with Graham? I don't think that's something I will ever be ready for.

"As ready as I'll ever be," is what I settle with.

"I'm surprised you're going, but I'm proud of you. My little girl is finally growing up." Hazel changes her tone in the last sentence to sound like a mom sending her daughter off into the big bad world.

I haven't told Hazel about my feelings, yet. I'm not sure how to phrase them properly. I'm hoping if I act nonchalant enough today, Graham will lose all interest, and I won't have to say anything.

"How were sales today?" I point to the bag on her shoulder.

"Well, I managed to sell a few tarts—they were the big hit today—but not much of anything else."

"I'm sorry, Hazel."

"If I could just get one person to try them, someone with the right taste buds and perfect tongue to taste out the talent, I would be shot straight into stardom. Then, I can finally open that bakery like I want."

It is Hazel's dream to open her own bakery. Well, after working two years at a fine dining restaurant as the pastry chef. Then, with her name out there and a few bucks under her belt, she will open her own bakery.

It has been her dream since her father first taught her how to make the gooiest chocolate chip cookies. All of which she snuck away for the two of us to devour in secrecy.

She is following her passions in food while I am following mine in sound. And we are doing it together.

I don't know how I would brave this world without Hazel. She is what keeps me going and what makes it bearable to not have a romantic partner at my side. When I get lonely, I just need to call Hazel.

She can't wrap her arms around me and snuggle or kiss the top of my forehead or whisper sweet nothings in my ear, but she can distract me from the loneliness with her crazy stories or mind-blowing treats.

"It will happen one day." I pat her arm.

"Yeah, yeah. So…tell me all about you and Graham."

"There is no me and Graham." I pick at the sleeve of my coat and focus my attention on our feet.

"Please, I see you constantly smiling at your phone and I can hear you whispering things or laughing when I pass your room."

"Stalker."

"Can't help it that we live together. Besides, you haven't told me about the date yet."

"There is nothing between Graham and I."

"Not what I asked."

I kick at a pebble on the sidewalk, putting all of my attention on the tiny stone.

"Look, I will stop talking about it if you just answer one question." When I look at her with a raised brow, she continues. "Do you want to go on a second date with him? Be honest."

An image of Graham pops into my mind. Him leaning against the counter of the bar in his all black uniform (a simple t-shirt and pants) as he leaned closer to me. So close I could smell the spice oozing from him.

I have never been a fan of spice or cologne, it often made me curl my nose in disgust, but on him, the scent was different. Foreign. Underrated.

Is he attractive? Certainly. He has a symmetrical face and dashing features, and I have seen many women fall at his feet in the limited time I have known him.

But is that all he is?

His voice, the same one that drew me in and tied me down, floods my head with the words "beautiful" and "trumpet".

Never have those words sounded as lovely as they do from his lips.

When we were in the living room of my childhood home, his voice echoed in the small space. His laughter engulfed me like a blanket.

Every fiber of my being is fighting, begging me to say "no", but it would be a lie to say my heart rate doesn't pick up at the mere mention of his name.

Trumpet.

No. I won't let this go any further than friendship.

I shake my head. "It doesn't matter." An answer to Hazel's earlier question.

As tantalizing as his voice is and enrapturing his words are, a voice can't stop me from falling too hard. A voice can't piece my broken heart back together.

Words damage and bruise, they don't mend and heal.

We pass a man crouched on the side of the street with a half empty bottle of beer in his hand. He's sitting in the shadows of the sunny day, but he's tanned with wrinkles and worry lines.

A part of me feels connected to him in a way. I can understand why he uses a temporary Band-Aid.

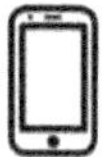

"This is an interesting choice," Hazel holds the door open to the restaurant for me.

It is one neither of us have been in before. A local restaurant too expensive for our taste. Usually, the both of us would have declined such an outing. Why waste money on something like this when we could use the same amount to buy a week's worth of groceries?

But Graham said all expenses are paid for. No ifs, ands, or buts. He didn't have to tell us twice.

"It certainly is," I agree.

The restaurant is dimly lit by a few lamp-like lights dangling above the tables. There is a soft piano tune humming from the corner. Voices are the lowest I have ever heard in such a public place and there is no clanging of dishes or scraping of forks.

Everything seems too delicate, too perfect, that I worry my squeaky boots against the linoleum flooring are only going to ruin the perfect facade

"How many?" A hostess asks Hazel and I. There is a polite smile on her face, stretching her lips wide and I wonder if it is something they train people to do or if hostesses are born with the ability.

"Oh," Hazel answers. "We are part of a party. I think they are already here, actually."

The hostess moves to stand behind a podium.

"Name?"

"Um, Graham…"

"Fischer." I quickly supply.

"Ah, yes. Mr. Fischer and Mr. Young are this way." She grabs a few menus and waves her arm towards the tables. "Please, follow me."

We do exactly that, our arms interlocked once again. When Hazel or I notice some new detail or something intriguing, we aggressively tap the other's arm to share the excitement or amusement.

She taps mine to point out a group of men in suits at one corner table. I tap hers to show the piano in the center of a dining space. She taps mine to point at a tiered chocolate dessert at a table. We continue this until the hostess stops at a table in the center.

"Here you are," she places our menus on the empty spots of the table.

I'm too focused on the guests occupying two of the chairs to so much as nod a "thank you".

There is a man I have never seen before seated across from where I stand. His dark hair is the perfect accessory to his semi-tan skin, like a dusting of an air brush across his flawless skin. When I say semi, I mean it is like a dusting of an air brush across his flawless peach skin.

The next thing I notice are the muscles straining beneath his dress shirt. He is handsome—that much is evident—but my eyes are only on him for a minute before they find the pair of emerald ones staring directly at me.

Graham's mouth quirks up and a blush instantly crawls up my neck. He's also clad in a casual dress shirt and his hair is combed in a different style. Did he dress up for lunch? Surely, he didn't go to the construction site like that. My stomach flips at the thought.

"You made it." Graham stands and pulls out my chair. Jason does the same for Hazel.

I don't realize until I sit down that Graham has me sitting in the seat right beside him. The seat he pushed in a little farther from Hazel and a little closer to him.

Why did I walk on the right side of Hazel?

"Yeah," Hazel speaks up. "We definitely wouldn't miss out on free food."

Graham is smiling at her comment, but his eyes are on me the second his butt hits his chair again. "This is Jason. Jason, this is Hazel and Piper."

Jason nods at each of us. He looks to Hazel first, "the girl who makes delicious cupcakes," then to me "and the woman with the bea—" He grunts before he can finish and gives Graham a stern look.

The two have a silent conversation between them, one I can't read, and Hazel half chuckles, half scoffs beside me like this is all some big joke. I missed the punchline.

I lean towards her to whisper, "what is happening?" but from our positions, I'm too far away and Graham and Jason are able to hear my question.

"He stutters sometimes," Graham comments. "It's a condition."

Jason scoffs.

"You're a doctor, right?" Hazel changes the subject and I couldn't be more grateful.

"Yes." Jason's response is short, clipped, like he can't wait to be done with this entire outing. A sense of calm washes over me at the idea that I am not alone in this.

Jason may not be as intimidating as Graham made him out to be.

"Good afternoon." a waiter stops between Graham and Jason, looking between Hazel and I and ignoring the two men. "My name is Michael, and I will be your server tonight. Are there any drinks I can get you started with?"

His pearly whites are on display in his charming grin. He lazily glances down my frame before forcing his eyes back up to mine.

My entire skin is flushed under his gaze and I feel something crawling across me. Similar to the idea of being trampled on by bugs with thousands of little legs.

Graham coughs, not bothering to cover his mouth, as he faces the waiter beside him. Michael shifts on his feet and brushes his shirt.

"Sorry," Graham notes, but his tone is anything but apologetic. "Still getting over some hay fever."

Michael takes a step back with a trained, polite smile on his lips. Hazel giggles from beside me and I find it contagious. When a small laugh escapes my own lips, Graham grins.

Eventually, Jason speaks up first, giving the waiter a complicated order. He asks a dozen questions about the appetizer, only to decide on something else. If the waiter hadn't been ogling me only moments before, I would feel bad for him.

After all of our orders are in and the waiter has disappeared, Graham turns to Jason. "What was that about? You never say more than two words, let alone ask questions."

Jason shrugs. "He seemed like he needed to experience annoyance." I like him.

"I second that." Hazel chimes in. "So, Jason, what field are you going into?" Hazel is doing this thing with her eyes and a tilt of her head. It's the same move she made on the man who *used* to bring us baked ziti every month. Now the man purposely avoids us in the halls.

Poor Jason doesn't squirm an inch under her gaze. He hasn't even looked in her direction. He has no clue of the trap she's setting.

Graham, however, is studying her with a small smile dancing on his lips. I wonder if she has ever used that move on him. If she has, was it successful? Would Graham fall for such a thing?

Of course he would because Hazel is the epitome of female charm. She is funny, beautiful, intelligent, and not scared to go after what she wants. Plus, she doesn't have a boatload of issues weighing her down and preventing her from pursuing a guy.

Hazel is the perfect pair for someone as great as Graham.

Nausea forms in my stomach.

"You might rip your shirt if you tug it any harder." The words are a whisper in my ear and a breath fanning against my skin.

When did he get so close?

"I definitely wouldn't mind, but I'm not sure how quickly we can find you an extra shirt."

I hadn't realized I had been playing with the hem of the only dress shirt I own. It's one that wrinkles easily, if not already noticeable by the few creases in the fabric.

I'm surprised he even noticed my actions with how entranced he was with Hazel.

"Jealous?" It's only one word but it throws me so off kilter I'm not sure it's what he said.

"What?"

He smirks playfully like I am the funniest thing he has ever seen. "I find Hazel's flirting amusing and I have always loved to watch Jason squirm, but that's all it was, Trumpet. I was merely watching the show."

Confusion sweeps over me for only a minute, trying to decipher why he is granting me this information, until it suddenly clicks. He heard my thoughts. No, I said them aloud.

My eyes track Hazel and Jason, expecting them to be staring at us, only to find them lost in their own conversation. Hazel has settled back against her chair, all signs of flirtation wiped from her features. Jason is actually looking at her. They have found common ground.

It's amazing how quickly Hazel can change. She would be a great actress in another life.

"Thank you for coming by the way." Graham pulls my attention back to him, although I'm not sure it ever fully left.

"Did you think I would ditch you?"

"I would be lying if I said it didn't cross my mind."

"Please. I would never miss an opportunity for free food."

"A knife straight to the heart, Pipes." He acts it out.

A grin is stretched wide across my lips, but I shake my head. "Why did you pick this place?"

At that, he settles back in his chair like our conversation no longer needs to be kept quiet. Something wedges its way into my chest. Cold chills trace my spine at his body leaning away from mine.

"Would you believe me if I said it was a spur of the moment decision?"

In a place like this? "No."

"I wanted to impress you."

A blush creeps across my skin and I'm suddenly relieved he's not so close anymore. "Why?"

"Depends. Is it working?"

"I guess you'll have to wait and see how the food lives up to my standards."

"I'm a very patient man."

I try not to scoff but fail. "That's not how I'd describe you."

"Are you calling me impatient?"

"Among other things."

"You haven't seen just how impatient I can be when I lose all control."

I have a feeling we aren't still talking about the restaurant, but I'm not sure how to approach it. What is it about Graham that turns me into an entirely different person?

Normally, I would stay quiet and to myself when out, especially around new people. Hazel would find ways to pull me into a conversation, so I don't have to put in much effort. Trying to start and continue a conversation outside of the people I know, to me, is the equivalent of running through the streets naked. There is no shot of courage strong enough to make me do that.

With Graham beside me, though, he seems to pull the conversation *from* me. Since the first day we met, he has had no trouble in making me talk. Not that there has been much resistance on my end.

"I'll be right back," he notes before departing from the table and I realize Hazel has left too.

I think she whispered to me about going to the restroom, but I was so lost in my own head to really take notice.

That leaves two of us. Me and a person I have never interacted with before.

I open my mouth to say something, anything to end the awkward quiet between us, but he beats me to it. "He's not as bad as he seems."

"What?"

Jason leans back and folds his hands on his lap under the table. "He can be obnoxious and too pushy at times, but he's not a horrible person."

"I'm sorry. I think you lost me. Who are we talking about?"

He studies me for a moment, but I don't feel scrutinized under his gaze. He studies me as though he is checking for injuries, any sign of harm. "We have been friends since we were kids." He continues, disregarding my question. "I've watched him fall for girl after girl. He gets in way over his head and goes too fast too soon. Let's just say if I were an author, I would have lots of material to work with…" he trails off with a light laugh.

"He can be impatient and too much all at once, but I have never known someone more caring than Graham."

A wave crashes over me. He's talking about Graham. He is talking *up* Graham. What exactly did Graham tell him about us?

"I'm sure you know this since you two are dating."

"We—" I clear my throat. "We aren't dating."

"Yeah? Does he know that?"

"We've only been on one date."

"Did you not hear me just say how Graham gets in over his head?"

The waiter interrupts before I have a chance to say anything and I couldn't be more grateful. He sets our drinks down. If he does it slow enough, Hazel or Graham might just reappear.

As if the universe is against me, Michael departs and Jason picks back up like we were never interrupted.

"From the second you sat down, all of your attention has been given to him. Even if you weren't lifting your head, I could see you reacting to every word he said."

"You were watching me?" I'm offended and it comes off clear in my tone.

"I was observing you. I can't take another weekend of him binge watching rom-coms."

I want to smile at the idea. Graham likes romance. *Comedic* romance.

"Something tells me you are different, though."

"Different how?"

"I don't know. I haven't quite figured that out yet." His head tilts to the right and he studies me some more. I wonder if that's something he does often: study people.

Can he read every emotion flicking through me right now?

"We aren't dating." I repeat.

"You said that already."

Not to the right person apparently. I *have* to turn him down despite every nerve ending of mine fighting me on it.

Jason continues, "All I'm asking is for you to—"

"Be patient with him?"

"No." He scoffs like the idea is unbelievable. "Give him a run for his money. He needs to learn that not every girl is going to fall at his feet."

I can't help the small laugh that bubbles out of me. "All I'm asking is for you to be honest with him. Don't beat around the bush and lead him on. If you genuinely like him, or even just respect him, be honest. He may be tough on the outside, but he cries." Then, as an afterthought. "A lot."

The thought sends a pang to my chest.

"Do you tell all of Graham's romantic interests this?" I joke.

He smiles softly. "Only the ones who need to hear it."

I wonder if he would feel the same way if he knew how much I am fighting every instinct in admitting to Graham just how much I *want* to jump into things with him. If he knew how I will fight those instincts and turn Graham down no matter how much I find the word "no" to be distasteful…would he still feel the same?

CHAPTER TWENTY-FIVE

PIPER

I'm late. I'm never late. It's the one thing I pride myself on because out of my entire family, I am the only one who shows up on time, if not early. Yet, here I am, rushing to work.

I slept past my alarm because I couldn't pull myself out of the dream playing behind my closed eyes. He was in my head and making me admit things I have never told anyone before and making me wonder just how stupid my "no dating" rule may be.

He leaned in close, so close I could hear his breathing and his heart beating at an erratic pace. Graham's voice found his way to me and I snuggled further into my sheets because of it. Opening my eyes and climbing out of bed seemed as torturous as listening to screechy bagpipes.

"Good morning," a familiar voice calls out to me.

I stop when a pair freeing green eyes and mussed blonde hair appear in front of me. He's here. Outside of my office. I must still be dreaming.

"Morning," I hesitate.

"You okay? You look like you saw a ghost." He stops a foot from me.

"I think I have," I mumble.

"What?"

"Nothing. What are you doing here?"

He smiles and my knees almost give out beneath me. "I wanted to bring you this." He passes a cup to me. "Sun's Cafe" is printed on the front, right above a phone number and the name 'Chelsea'.

"Does the phone number come with it?"

He scrunches a brow. I hold the cup up for him to see.

"One second." He snatches the cup out of my hand and walks to the truck parked alongside the road beside us. I peak past him, noting the carrier of drinks on his passenger seat.

Graham resurfaces with a different cup in hand. "Here."

I slowly accept the cup and take a sip. A minty taste greets my tongue. I only get this beverage on occasion, when I am feeling too down in the cold or am willing to treat myself on a good day. Both occasions are rare.

"How did you know I like this?"

He shoves his hands into his coat. "Wild guess."

I bounce on my tiptoes. "Are you in the delivery business too?"

"What?"

I nod towards his truck. "The drinks."

"Oh," he rubs at the back of his neck. "I wasn't sure what you like so I wanted to be prepared." My heart does a summersault. I use the cup to shield my smile.

"What else did you order?"

"Doesn't matter." He says it sheepishly. It sends a surge of confidence through me.

I move towards his truck and open the door. He stops me with a hand on the frame.

"Why are you being so secretive? How many did you order?"

"Just a few."

I narrow my eyes at him. Then, I look over his shoulder and shout "Hey, Hazel" to her ghost. Graham loosens his hold on the door and turns. I yank the door open where I find a total of three drink carriers littered on this side.

Graham gently nudges me away and closes the door. I'm laughing too much to care. "You ordered the entire menu." The words are a chuckle on my lips.

He's rubbing furiously at his neck. "Not the *whole* menu."

"Well, thank you, Graham. I think you just made my day." It's not a sentence I take lightly, but after the words fall out, I know I mean it.

Graham drops his hand and shoves it into one of his coat pockets. "You're welcome."

He takes a step closer and my back hits the cool frame of his truck. When did we get so close? My heart picks up its pace as it jumps to see over the wall around it.

"I was thinking…" His words are slow, purposeful and I am on the edge of my seat. "If you're interested, I'd like to—"

He's within a foot of me. He leans a hair closer and it's like he stepped on a trip wire, heightening all of my senses. He's too close. Too close and I can't breathe with him *this* close. Instinctively, I shift from my spot and put at least six feet between us.

"I need to go." I tell him, but it comes out breathless. "I'm late for work." As I start to back away, "thank you for the tea."

His face falls, but he doesn't utter one word. Just nods and waves me away.

When I unlock the door to my apartment, Hazel is sliding across the floor in her fuzzy Christmas socks to meet me at the door. "You're home."

"Am I not supposed to be?" I joke.

"No. I mean, yes, you are. Sorry, I'm just so excited."

"Excited for what?" I set my shoes on our shoe rack and pass her to slump on the couch in the living room.

I used to despise this couch. It is a mustard yellow and Hazel found it in a thrift shop. We had to scrub it for days before bringing it inside and scrubbing it for another three. Now, I find the sinking cushions to be the epitome of falling into a cloud.

"For you to tell me all about your date with Graham." She wiggles her eyebrows as she plops down beside me with her legs crossed. "We haven't had much time to talk since then and you have given me no details."

She's right. Even though it has been a week and we went to lunch with Graham and Jason the other day, I have had no time to talk to her. We haven't even been able to meet for our usual lunches. She's been busy baking and I have been…distracted.

I point to the icing covered whisk in her hand. "Don't you have something to finish?"

"Oh," she lifts just high enough for her to chuck the whisk into the sink. "Perfect shot."

"What if that had splattered everywhere?"

"Then, I would clean it. I'm the only one who cleans anyway."

"Not true."

She pins me with a look.

"Not *all* the time."

"So…tell me about Graham. Where did he take you? What did he wear? What did he say? Did he—"

"Can we do one question at a time?"

"Fine. Let's start with where you went."

My fingers find the hem of my shirt and I lazily trail the tips over it. "Mom's house."

"He took you to his mom's house?"

"No, we were at *my* mom's house."

"Okay, I know you aren't a fan of providing relevant information, but I desperately need some context right now."

I sigh and turn to face her. "I forgot I had to babysit Kyle the other night so Mom and John could have their monthly date."

"Oh. It was the fifth, wasn't it?"

"Yeah. Anyway, I had to babysit so that's where we went."

"He went to the house with you?"

"Yes."

"And he stayed there the whole time?"

"Mhmm."

"And he didn't complain once?"

"No."

She's giddy. I fear what comes next. "Piper, you know what this means, right?"

"He's a nice person?"

"He's in love with you."

Love? My heart nearly vomits at the thought. "We just met Hazel. And we've only been on one date, if you can even count that as a date."

"So? Elizabeth and Mr. Darcy barely knew each other, and he fell in love with her instantly."

"Different time period and fictional characters."

"Okay, Mrs. Party Pooper. Let's say he's not in love with you. But he really, *really* likes you." She pokes my arm. I try to hide the smile fighting to break through, but her excitement is contagious. "You're blushing."

"I am not."

A timer goes off. Hazel quickly jumps up to fetch something from the oven. She doesn't bother grabbing oven mitts before reaching her hands inside.

"You actually set a timer?"

"Oliver said he could taste the bitterness in my food from being slightly overdone."

"*Oliver?*"

"Oh, that's right. I haven't told you about him." She finishes what she's doing and plops back down on the couch. "Man, so much has happened in the past week."

I snatch a chip from the discarded bag on the coffee table. They are stale, making the crunch louder than necessary.

"So the other night I—well, let's just say I was a little down about my desserts and happened to be sitting in the alley between that exotic restaurant and that floral shop you love."

"The one covered in vines?"

"That's the one! Any who, I heard this loud bang and when I looked up, there was Oliver. He is quite handsome, might I add, especially in the chef's uniform he was wearing."

She takes a pause to bite into a handful of chips. When the chunks are half-chewed, she resumes. "Turns out he is the owner of the restaurant I happened to be sulking in the alley of." I make a mental note to remember the sulking part afterwards. "He tried a bite of my desserts, gave some very harsh criticism, then offered me a job. Me? Can you believe that Piper?"

"That's incredible, Hazel. So when do you start? What do you do?"

"Well, that's where it kind of turns sour. I start as a dishwasher and my first day is tomorrow, actually."

"Wait. He tried your desserts and offered you a dishwashing position?"

"Yeah. He said I still have some learning to do, but he sees potential and wants to have me on board his team."

"That's amazing, Hazel," I tell her and mean every word. I wish I had one of those poppers to explode in celebration. Instead, I return her beaming smile.

"I know! But enough about me," She grabs the blanket from the back of the couch and deposits it on our laps. "Tell me more about your date."

"What exactly do you want to know?"

"How did it go? Give me the highlights."

"Well, he built Legos with Kyle and then we all ate dinner and played a game. Then, he drove me home."

"I don't want a summary of events. I want the gritty details. What did he say? What did you say? Was there any intimacy involved?"

"Hazel." I playfully shove her.

She feigns innocence. "It's a valid question."

"We were at my mom's house with my brother upstairs."

"So you're saying that something could have happened in the right environment."

"I'm saying you are crazy."

Even if Graham and I were in the most romantic spot, I wouldn't go that far with him. No matter what I'm feeling in that situation, I won't do it. I don't plan on having sex with someone until I know I can trust them. Even if that day may never come.

She laughs through her chips. "Okay, moving on. What *did* you guys do?"

I stare at my hands in my lap, thinking back to last night. A sudden warmth fills my chest at the memory. "We talked."

She's looking at me with a small smile playing on her lips.

"What?"

"You're happy." She states rather than asks it, but I don't refute her words. I'm not sure I can. "Will there be a second date?"

"He did ask me out again." It was before he dropped me off at my apartment building. I had somehow fallen asleep in his truck and when he put the car in park, I stirred awake.

I turned to find his eyes on me and a lazy smile on his dashing face. "You can keep sleeping," he said.

"Why? So you can keep watching me?" Even when I was half asleep, I felt the urge to tease him.

"I thought about it."

The moonlight beat against the opposite side of the street from where Graham, shielding my blush in the shadows. My hands fiddled with the bag on my lap.

"Is it too soon to ask you out for another date?" Graham whispered in the space between us.

"You still want to?" I don't know why I expected him to call it quits, but I did. Maybe it's because I never let anyone get this close, this far, before.

He chuckled, low and deep. "Yeah. I really do, Piper." My name with his voice coiling around it is my favorite sound.

"What did you say, Piper?" Hazel's voice brings me back to the present. She's staring at me impatiently.

My voice is barely above a whisper when I admit "I said I need to think about it."

"And? Have you thought about it? I'm surprised you guys didn't go out again before the four of us met for lunch. Although, you two already seemed pretty chummy." She lays her legs across my lap and settles back against the arm of the couch.

"We weren't 'chummy'. I don't even know what that word means."

"You don't need to. So, second date?"

I pick at her sweatpants, needing something to busy my hands with. "I don't know."

It's the truth. I don't. I know there shouldn't be a second date. If I go out with him for a second time, I might want to go out with him for a third or even fourth time and then all of it will get foggy in my head until I don't know what's happening anymore and it's too late. You can't have self-control when you let it go.

"Do you like him?"

"I already answered that, Hazel. It doesn't matter if—"

"It does, though. Piper, if you like him, if you really like him, why would you deprive yourself of that opportunity?"

My blood starts to boil and I feel the urge to dig my fingernails into the palm of my hands. It's not Hazel I'm irritated with. She doesn't understand why I can't date Graham. Why I have to stop after one date. She doesn't know why I'm so scared that no matter how much the cold makes me cry in the middle of the night, I will not allow someone to share the bed with me. I will not let someone wrap me in their arms and whisper promises I know they won't keep. I won't do it.

"I'm not like you, Hazel." It comes out harsher than I intend. I take a deep breath. "It's not that simple. Either way, Graham and I are better as friends."

She grabs one of my hands and drags my attention to her. "I'm sorry. I wasn't trying to belittle your feelings. I just want you to be happy. You deserve the world and so much more, Piper."

Her words are supposed to be endearing, but all I feel is this hollowness in my chest. "I know, but I am happy." There's sympathy in her eyes as she tilts her head. "I promise," but I know how easy it is for someone to break their promise and not keep their word. I have done it far too many times.

CHAPTER TWENTY-SIX

GRAHAM

The excavator rumbles as it scrapes the pile of dirt a few feet from me. I watch intently as it sinks into the ground and scoops the chunks up. When the bucket raises, my eyes catch on fiery red hair on the other side of the fence.

I cross my arms over my chest, smiling, and wave at her. As if noticing me for the first time, Piper shakes her head and backs up. She hurriedly walks down the sidewalk.

I jog from my spot over to her before she has a chance to get out of my line of sight. "Hey," I call out.

She turns a fraction, "Hey," but doesn't stop walking.

"You can't just ogle me and then ditch as if nothing happened."

At that, she stops. "I wasn't ogling you."

I lean my hands on the wire fence, hating how it separates us. Her image is fragmented around the design of the wires. No matter how I adjust, I can't see her properly. "Right. You like to stand outside of a lot of construction sites. I bet its premium entertainment."

"It is. I even considered bringing popcorn."

"Of course. No show is complete without popcorn."

Finally, she looks at me.

I'm grinning like a fool. "I was worried you were losing interest."

"What?"

"You haven't been answering my messages much." She plays with the hem of her coat. If we weren't separated by this fence, I would reach out and tuck the fallen strand of hair behind her ear.

"I've been busy."

I nod. "Well, since I have your attention, I was thinking maybe you and I could go out again."

"Why?"

A chuckle escapes me. "Generally, when the first date goes well, you go on a second date." She's hesitant and doesn't so much as crack a smile. "The first date did go well, right?" There's a sour taste on my tongue like I ate a lemon.

"Yes. I mean, it went alright."

"Good. Then, how about a second date?"

"You already asked me this the other night."

I did and I gave her a week to consider. A week to weigh all the pros and cons. I even settled for a group outing instead of a second date in the meantime. "Yeah, and if I remember correctly, you said you would think about it. So? What's the verdict?"

We had a great time so I don't see any reason she would say—

"I don't know."

"Is it because of my competitive nature? Look, I promise no Uno this time. And since it will be just the two of us, I will have much better game."

"I thought you said no games."

"None in the traditional sense."

She studies me. I wonder what she's looking for. Maybe a flaw to use as an excuse? Either way, my heart has stopped in anticipation of her answer.

"I'm not much of a relationship person, Graham."

Not the response I expected. "It's just a second date." When she stays quiet, I add. "Just give me one more chance, one chance to really show you what dating me could be like."

"We already went on a date, though. Were you pretending to be someone else?"

"No, but I'd like to show you the side of me that's not kid-friendly."

Her face reddens the same shade of her hair. I bite my lip to keep the smile at bay.

"Please."

"Why are you asking me out? What about the girl you asked for advice on earlier?"

"What?"

"You messaged me and asked how to win the woman who caught your eye." Her gaze is ducked. I lower my head to try and find her eyes.

Is that what all of this is about? She thought I was interested in someone else? I need to amend this so she knows just how much she is the only one I am after. "Just let me take you on the second date."

She opens her mouth, but I'm already backing away. I shout "Sorry. Can't hear you over all of the noise. I'll send you the details later."

I turn around so I don't have to see her walk away. I'm not sure I will be able to focus or stay on task if she's around any longer.

"Who's the girlfriend?" Vince pats my back when I make it back to where he's standing.

"What girlfriend?" I shout over the sound of the excavator and Jeff's commands in the background.

"The girl you ran off to. The one with the fine—"

I interrupt with a firm grip on his shoulder before he can say anything that would result with my fist slammed into his face. "She's…not my girlfriend."

The words are reluctant on my tongue. Technically, we didn't label anything and we only went on one date. One date I think went pretty well. As much as I would love to call her my girlfriend and own the title of boyfriend, I don't want to push her any more than I already have.

The last thing I want to do is make her uncomfortable. Especially when she is just starting to let me in.

"Just a hookup then?" Vince's question sends a burn of irritation up my throat.

Piper is not a woman you meet for "just a hookup", not that anyone woman is. She is the woman you want to have deep conversations with and snuggle on the couch with and eventually show off to your mother to say "look! Can you believe I was able to convince her to look past every flaw of mine and pick me?"

Piper isn't a demo you listen to and then throw away. She's like a never-ending symphony and my ears are tuned in until the big finish.

"Watch your mouth, Vince," I warn.

He raises his hands in mock defense. "Hey, just a question. Don't get your panties in a bunch, Fischer."

I grumble a silent curse as a few violent scenes play out in my head. I'm not a violent person. I didn't get in trouble in school for fights. I always broke them up. But the idea of a fight is sounding pretty good right now.

Swallowing all of those emotions, I resume work. I can't afford to lose this job over Vince's disrespect.

I'm walking to the trailer to clock out for my break when I hear Jeff call out to me. I turn and wait for him to reach where I stopped. "Sir," I greet.

"Any chance you're available tomorrow around three?"

"Yes. Do you need me to stay longer?"

He sighs and starts to walk towards the trailer. I follow beside him. "No. Madeline is having some trouble with school again and I was hoping you could help her."

Madeline is his daughter. She's a freshman in college, meaning she's only a few years younger than me, and is studying to be a marketing consultant. She has to take a few literature courses in the process, which is far from her strong suit.

I've helped her study before, despite the irony of a non-college student helping a very intelligent college student. She's quick to learn and the books she reads in class are great recommendations for myself.

"No problem. I just have to be gone by four-thirty so I can head to the bar."

"You still work there?"

I nod, not wanting to delve into this anymore than needed.

He opens the trailer door and steps inside. I have to be quick to grab the door from him before it shuts between us. "You know, I really don't understand you."

The fridge is stocked with the same cans of soda and day old string cheese. I shut it and open my locker to grab the granola bar I stole from Jason this morning.

Stolen food always has a sweeter taste to it.

"Why work this hard when you are so smart. You could be *my* boss. Hell, with your brains and stubbornness, you could be the boss of my boss."

I smile at the compliment, but power is never something I craved. "I don't think you would like working under me, Sir."

He pulls out a chair and starts scribbling on a clipboard. "Can't get any worse than the current one."

I munch on the bar in the quiet space between us as I study Jeff. He's paler than he was yesterday and he's definitely losing some weight. I wonder if Madeline knows about his condition. If she's taken the time to care for him. I make a mental note to approach the subject when I see her tomorrow.

I grab a water from the fridge, one I purposely hid in the back, pass it to Jeff, and plop in the seat across from him.

"Thanks." He chugs a big gulp of it before staring me down. "Seriously, why didn't you go to school? Choose a better life?"

My mouth opens to respond when he raises his hand to stop me. "Don't give me that crap about how you are living a great life now or you like to keep busy."

"It wasn't in my plans," I shrug.

"Well, I hope you're regretting it. Maybe it would finally knock some sense into you."

A forced laugh escapes me. It's the only response I know how to give. The one I've practiced and perfected year after year since the day I told my parents I wasn't going to college.

"Why not?" Mom asked.

"Do you not know what your major will be?" Dad interrogated.

I knew I would pick English. It is my passion, but that's not a big enough reason to waste four years of my life that I could be spending earning enough wealth to take care of my family. Just like my grandfather.

After they let all of their questions out, I gave a shrug of a laugh, wrapped an arm around my mom's shoulder, and said, "It's not that. I'm just not the college type."

It was a lie, one of the few I ever told them, but after that, they continued to spiral out of me like vomit. I laughed and shook all of the questions off each time they arose. "It's not for me," I would say. "I like where I'm at." "I'm better with my hands than my head." "I like to stay busy."

Only one of those is the truth.

I can always tell Mom wishes I chose a different path. I can see it mixed in with the pity swimming in her eyes. I hear it every time someone makes a comment about how I could be doing so much more with my life.

Each time I shut them down.

If they knew how much I regret my decision, how much it keeps me up at night, how much I feel this hollowness in my chest for not chasing the one thing that actually made me feel complete...I can already hear the "I told you so" on their lips.

"Hey, I brought—"

I slam the face of my computer down as Jason makes his way to the living. His half sentence hangs in the air between us as I turn to see the pizza box in his hand.

"You got pizza? What kind?"

He set the box on the table and crossed his arms. "Why did you slam your computer?"

The device is burning a hole into my lap. I had been researching online colleges that would be affordable and accessible for me to get a degree in English education. I wasn't going to pursue any of the leads, but curiosity got the better of me. That, and my talk with Piper the other night keeps stinging the back of my mind.

She made it sound like I still have a chance. Like it's never too late to rewrite your future. I just have to reshuffle my cards...

"Nothing." I tell him and stand. I open the box and grab a slice. I devour a large bite of it. "Thanks. I was starving." I pat him on the chest, but his expression has yet to change from its skeptical state.

I can't have him asking questions. He has this way of pulling information out of me and hitting every insecure mark on my body. He would make a great torturer.

"How did your date go with Jasmine?" Conversation shift. A dramatic one always does the trick.

He releases a big groan before copying me in devouring a slice of pizza.

"That good, huh?"

"It wasn't a date."

"Right. The tabloids got it all wrong." It's a lie. There were no pictures or story about the two of them in the headlines, but I love the raised eyebrow and wide eyes it earns me.

When he sees the grin on my face, "Jerk."

"You love me."

He groans through another bite. I sit opposite him. "How is Piper? She break up with you yet?"

Ah, the sweet, sweet brotherly love I have come to know from him. "She's madly in love with me, I'll have you know."

He scoffs.

"You're just jealous girls don't fawn over you like they do me."

He's quiet for a moment, savoring his pizza a little too long. "Don't hurt her, Graham."

I stop chewing. "I—"

"She's nice and a good woman. Probably way too good for you." If only he knew how much I have been telling myself that for the past few weeks. "She is also the type that will run away the second you push too far." It's a warning.

"I'm not going to—"

"Elizabeth. Ninth grade. Taylor Swift on the speakers. A dozen roses in the classroom."

I cringe at the memory. After the entire class focused their attention on her, her face turned a beat red. Except, it wasn't out of shyness or even embarrassment, it was out of pure anger.

Before I had time to process, the roses were torn into pieces and thrown at me. I still can't listen to Taylor Swift without the sting of the thorns floating back to me.

"That was one time and—"

"Mariana in the tenth grade. A peach—maybe it was blueberry—cake in the shape of a heart with your initials in icing on top."

"Okay, that one wasn't even that bad."

"She went to the hospital."

"She shouldn't have ate the cake if she was allergic."

"You forced her to take a bite."

I rub the back of my neck, not sure how this conversation turned into my personal roast. These are memories I planned on shoving down and never acknowledging for the rest of my life. Unfortunately, Jason had been a witness to each one.

"All I'm trying to say is: don't push Piper. I like her and you better not ruin it."

Jason has never approved of any of the girls I fawned over. At least, not until each one blew up in my face. Then he praised them for showing me where I stand. Quite the best friend he is.

Yet, he is a fan of Piper. *My* Piper.

My heart swells with warmth, but there's this sinking feeling in my gut.

As much as I hate to admit it, I do come on too strong. I have thought about endless ways to woo her, each one being more elaborate than the previous. If I like a girl, I want her and the rest of the world to know it.

Piper, though, has turned me down without me even having to go through the effort of putting on a big show. Maybe that's what stopped me from going too far too soon.

That and the thought of losing her because of my idiocy sends a knife straight to the chest.

Piper. Trumpet. She's…*special* doesn't even begin to describe how out of this world she is. There are twenty six letters in the alphabet and one million words in the English language, but I can't find one to describe her. One that matches just how perfect she is.

I've fallen for her. Hard.

"I know," I tell Jason and it's the truth. I'm holding back with as much strength as I can muster, and I will continue to do so until I hear her voice give the order to let go.

CHAPTER TWENTY-SEVEN

GRAHAM

"Where are we going?" Piper buckles her seatbelt over her dark green sweater and black coat.

"It's a surprise." I turn my attention to the road and move us into the traffic.

"You aren't taking me to some stranded field to leave me for dead, are you?"

"I'm not that cruel." Then, after a beat, "it's the middle of winter."

"I knew you were suspicious," she says with a sigh as she crosses her arms and leans back against the seat.

A laugh bubbles out of me. "No deserted fields."

"An abandoned building? Maybe some dark alleyway?"

"No to all suspicious locations. Although, I'm starting to wonder if you watch too much crime tv."

Piper shakes her head. "Oh, no. Only a healthy amount."

"Of course," the sarcasm is brewing between us.

"Can I ask you a question even though it might bite me in the butt?"

"Sure."

"You've told me before that you don't date. Why?" More importantly, why me?

She's quiet, lost in thought, and I wonder if I'll ever get an answer when she says, "Why would a deaf person go to a concert?"

"You lost me."

"If you know what's going to happen and that outweighs all of those 'fuzzy feelings', which means you barely feel anything, if at all, because of the knowledge, why would you pursue it? Why go to a concert you know you can't hear?"

"Isn't there more to a concert than the music?"

She turns her head towards me. "Something tells me you have never been to one."

"There's more than the sound, isn't there? A concert is packed with diverse people and even if you can't hear what is on stage or the screams around you, you can still feel it. You can see it."

"But a moment of bliss isn't worth a lifetime of regret."

Our gazes meet for a brief second, a minor minute when we are stopped at a light and I am able to give her my full attention. Her eyes are glossy, but not in a beautiful way. More of a delicate dam that could overflow with even the tiniest drop.

A car honks and we are jolted out of the spell. I put my foot on the gas.

Piper clears her throat. "Is it my turn to ask a question now?"

"Ask away, Trumpet."

"If you could rid the world of any emotion, what would it be?"

"Pass."

"You can't pass."

"Then my answer is none."

"Come on. I answered your question. Answer mine."

I sigh and drum my fingers on the steering wheel if only to give me time to think.

I could say depression. It is a life-altering feeling that can shape a person and their relationships. It is drowning in the ocean even with a life preserver within reach. One can't escape. But it connects us to others in our most vulnerable moments and builds relationships where we least expect it.

Grief is a close second, but I think it is more of a positive, than a negative. If you grieve over someone, it only means they were special. It symbolizes just how important they are and I would never want to not grieve over someone I love.

As we pass a restaurant known for the birthday parties it holds, I know what my answer is. "Loneliness."

"There are lots of people who are comfortable being alone." Piper phrases it as more of a question than a statement.

"There is a difference between alone and lonely." What I don't say: "I have proof."

"I think loneliness can be good." I raise a brow at her statement to which she waves her hand. "Not that being lonely is good, but the feeling it brings. I mean, if you are lonely, it grounds you and reminds you of some things you can't do alone. Some things you might not *want* to do alone. I mean, there's a better way to put this, I just—" She catches the smile on my lips. "I'm sorry. I'm rambling."

"Trumpet, you can ramble for days and I would still pay to be part of the audience."

Her cheeks flush the most beautiful shade of red and in that instant, I suddenly have a new favorite color. "You're insufferable." She plays with the hem of her shirt and I wonder—no, I need to know what questions she's holding back.

I bite cool my features. "My turn. Biggest fear."

"Getting deep now?"

"You asked about the worst emotion."

"Point taken."

She's quiet, studying the landscapes we pass by through the window. "Well?"

"You want the truth?"

"Always."

"I…You go first."

"What happened to passing not being allowed?"

"I'm not passing, I'm merely giving myself time to think."

"Right. I'll go first then." I take a moment to consider even though I knew the answer to this question the second I asked it. "Biggest fear? Not living up to my grandfather."

"Does he have high expectations for you?"

"No. In fact, I'm pretty sure he had the lowest standards for me." I ignore her stare because I'm worried what I'll find in it. She wants honesty and I'll give her honesty, but I can't do it while looking into her eyes. "He spent his entire life working his butt off to give his kids and grandkids the life of their dreams. He was cheap. I think his sock drawer only contained seven pairs and each one had holes." I smile at the memory.

He used to always tell my grandmother, "it adds character" and she would swat him on his arm.

"He didn't ask for one thing in return. But when it came to us, especially Grandma and Mom, there was not one thing he would deprive them of. He wanted to give them the life he never had. He wanted them to never have to worry about a single thing."

I trail off as I make a right onto a dirt road. I hadn't realized how much I delved into until I pause to take a breath.

"Anyway," I get back to the point. She doesn't want to know about all of that. "He worked so much that he was able to save a boatload of money for us to inherit. I technically wouldn't have to lift a finger if I tapped into it, but—"

"You want to make your grandfather proud."

I let my foot ease up on the gas so I can turn to face her. When I catch her eyes, I nearly put the car in park just to wrap her in my arms. There is no pity, no sorrow, only understanding. Like she knows how heavy this entire thing is on my shoulders and she doesn't blame me for working endlessly. Like she can feel in my heart just how much effort I put into everything I do and just how much weight sits on my shoulders because of it.

She knows that I gave up my dream, even though I might regret every second of it, just so I can do the same that he did. It's such an intense connection that I wonder why I ever doubted her. Why did I ever think she would pity me?

"That's very admirable, Graham," she breaks the quiet between us.

Her hands rub her arms as she looks away. I turn the heat up a notch higher and adjust the vents to blow on her.

"Thank you," I finally say and, because I need something to be off the topic, something to keep me from spilling my guts to her even more, I ask "What about you? Biggest fear?"

Her fingers stop fiddling with the hem of her shirt, but her attention is on the scenery outside the window. "This."

I don't ask any follow up questions. Instead, I wait. I wait for her to be ready to dive more into it because she was patient with me and I am more than willing to wait as long as it takes to finally be able to hear the thoughts racing through her mind.

"Everyone I know has dated and fallen in love. Whether it be with the wrong person or right person, they still put themselves out there. I never understood why. Why risk everything on someone when you have no idea if they are the one? I mean, you are madly in love one second, just to fall out of it the next."

She takes a breath. The only sound is the hum of the truck and the crunch of the tires on the road.

"But then I watch the stupid romance movies and listen to the gushing stories people tell me about how sweet their partner is and how wonderful it is to be held by someone and hugged and kissed and—I start to wonder if maybe that's why it's worth it all. If maybe all of the heartache and fear is worth it because at least you have someone that notices you and will wrap you up in their arms after a long day or just because they want to."

There's more to it. I can tell by the way she shrinks into the seat.

If there was a way I could prove to her that I could be that person and the only risk would be me falling head over heels for her, I would sell my soul to do it.

"It's scary." I finally mumble, earning a soft glance from her. "Putting yourself out there is one of the hardest things to do." I say it as gently as possible and I mean every word of it. It is scary. I should know. "And I'm honored…" my hand finds hers and I slowly interlock our fingers, waiting for her to tell me to stop. She doesn't. "…that you decided to open up to me. I promise not to make you regret it."

She stares down at our interlocked hands like they are the newest phenomenon. Am I squeezing her hand too hard? Oh, God. Are my palms sweating? Did I just mess this—

"I've never held hands with someone before." Her voice is small, astonished.

My whole body is frozen, waiting for her to decide what happens next. If she lets go, I will respect her decision and keep my distance. If she holds on…

She squeezes my hand ever so lightly as though she's testing it. What she's testing, I'm not sure.

My heart beats frantically in my chest and I fight every urge in me to pull over.

"Is this okay?" I finally ask because I can't stand the silence. I need to know what is running through her mind.

Piper mumbles something inaudible under her breath before squeezing my hand one last time and letting go.

CHAPTER TWENTY-EIGHT

PIPER

Graham pulls the truck to the edge of a field, right outside of a red barn. "Wait there," he tells me and steps out. He rounds the truck to my side and opens my door with his hand outstretched.

I place my hand in his and carefully step down. "You really have a prince charming complex, don't you?" I joke.

"Only when it comes to you." The door slams shut behind me. "Give me one sec."

Graham digs for something in the bed of his truck.

I shove my hands in the pocket of my coat. My eyes trail his frame. This may be the last time I see him like this. I planned on confessing to him in a more comfortable, easily escapable environment, but I couldn't find the heart to say 'no' to this date.

Maybe it will be a good way to end: one last date. Although, I should slip a twenty into his glove department later to cover the gas he used for this date.

Who wants to look at a draining bank account after being rejected?

When Graham resurfaces, he has a duffle bag held tightly in his grip. "Ready?"

"Would it change anything if I said 'no'?" I'm half joking, but when he speaks, it's full of hesitation.

"Of course. I would start the truck back up and take you home."

Suddenly, the chilly air isn't as freezing as it was only moments before. He's not going to make this easy.

"Graham," a rougher, weaker voice calls out. We turn to an older gentleman making his way to us. He's not wearing nearly as many layers as he should and there's a cap on his head with the title "Moon Farms" scripted on it. "I was wondering when you'd get here."

"Ran into some traffic," Graham says as he goes to wrap an arm around the man in a side hug. The man is all smiles and I can't help the little flutter in my chest at the sight.

It's times like these that remind me just how loveable Graham is. Not that *I* love him, though. Just that it is clear why someone would.

"Well, the barn is all set up for you and your…lady friend." He emphasizes *lady friend* as though it's an inside joke between the two and Graham rolls his eyes. "Is this her?" He motions to me.

Graham nods, slowly, probably trying to gauge my reaction, before introducing us. "This is Piper. Piper, this is Al. He owns the farm and has been a family friend for years."

"Please," the two stop a few feet from me, Graham coming to stand back beside me. "I practically changed his diapers."

I smile and it's not forced. The image of Graham as a child is one I long to see.

"It's nice to meet you, Piper." He extends a hand in which I accept. His other hand folds over mine gently and shakes before we both release.

"It's nice to meet you too."

"Please, tell me. Did he bribe you?"

I laugh awkwardly, not sure whether it's a joke or not. Or what Graham would have bribed me to do.

"I'm just kidding. Graham is a sweet boy. Although, I would watch out for any roses. It's a sign of bad luck."

Graham doesn't say anything. Just shakes his head as he rubs the back of his neck.

"You know, he's said a lot about you, Piper, and I must say, you are just as beautiful as he described."

My breath falters and there is a hitch in my heartbeat. Graham told people I am beautiful? And we're just going to discuss it like it's a normal conversation piece? I have too many layers on.

Graham must have noticed me wafting the collar of my shirt because he glances at the action before patting Al on the shoulder. "On that note, we really should get started before the day is wasted."

"Of course. If Elaina knew I was out here, she'd probably have my head. I'll let ya two get to it. Everything's all set up and if you need anything, just holler."

"Thank you, Al."

As Graham starts to guide me towards the barn, I give Al a little wave in which he returns with a small smile and wave of his own. "It was nice meeting you."

The barn is freshly painted, more evident the closer you get to it, and when Graham opens the door for us to step in, I halt in place.

I expected chickens, maybe goats—some kind of animal and lots of hay. Maybe some cow poop lingering somewhere, but the barn doesn't look like it has been touched by a person, let alone an animal.

It is a sitting room with bookshelves lining the walls and a wood stove in the corner. In front of it are two recliners and a very spacious rug on the floor. In the center of the room is a giant table, fit to be Arthur's round table with how elite it appears.

My gaze travels upward to the twinkling Christmas lights hung on rafters and adding to the soft glow from the fire.

"Here," Graham breaks the spell by motioning to take my coat. I shrug it off and pass it to him.

"What is this place?"

After disposing of our coats and scarves, he comes to stand beside me. "This isn't even the best part. Come here."

He leads me to a ladder hanging to the above ledge. He starts to climb. When he is almost halfway up to the top, he glances back down at my solid frame still at the bottom.

It takes a full smile on display with one of his hidden dimples, just for me, and a pleading "I promise no funny business," before he has me convinced to climb the ladder after him.

My hands are shaky on the frame because my boots are a little slicker than what a wooden ladder is meant for, but Graham's outstretched hand as he leans at the top, has my nerves calmed to a rolling boil instead of the sizzling broil they were in.

He helps me up when I reach the last few rungs and I am immediately awestruck at the sight. There are even more rows of books with little tea lights littered on shelves at the edge and a middle shelf of snacks in the center. Except, the snacks aren't from a factory but are baked goods that look suspiciously familiar.

"Are these...?" I point to the pastries.

Graham rubs at the back of his neck. "I may or may not have called in a favor."

That's what she was doing yesterday morning when I came out to the living room and she practically shoved me back into the bedroom. Except, she said she was in the process of catching a mouse and couldn't handle having to search any other areas. I knew she was up to something when the delicious peach scent wafted under my door.

"If you don't want to eat it though, I completely understand. If you don't want to do any of this, that's completely okay. I may have gone a little overboard. I just—" He stops with a sigh when his eyes meet mine.

I'm grinning like a fool. I know I am, but I can't seem to bring the corners of my mouth down. They refuse when this amazing man is standing only a few feet from me inside this barn—this heavenly barn— he decorated and set up just for the two of us. Just for *me*.

A lump forms in my throat from how incredible this man is and how hard it is going to be to utter those few words I rehearsed in the mirror earlier. I swallow it and turn away, blinking back the water in my eyes.

"It's amazing, Graham." I whisper. "How did you do all of this?"

"Well, the books and stuff have all always been here. Elaina and Al love books, but there wasn't enough room in their house for the collection. They are family friends of my grandparents', so I used to come out here often as a kid. Still do on some weekends to help them out a little or trade a book or two."

I run a finger down the length of the bookshelf, wandering, as he talks.

"Anyway, all I really did was hang a few lights and convince Hazel to bake a few things. Although, she didn't really need much convincing when I told her what it was for."

I make a mental note to chastise and thank Hazel later.

"Do you…like it?"

"I love it."

He exhales a breath and claps his hands. "Well, this is only the beginning."

"What? Is there a secret door somewhere too?"

The corner of his mouth lifts. "Now, I can't go giving away all of the secrets." He points to the treats. "Pick some of your favorites and I'll carry them down so we can sit by the fire where its warmer."

I do as he instructs and follow him back down the ladder. Graham gives me his hand at the bottom to help me on the last rung. When I'm on steady feet, I expect him to release my hand, but he doesn't. Instead, he interlocks our fingers—for the second time in one afternoon—and guides me to the fireplace.

Only when we are at the chairs does he let go. My hand is suddenly cold and idle. I shove it into my pocket. "Sit wherever you like."

I plop down in the recliner to the right. Before I have time to register, Graham lays a blanket over my lap and passes me one of the pastries I grabbed.

He sets up a pitcher of hot water and mugs on the table between us. He's so invested in his actions like every part of him is loving this. Loving being here with me. Why does it have to be him?

He took me to a spot that means something to him. A spot that he might not show very many people. A spot where the owners know my name because Graham told them about me and told them I'm *beautiful*.

There are so many questions I have for him. So many things I want to say, but the only thing that leaves my mouth is "Why are roses a sign of bad luck?"

Graham stiffens for the tiniest second before he straightens and carefully passes me a mug. It's hot cocoa. I inhale the chocolatey scent, fighting the moan in the back of my throat.

He sits in the other chair, bringing his own mug to his lips. "Any chance you'll believe me if I say they are cursed?"

"Of course. If I'm given a proper back story."

I try not to melt at the playful grin on his lips, but I can't help the warmth in my belly. "Do you remember when I said I can be a little forward?"

"Yes." I also remember Jason mentioning something along those lines as well.

"Well, I wasn't kidding. I have a history with women where I go all in too soon. There was this time in school when I was trying to impress a girl I liked. I blasted music through the intercoms and had a huge bouquet of roses."

"Oh, no."

"Oh, yes. Let's just say she is not a fan of attention and the roses ended up as violent confetti rather than a gift."

I bite my lip to keep from laughing.

Graham raises a brow. "You want to laugh, don't you?"

I nod slowly, worried that if I open my mouth, it will escape.

He turns away. "Go ahead."

A wild laugh that nearly has me kicking the air releases. My stomach hurts and I am so amused that I can't remember the last time I laughed this hard or felt this *good*.

When I come up for air, Graham's eyes are on me with an intense look. It sends a shock wave down my spine. He's feet away from me and yet, I feel like I can hear him breathing.

Or maybe that's my heart pounding in my ears?

"I love that sound." His voice is merely a whisper of a breath.

"The crackle of the fire?" It's the only thing I can hear over the erratic beats in my chest.

"Your laugh."

A blush creeps up my neck and I turn my face to hide it, pretending the fire is the source of the new warmth.

"So," he clears his throat. "Hazel said you despise strawberries."

I pick at the peach pastry in my hand, tearing off a piece at a time to shove in my mouth. "I don't *despise* them. They just aren't my favorite. They are too sour." "I've never heard someone call a strawberry sour. Are you sure they were ripe?"

I narrow my eyes at him. "Everyone has something they don't like. I'm sure there's a fruit you can't stand the taste of."

"There is, actually, but only because I'm allergic." "What is it?"

He motions to the pastry in my hand. "Peaches."

My stomach sours at the thought of him accidentally poisoning himself in the process of bringing these here. How could my favorite be his death sentence?

"Although, I haven't tried it since I swelled up like a tomato when I was three. For all I know, I could be cured."

"Is eating poison a past time of yours?"

"Depends on how I get to taste it." His gaze flicks to my mouth.

I shift the blanket. God, it's hot in here.

I have never been kissed before or taken the initiative to start a kiss. It's something that accompanies dating and I don't date. That, and it's something I want to have with someone special.

It is what I keep telling myself every time I felt a pang in my chest when I have to turn another boy down or see a happy couple walking the streets. I can't have what they have. Not yet.

I made the right decision because not everyone has a soulmate. Some people are just meant to be alone.

Graham's intense gaze and the way his attention has yet to fixate on something else, *anything* else in the room, is making all of those thoughts blur. So much so that it scares me.

I need this tension to ease.

"So did you bring me here just to eat treats in front of a fire in the barn?"

He shakes his head and stands. "No, although we can spend the whole time doing that, if you want." He digs around behind the chair and when he resurfaces, he holds a stack of books in his hands. "I figured we could read. Together. Well, you reading while I'm reading. Separate books, but in the same space." He's rubbing at the back of his neck.

"Is this your big move?" I joke, trying to ease the nerves from him. "How you get the ladies to fall for you?"

"Depends. Is it working?"

I ignore his smirk. "I'm not much of a reader."

"I know. I mean, you told me. That, and I remember your complaints about *Gatsby*."

He recommended the book to me, but I couldn't focus long enough to get past the first page so I read summaries online. This, he doesn't know, though.

"Anyway, I had a plan B set in motion."

"A plan B?"

He sits, setting the stack on the stand between us. "Well, I was thinking—if it's not too weird and you want to—that I could maybe read to you? That is, if you want to.”

He doesn't look at me and I know it's out of worry. He's worried I'm going to laugh in his face or turn him down. If only Graham knew how much the idea of him reading to me sends a spark through my veins. If he knew just how many times I have replayed his messages to hear his voice on repeat…

“On one condition,” I say. “I get to pick the book.”

His lips are stretched wide and I've never felt more special with a grin aimed just for me. “Deal.”

CHAPTER TWENTY-NINE

PIPER

I made a mistake. Not a simple mistake in which I can pull out one of those big erasers and wipe it away. Not even a mistake in which I can apologize to someone and move on. No, I made an irreversible mistake. One I will never be able to come back from.

I let myself fall for Graham.

The exact moment of when or how it happened is unclear to me. Maybe it was two days ago when he brought me to a barn lit warmly and covered me up by the wood stove as he read a romance novel—in which he impersonated each character—to me.

Or maybe it was on our first date when he willingly went home with me and spent time with my brother, even though Graham works all hours of the day.

It could have even been all the way back to our first meeting in the cafe when he jumped in to save me from a ridiculously embarrassing moment. Without even knowing who I was.

Or maybe it was the times in between. Sending me voice messages about little nothings. Opening up to me about his career and his family. Bringing me a surprise mocha.

I don't know why or how or when it all happened, but as I stare down at the message Graham sent me a few hours ago—one about how Pandas are called an embarrassment and how that fact is both sad and humorous—and my unread message below it, I can't help but feel that stupid longing in wanting his message to come again.

Why hasn't he answered me?

It's been at least five hours and he usually is quick to respond. I know our conversation is nothing important and I know I am turning into one of those cliché girls that waits by the phone for their crush to call them, but every nerve ending of mine is on fire.

We shouldn't even be talking. I was supposed to end things yesterday. I had it all mapped out, but somehow…

I couldn't bear to tell him the same words I am scared to hear.

My father's sentence to my mother floats back to me. The dimly lit stairwell I was crouched in. Their shadows on the floor. The door shutting after his departure. Mom's sobs breaking the first silence I ever acknowledged.

I promised myself to never be in the same situation. In a matter of weeks, the promise is broken.

"Hello?" I speak into the phone warily. I feel pins and needles pricking my skin.

"Hey, I—are you okay?"

"Yeah. Why wouldn't I be?" My words are clipped, short, but I try to keep it light and airy to ooze the perfect confidence.

I'm okay. I'm okay. I. Am. Okay.

"You don't have to be polite with me, you know? You can be honest."

I stay quiet. I should have never picked up the phone a year ago.

"If you can't do Saturday evening, I can make some adjustments. Or we can meet another day…" He's referring to the third date he asked me out on. I swear the word "no" was on my lips, but his green eyes gave me visions of a life I only ever dreamed about.

Finally, as though it's an afterthought, I find my voice again. "Another day might be best. I have some things going on Saturday and I'm not sure I will have time."

"Of course. No worries. How about I make a plan and I'll message you with it later?"

"Okay." It's the same word I texted him earlier. The only word I ever texted him. It's supposed to be a confirmation, a reassurance, but it's laced with so much anxiety.

I realize I say it more to myself than to him.

Okay: you're overreacting, Piper.

Okay: he didn't lose interest.

Okay: he is not your father!

"Okay," he says with a breath of enthusiasm.

If only he knew how not 'okay' I am.

287

CHAPTER THIRTY

PIPER

I check my phone for the sixth time in a row. Graham and I have plans to meet later this evening for our *third* date. This will be the last one. I have been pushing it off, but it's time. That, and my stomach has been in so many knots I haven't been able to keep any food down.

"Will you please put that thing away?" Hazel begs from beside me.

It's another day of us selling her treats and they seem to be doing a lot better this time. We had to come out a little later today so she had time to make her shift at the restaurant.

She pulls the device out of my hand and shoves it into my back pocket. "It's sucking the life force out of you."

"Sorry. I don't know what my problem is."

"It's your first time dating, Piper. It's understandable that you don't know how to act."

Act. Is there a right way to act when you are dating? Isn't acting fake? Am I supposed to be fake?

If that's the case, I've failed this entire time.

My phone vibrates in my pocket and I am quick to yank it out, ignoring Hazel's sigh beside me. When I place the device close to my ear, I listen to Graham's message and all of the anxious butterflies seem to float away.

He's looking forward to our date, he tells me. He wishes it could come sooner.

I slip the phone back into my pocket and feel a wave of normalcy wash over me.

I'm worrying over nothing. Graham isn't like other guys. He makes me feel—well, I'm not entirely sure on that part yet, but I know he's different. He has to be different. There's no other way around it.

In another universe, I might want a relationship with him.

"Have a wonderful day!" Hazel tells the woman who walks away with a cookie in her hand. Out of the corner of her mouth, "These are really selling today."

"Did you lace them with something?"

"Are you saying my desserts aren't good without being laced?"

I raise a brow to mess with her. She shoves my shoulder and I laugh.

"Oliver helped me with a new recipe I was trying out."

"*Oliver?*" She's mentioned him once or twice. Her boss, the same man that found her on the street crying and gave her a job.

"Oh, stop. Not every guy is a potential suitor."

"Says the same woman that tried to seduce Graham *and* Jason." Our shared dinner floats back to me.

"Hey, you hadn't met Graham yet and we knew almost instantly that that is an avenue neither of us want to take. Could you imagine? *Me* with Graham? Ugh. I think there's some bile in my mouth." She places a hand in front of her mouth, feigning nausea.

"And Jason?"

"What can I say?" Hazel adjusts the treats on display to cover up the empty spaces. "He's cute. And tall. And smart. Plus, being a doctor is a whole new ballgame."

"And being a restaurant owner isn't?" I don't get to tease her about guys much because she is usually all for it. With Oliver, it is so easy to push her buttons.

"Oh, look. More customers."

I grin and straighten, readying myself to answer any and all questions these people might have.

Is it gluten-free? Is it vegan? Does the peanut butter croissant have peanut butter in it?

I smile through every painful conversation, dreaming of when I will finally be able to see Graham again.

"Mom, I will be there for dinner this weekend." I say through the phone.

She called when the rush died down so I offered to get Hazel and I some hot beverages while Mom yapped away on the phone. Walking gives me strength to handle these talks.

"Give me one good reason why you can't come tonight, Piper." She called to ask if I was available to have our family dinner tonight instead of Sunday. Her and John plan to go on a Sunday trip while Kyle stays with his grandmother. She's asking if I'm free, but her tone is more of a demand.

"Mom, I just can't, okay? I will be there Sunday, though, and—"

"Piper Brooks. What could possibly be more important than time with your family?"

The urge to throw that same question back at her is strong.

Graham is kind and special and I love spending time with him. If I had to choose, an evening with him sounds a lot more fun than an evening at home with people who only see me when it's important.

Graham makes me feel important. Makes me feel heard.

Which is not something I expect my mother to be able to understand or even comprehend.

"Plus, your brother has been causing quite the ruckus, and it would be good for him to see his sisters every now and then. You know, he barely sees you anymore."

"Mom, I—"

"I just don't understand what is so important that you have to—"

"I have a date." The sentence tears out of me before I have a chance to even process it. I'm two blocks from the cafe and I can feel the eyes on me.

I've never backtalked to my mother before. Never spoke up. I've always let her words drown my mind until it turns to mush and only her will and her answer is present. My chest hurts, but my shoulders feel a tad lighter.

"You have a…date?" she says the word as though it's poisoned.

"Yeah. I mean, didn't you want me to date?"

"Yes, I do. Of course, I—" she takes a breath, the inhale is strong like she's trying to suck in a room of patience. "This is great Piper. Who is the man?"

I hesitate for the briefest moment. The cafe is visible, only a few steps away now. I could easily say I have to go and end it here. But my mind outweighs my heart. "Graham."

She's quiet, something my mother hasn't been since that night everything changed. The night she was forced—shocked into silence.

"Mom?"

"I thought you two were friends?"

"Well, we are. We haven't technically—" put a label on it? God, this all sounds so childish.

"Is this your first date or…?"

"Why?"

"Well, this is a very important distinction, Piper. If it's your first, then I need to head over to pick out your outfit. Oh, I'll call your sister too. Is Hazel available? She always has the greatest sense of fashion when it comes to these things."

And Mom is back. I drown out her words, rolling my eyes despite the fact she can't see me.

I push the door to the cafe open, the rush of sounds swarming me. I'm about to respond to Mom, tell her that it's not necessary to get this hyped up, when the door shuts behind me and I stop in my tracks.

He's here. Sitting at a table in the corner and staring out the window. I lift my hand and make a motion to move towards him. I don't usually do this kind of thing. In fact, I purposely avoid people I know when I see them in public. Even Hazel sometimes. It leads to awkward greetings and then you do this weird shuffle of "are we going to spend the rest of our time shopping together or is it okay to part here because I don't really want to buy undergarments with my mother"? It's uncomfortable and unnecessary.

But I want to talk to Graham. I want to see him smile when his gaze finds mine. I want to hear about his day. At least, while I still can.

So I lift my hand and start to motion to him, but a figure blocks my path. I instantly drop my hand and stop in my tracks.

A woman, a beautiful woman, takes the seat across from him. He smiles that Graham smile, but it's not at me. He talks to her and she laughs at something he says. He's telling jokes, but I don't get to hear the punch line.

Everything around me has drowned out like I'm swimming in the depths of the ocean and there is only a ringing pressure in my ears. My chest aches and I feel the need to rub a fist on the bruised spot.

Someone bumps into me, muttering about how rude it is to stand there, and the world seems to shift back on its axis.

"Piper!" Mom screams in my ear. She's still on the phone and I was too caught up to even notice.

"I'm sorry," I whisper to the woman I bumped into before making my way out the door. I keep my eyes off Graham the entire time. I can't do it. I can't handle it. Not when it hurts this much.

"Mom," I finally speak. "I have to go. I love you."

I don't wait for her to answer before I hang up and slide the phone in my pocket.

That night is flooding back to me and I'm having trouble focusing on where I'm walking. Everything is becoming a blur. It's as though I'm walking in a fog, a haze of memories I never wanted to resurface, and the only sound guiding me is my father's voice and my mother's broken cries.

I place my hands over my ears as I walk. I'm not even sure when I made it out of the cafe, but I'm on the sidewalk and filing in with the crowd.

All I can see and all I can hear is that night on replay in my mind.

CHAPTER THIRTY-ONE

PIPER

I was in high school at the time. Back then, I still loved music. It was something my father and I shared and I constantly practiced just so I could impress him with any new skill I learned.

That day, I spent hours after school rehearsing a song I wrote on the piano. My fingers were cramped from the endless playing and Sarah yelled once or twice for me to "shut up".

None of it stopped me, though. The look of pride and warmth in my father's eyes when I did something new, was worth any pain.

The sound of his car pulling into the driveway halted my playing. I ran to my bedroom window, saw him walking to the house, and lit up. I quickly scrunched my sheet music into a pile and raced down the steps. A faint burning smell filled my nostrils as I approached the kitchen.

"Dad," the word was on the tip of my tongue, but it didn't make it out when I heard my mom's voice instead.

I stopped in my tracks, two steps from the bottom, and stayed hidden by the wall between the stairwell and kitchen.

"I don't understand," she said. The exasperation and disbelief evident in her tone. I imagined her putting a hand on her hip while the other rubbed at her forehead.

"Carol…" My father's voice was devoid of all emotion. My heart dropped to my stomach. I felt like I could puke. "I don't love you like that anymore."

My knees caved in below me and I fell to a sitting position on the step. The sheet music crinkled in my loose hold.

The rest of their conversation was tuned out by this loud ocean in my head. It was as if wave after wave beat against my skull.

When the front door closed shut and the engine to my father's car started, my mother's sobs found their way through the chaos in my mind. I sat, frozen on the steps, listening to the sound of a heart breaking.

It wasn't the first time I heard someone cry over the person they love and it certainly wasn't the last, but this was different.

My father and mother were an epic love story. When they met, everyone else paled in comparison. They have been together for years and were best friends before that. How could all of that history, all of those emotions, just vanish?

CHAPTER THIRTY-TWO

GRAHAM

"Hey," I place a gentle hand on Piper's elbow, beckoning her to turn and face me. When she does, I smile. "I thought it was you."

She drops her hands to her sides, shaking out of my hold. "Hi."

I try to meet her gaze, but she dodges each attempt. Something sour settles in my stomach. "What's wrong? Did something happen?"

"No." It's only one word, but it feels like there is so much weight behind it.

"Piper, you can talk to me." I need her to look at me. If she would just look at me, if I could just see her face, then I could reassure her that everything will be okay.

"Is it about Melanie?" I think back to when I saw Piper in the cafe just a moment before. I heard a muttered 'sorry' and glanced up from Cindy across from me to Piper exiting the cafe. I excused myself and rushed out after her. I assumed she hadn't seen me since she didn't say hi, but maybe she had. Maybe she thought wrong of the situation.

"She's my boss' daughter and she asked for some help with her literature class. If it bothers you, I can—"

"No." Her tone is sharper. "It doesn't bother me, Graham."

"Okay. That's great, then. I—"

"I don't think we should continue."

"Oh, do you have somewhere to be? I can walk you there. Just let me tell Melanie and—"

"No. I mean, this" she motions between us. "Us. It needs to end."

I know what she's saying. I know what these words mean, but right now I can't seem to comprehend their definitions. "I'm confused."

Finally, she looks up at me, but it's with a boarded expression. I instantly regret ever asking to meet her gaze.

"I can't date you, Graham. I don't date. I think it's best that we end here."

"I don't understand." My eyes shut for a second, trying to process the information. "I—I thought we were on the same page. I thought—was I just imagining everything?"

She told me before she doesn't date—this isn't new information—but I thought that I might have changed her mind. I thought she might actually feel the same way about me that I feel about her. I mean, just minutes before her voice sounded so cheery on the phone. Was it all an act? Was she trying to tell me this all along and I just ignored her?

No. She clearly is into me too so what—

"You weren't imagining things, Graham. I led you on and I'm—I'm sorry for that, but I think it's time we end things."

"Why?"

Piper takes in a large breath like she's gathering her strength. "Graham, I—"

"Just give me one good reason." If she wants to end things, fine. Despite how bad my chest hurts right now and how clouded my mind feels, I never want to force her into something. If I'm going to let her go, I need a reason why. "Tell me why and I'll leave you alone."

"I don't date."

"I need a real reason, Piper."

"I don't have any other reason to give, Graham."

I cross my arms over my chest. "You went on dates with me, Piper. If you don't date, if you don't feel what I feel, then why? Why go out with me? Was it all just one big lie?" I hate how accusatory my tone is and the reaction it is causing her. As though my words are whips lashing at her face.

I hate it. I hate it. I hate it.

"None of it was a lie, Graham." Her words are soft, broken.

"Then why not keep going? I thought we had something special. If none of it was fake and we both felt what we felt, why end it?"

"Graham."

"No. I deserve an explanation."

She takes a breath, steadies herself. Her eyes are watery—a sight making my chest hurt. "I didn't know you before, but now that I do…"

"Isn't that a good thing? I mean, you know me. You can trust me." I try to reach out for her, but she steps out of reach.

"No, Graham. It's worse."

"Why? Am I that hard to love?" The question burns my throat. It's the same question I wanted to scream at every girl that turned me down. The same question I wanted to ask my parents when they fawned over Jason instead of me or said that I'm already too much for them to even consider having another child.

It's not a question I thought I would ever ask aloud, especially to the one woman I never thought I would have to.

And yet…

"That's just it." Her voice is louder, and I can feel the eyes on us from the passing strangers. I want to pull us into the shadows where only I would be able to hear her, but I'm scared of seeing her shy away from my touch. Again. "It's really easy to—to like you. So much so that I didn't push you away every time you got too close. I let you in when I should have been boarding up my walls higher. You are so perfect, so sweet, yet so infuriatingly maddening and I don't know why, but you make me—you make me feel warm."

"I'm confused." Those are all good things, maybe even compliments, but why do they sound like a curse coming from her lips?

"I promised myself I would never fall in love. I would never let someone get that close. I thought—I let you get close because I thought we would never actually become anything serious. I was foolish enough to think that what I feel for you is simply infatuation. I knew that if I didn't let myself go too far, if I could still pull away at any moment, then I would never get hurt. But now—I can't date you Graham."

I don't know what to say. Her words are too fast for my brain to catch up. My chest is so sore, I feel the urge to claw at it. My bones feel hollow in a way they never have before. "Piper—."

"It hurts too much." Her voice is broken, faltering at every syllable as though she's biting back a cry. "It hurts too damn much and I am not strong enough. You deserve someone who can give you the world, Graham. You should be with someone who deserves to feel as special as you made me feel."

I open my mouth to tell her "Okay." I'll leave her alone. I'll do anything it takes so long as I can erase the tremble in her voice and the quiver of her lips. So long as the fear in her eyes vanishes, I will become a ghost. I will put my feelings aside and leave as long as she promises to smile in my wake and maybe even laugh.

Before the words have the chance to even form, she's sauntering away and I'm too locked into place to chase after her.

CHAPTER THIRTY-THREE

PIPER

It's been twenty-four hours, maybe more, since I ended things with Graham. Not that there was anything to end in the beginning, anyway.

We went on a date or two and we talked every day, but we weren't in a relationship. He never pushed me to label what we were. He only asked that I give it a try. And I only made him regret ever giving me a chance.

I bend and spit the toothpaste into the sink. I've been staring at my reflection in the mirror for the past two minutes, while I have been aggressively brushing my teeth. A hint of red is mixed in with the white toothpaste in the sink and a metallic taste is present in my mouth.

After I rinse the rest out, I sigh and find my face back in front of me. There are bags under my bloodshot eyes. My skin is pale against my red hair, making my freckles less prominent.

I haven't been able to stop thinking about Graham and the words I threw at him. The confusion in his voice and the vulnerability in his step are on constant replay.

Watching his smile fall was the saddest movie I have ever been an audience to.

When I said those things and told him we shouldn't see each other anymore—whether it be as friends or more—I spoke the truth. I said what I had to say to get rid of the sick feeling in my stomach. The memory of my parents came flooding back and all I could see was Graham and me in their place.

I don't love you anymore. I don't love you anymore. I don't love you anymore. I don't love you anymore. I don't—

"Piper!" Hazel's cheery voice breaks into my thoughts.

I unclench the sides of the sink, stand, and exit the bathroom and the smallest smile I can manage plastered on my face. She doesn't need my problems to add onto her shoulders.

When I make it to the kitchen, she is plopping a cardboard box onto the counter with fruits poking out of the top. *Graham.*

A lump forms in my throat.

You wanted this, I remind myself. I made my bed, so I have to lie in it. The same way I always have.

"Hey, guess what I—" She stops the second her gaze lands on me. "What's wrong?"

"Nothing." I lie as I rub a hand down my arm as though I were smearing something away.

"What happened? Is it your mom? Is she trying to set you up again? I knew it was suspicious when she asked me to pick out some dresses."

Mom. I completely forgot about our conversation and how I willingly—stupidly admitted I was going on a date with Graham. A third date.

How am I going to tell her that he isn't in the picture anymore? That I pushed him away just like all of the others.

"Hey," Hazel's hand finds a spot on my arm, an inch away from where Graham's hand was. I can still feel the imprint of his callouses even though he only touched me for a second before I shrugged him off. "What's going on, Piper?"

God, I'm a jerk.

"Nothing." The lie sounds broken on my lips. The thump in my throat has grown larger and it's hard to swallow without the stinging in my eyes.

Why am I upset? I wanted this. I needed this.

Why can't it just be easy?

I don't realize how hollow my chest feels until Hazel has me pulled to her in a hug and her arms are holding me tight.

"Tighter," I want to tell her because maybe if she squeezes a little harder, all of this pain will be crushed into oblivion.

"Don't let go," I want to plead because maybe if she holds on, I won't break apart at the seams.

"Tell me I did the right thing," I want to beg because maybe I can bear it if she agrees.

I've only ever needed Hazel in my life—she's always been enough—but right now, her hug isn't strong enough to erase all the emotions coursing through me.

"I'm lonely," are the words I finally say aloud but they come through with a sob.

I feel her arms tighten around me as she whispers, "it's okay," in my ear. "I'm here"

For the first time in my life that fact isn't enough for me. I love Hazel, but it's someone else's arms I want wrapped around me. It's someone else's voice I want to whisper sweet nothings in my ear. I want someone and I am too scared to ever grant myself a life with them.

"You don't have to tell me anything you don't want to," Hazel reassures me from her spot beside me on the couch.

After I cried silently in her embrace, she led me to the couch, laid a blanket on my lap, brought me some icing from the fridge, and plopped down beside me with an arm draped over my shoulder.

This is the first time she spoke since hugging me and I think the only reason she did is because I let out a long sigh.

"I know." Thankfully, the word doesn't come out as shaky as I feel.

I let a steady quiet fall between us, not sure of where to start. I want to tell her everything. I want her to give me her honest opinion because Hazel's opinion is the one I value most in this world. But I know exactly what she's going to say and I'm not sure I'm ready for it.

"I don't have my date with Graham tonight," is what I settle for.

My face is turned from her, but I can hear the wheels moving in her head.

"Or ever for that matter."

"I'm sorry, Piper."

"Why? I'm the one who ended it." My tone is lacking of any emotion. I don't think even an electric shock would arouse the slightest feeling in my bones.

"You really liked him." Hazel's tone is soft, something that is only present when she is comforting me or feels bad for me. It's something I used to despise to hear in her tone. It often made me feel like a child. Now, it only causes another chip to break off my heart because I know *why* her tone is soft this time. I know what she's thinking.

"It's not enough."

"What do you mean?"

I'm not entirely sure, but I let my words fall out without considering anything. For once, I just let myself go. "I like him, but it's not enough, Hazel. There's no guarantee that he actually feels the same way I do and there's no guarantee that it is going to go anywhere. The only thing I know for sure is how much the not knowing hurts."

I stop, hold my breath, bite back the tears, and then continue. "I'm lonely, Hazel. I'm so…lonely." The last word is merely a whisper, and I have to suck in more air in order for me to manage my next statement. "But I can't be with someone. Not in that way."

Hazel doesn't say a word. Instead, she pulls me in for another hug and, for the first time, I welcome the silence.

CHAPTER THIRTY-FOUR

GRAHAM

One thing I have never considered before is how much it could hurt to have another person in my life. I always craved a sibling or another friend and even a romantic partner. I wanted someone who would love me for who I am.

I wanted someone who wouldn't shy away from how overbearing I can be. So much so that I may have ruined my only chance at it.

Piper is gone and I haven't had the courage to call or message her. Piper—not my feelings for her or my need to have her in my life in any way she will allow—is the one thing I have ever been sure of.

"You know, I'm not sure what hurts more." Sebastian leans against the wall behind me with his arms crossed, except one of his hands continues to move as he talks. "The fact that you are doing other things while I'm paying you or the fact that we are slow enough for you to do other things while I'm paying you."

I roll my eyes, something I never did before, until I remember who I picked it up from. I shift my weight to release the tension in my arms.

"What are you working on anyway? Better not be a job application."

"It's papers for school."

"School?" A slow grin spreads across his mouth. "Don't tell me you've finally decided to stop digging yourself into the ground."

"Working for you *has* been something like death."

He ignores my comment. "So? What's the plan?"

"Four or five years of online schooling—plus some outside requirements—and I will officially be a qualified English teacher."

He shifts to pat me on the back, hard. "My man. Glad you finally figured it out. Although, maybe I should be thanking the *woman with the beautiful voice* instead."

One time I tell him that she has a beautiful voice and he never lets me live it down.

My shoulders tense at the mention of her and I pretend to busy myself with skimming through the documents I practically have memorized by now.

"Don't tell me you let her go."

Technically I didn't, but it doesn't stop this gnawing feeling of regret in my chest. "No. She asked me to stop pursuing her." In other words.

"What did you do?" His eyes are narrowed at me.

Why is it always me? Why am I always the problem? I'm always too enthusiastic or not enthusiastic enough. I always get in way over my head. I'm too much of a handful for my parents to even consider a second child.

"I didn't do anything." My tone is a little snippier than I intended.

"Hey. It was a joke."

I don't say anything. Not sure I can without blowing up.

"Grab the next customers for me. I got to go out back real quick."

I nod and close my laptop to shove it away. The likely hood of being too busy to accomplish filling out the form is slim, but I'd rather not have any more questions or comments from Sebastian.

"Still haven't quit, I see." Jeff slides on the barstool in front of me, plopping his ring of keys on the counter between us.

"Sir." There's no energy left in me to say anything more, to joke back.

"No remark about how you like to stay busy?"

I shake my head. "What can I get you?"

"Grab me a Heineken." He points behind me. "What's got you in a rut?"

Forcing a smile on my face and shaking the thoughts layering my mind, I pop the cap from the bottle. "Not sure what you're referring to, Sir. I've never been better." Even I don't believe the lie.

"It's a girl," Jason slides into the seat next to Jeff.

"A girl?"

Jason holds a hand out to Jeff, to which Jeff shakes. "Jason. Graham's roommate and friend."

"Jeff. Graham's boss. Well, one of them." Jeff takes a sip of his drink. "What about a girl has him pouting like a lost dog?"

"She's the love of his life and he let her get away." Jason says this as he casually yanks textbook after textbook from his bag.

"The love of his life?"

I'm so astonished by Jason willingly socializing to bother speaking up to defend myself.

"Oh! Is this the girl that hangs by the fence?"

"What?" Now, my interest is piqued. Piper has been at the fence of the site *once*, but Jeff would have been too occupied to notice. Has she…?

"The red-haired girl who has been stopping outside the site every morning to eye one of my workers. I thought she was one of Vince's, but it makes sense she was looking for you."

Every morning?

That information should make my heart sing, but it only makes it bleed more.

"Tell me about her." Jeff looks between Jason and I, but Jason is long gone in the dictionary he has highlighted and annotated.

No one has ever been as serious about education as he is. Then again, he would probably call it a hobby.

"Is she smart? Please tell me she has a sense of humor. We can't have another Britney."

"I forgot about her." Jason pipes in.

"Yeah. The girl who couldn't take a joke to save her life."

"She also had those ridiculously long nails. How are you supposed to do anything productive with such freakishly long nails?"

I almost roll my eyes. "Her name is Cheyenne."

Jeff moves his bottle around as he talks. "Tomato, tom-ah-to. Anyway, tell me about the girl."

"There is no girl, Sir."

"Don't tell me you went overboard again, Fischer."

"Sir."

"Women need patience, you know?" My nails dig into the palms of my hands.

"Is it that hard to just let the universe take control?"

My chest burns and I bite back the words on my tongue.

"Why can't you just—"

"I get it. I'm a handful. I'm too much. I make people run away. I get it, Sir. I'm the reason…" —*Piper*— "all of those girls ran away. I know, okay? So can we please just change the subject?"

They blink in the wake of the storm falling from my lips. Jeff sighs, but Jason is the one who fills the space. "Graham, you aren't the reason Piper or any of those girls ran away."

"Yeah?" The word is a scoff. "You've told me otherwise our entire friendship."

The book slams shut as he turns all of his attention to me. "Can you stop acting like everything around you is shit? Excuse my language, Jeff." Jeff waves his apology away.

"I'm not— "

"Yes, you are. Every time you get one of these fantasies in your head, you break down at the minor inconvenience. Lindsey from the fifth grade didn't like the pudding you gave her because she genuinely didn't like the pudding. She had the biggest crush on you, though, and you were too wrapped up in the pudding to even care."
"Lindsey—"

"I'm not finished. The same thing happened with the Spanish notes you took for Michelle in the seventh grade and the ice cream date you took Lily on two years ago." His tone is so harsh it hits every scar on my body, reminding me of old wounds. "You have been too in your head about finding the perfect woman who will melt at everything you do. So much so that you missed every sign the one girl who might have actually been the one, threw at you."

When he finishes, he's out of breath, staring at me so intently. My chest is hollow at his words and the truth laced around them. Maybe I did miss every sign Piper gave me. No one just up and decides to end things. There were signs and I ignored every one of them.

I think back to our interactions. She didn't say "yes" when I asked her out. She said "okay". She pulled away every time I got too close. She stalled and avoided every question or discussion about relationships. I went to her house on the pretense of getting her mom to stop setting her up on dates. *She* didn't want to date and I pushed anyway. I pushed so much that she ran.

"Graham," Jason's voice is softer as he pulls me from the whirlwind of thought. "You get in over your head, but that's who you are. There's nothing wrong with that—except for the incessant crying—and the only reason I say all of this is because…"

His face is full of something I can't quite decipher. Pain? Disappointment? Empathy?

"Piper is different from the others and I know you thought she could really be the one. I'm sorry you lost her. And while you were oblivious to so many things with her, she did genuinely like you and you aren't the reason she ran."

Even though he says it with sincerity, and I have tried to burn the same sentences into my head for the past twenty-seven hours, none of it feels like the truth.

"He's right." Jeff finally joins the discussion. "I don't know the girl, but I know you. If she ran, it wasn't because she doesn't like you."

They both share a look before staring me down head on as if they are willing me to hear them. I want to, I really do. But hearing and believing are two different things.

Jeff clears his throat. "Enough about all this mushy stuff. Tell me about other stuff. Have you decided to quit yet?"

My gaze finds the laptop I shoved away. I wasn't planning on telling Jeff about my decision so soon, but… "Well," I finally say. "It's funny you ask that."

There's no need to dive back into the world of Piper. She's not ready for a relationship and I am too self-obsessed to notice. Either way, no matter what, I'm not going to push her again.

Instead, it's time to focus on reshuffling the cards.

CHAPTER THIRTY-FIVE

A ghost vibration from my phone jolts me from staring into the abyss. I pull my phone out of my back pocket only to find no message on the screen.

Forty-eight hours. Forty-eight hours since I ended all contact with Graham and not once has he tried to reach out. He respected my wishes, and I couldn't be less grateful.

A mug of steaming tea plops down in front of me without the delicacy it should have. Elias rounds our desks to get to his.

"What is this?" I stare into the dark brown liquid.

"Coffee."

"I don't—"

"Drink coffee. I know. With the way you have been checking your phone constantly and staring off into space instead of actually being productive," his tone is harsh, annoyed, but he huffs a breath and softens. "I figured you could use the hard stuff today."

I give him a small smile and bring the mug to my lips. "Thank you, Elias."

After rolling my shoulders and tucking my phone far away and out of reach, I scoot closer to the desk and get to work. It's hard with my brain keeping a separate tab open the entire time, a tab dedicated to Graham, but when I eventually make it into the studio to record, I let my actions erase everything from my mind.

It reminds me of when I used to play the piano. My fingers would take control of finding a rhythm and creating a symphony while my mind finally laid to rest. I didn't have to think if I didn't want to.

When music stopped meaning something to me, I found myself drawn to the music of the universe: the sounds around me. I would hide in corners or still myself so I could listen to the surroundings. Often, I would quiz myself on whose footsteps were within earshot or what actions someone did to create the noise I heard. Most of the time, I would win.

It's one of the things I love about what I do. It drowns out the rest of the world until all that's present are meaningless sounds.

When I'm in the studio, though, recreating every sound on the screen, all I can think of is the night I brought Graham to the roof. The night I shared a piece of myself with him. The night he asked about me and was interested in me and listened to me.

I walk out of the studio and into the hallway when Elias calls it. The second I step out, I regret it.

"Oh, stop." Lindsey's voice travels to me. I look down the hallway to see her back leaning against the wall, a phone pressed to her ear, and a blushing smile on her lips. "Honey, I'm at work." She whispers it playfully. "I miss you too. I know—I—" she breaks out in laughter.

My chest feels hollow and my head is dizzy.

I shove my hands into the pocket of my sweater and walk down the other end of the hallway towards the bathroom. When inside, I turn on the faucet and let my eyes leak everything they need to.

Kyle runs to the door when I enter the house. His arms wrap around my legs and I lightly tap his back in return. When Mom rounds the corner with a smile on her face, I try my best to reciprocate.

"You're late." She tells me before flowing back into the kitchen.

Kyle pulls away from me. "I'll be up in a minute," I tell him. He runs up the steps and I follow Mom into the kitchen.

"I'm early, Mom."

She's sitting at the dining table, scowling at a barely started jigsaw puzzle. "I'm not talking about now. I mean about your date."

Instantly, my fake smile drops, despite how hard I try to keep it in place. I slide into the seat across from her with my head down.

"You haven't been answering any of my calls, Piper. Please tell me you did not wear something like that on the date. As pretty as you are, there are such things as hideous clothes."

"Thanks, Mom."

"Why haven't you been answering my calls?"

"I've been busy."

"With what? Is it that hard to answer your mother every once in a while?"

"Mom, I—"

"I just don't get it, Piper. Is it Graham? Is he making you this way?"

That ignites a fire in my bones. "No, Mom. Graham—"

"I knew he wouldn't be any good for you. Well, that's alright. I will call up Denise and set you up with her son. I hear he's in—"

"Mom!" My voice is loud. Louder than it has ever been when I've talked to someone, let alone my mother. When I raise my head, she's staring at me with wide eyes and with her wine glass clutched tightly in her grasp. Softer, "I'm sorry. I don't mean to yell, I just—Please don't talk about Graham like that."

"What's wrong, Piper?"

"Nothing."

"Did he do something to you? Is he pressuring you?"

"Mom, I'm twenty-four."

"Doesn't matter. If he's hurting you in anyway…"

"He's not." A sad laugh escapes me. "I hurt him."

"What?"

"How did you move on so quickly from Dad?" My question is so frank it even throws me off guard. I watch her face change from shock to confusion to understanding.

"Your father and I…When your father left, I was devastated." She swirls a finger around the bottom of her glass. "I never told you girls this, but the night he left he—"

"Told you he doesn't love you." It's the first time I have said the words out loud. After I heard their conversation that night, I ran back upstairs, curled into a ball on the floor of my room, and never spoke of it to anyone. Even Hazel doesn't know the full story.

"How did…?" She studies me, then sighs. "You heard. I'm sorry, Piper. If I had known you were there, I would have—well, I don't know, but you shouldn't have heard that."

"How were you able to move past that, Mom? How were you able to marry another man?" My words are calmer, steadier than I thought they would be. Yet, my bones may crumble at any moment.

"I wasn't. For the longest time I shoved John away. And when we first got together, I continued to be skeptical of him. God, I even blew up at him for buying the wrong cheese once."

She takes a breath, stares into space, then meets my gaze. "But he never gave up. I went to therapy because I wanted to make it work. I missed your father a lot, Piper. Sometimes I still do, but he was never coming back and I couldn't spend the rest of my life alone."

"You weren't alone." She had Sarah and me. We were always here for her.

She lays a hand over mine on the table, lightly squeezing. "Yes, I was. I needed someone that would keep me warm at night. Someone I could talk to and laugh with.

Someone who would be by my side no matter what. John became that person and I wanted to make it work so bad that I decided to do everything I could."

I take in the information, trying to process everything. It can't be that simple. It can't be that easy as just going to therapy and moving on. If it was easy for her—the one who was dumped, betrayed—why is it so hard for *me*?

Why can't *I* move on?

"Now," Mom breaks into my thoughts. "Are you going to tell me what's going on?" I stay quiet. "Why are you asking about your father, Piper?"

I open my mouth to speak as I play with the hem of my shirt. The words come out broken. "I…" I suck in a breath trying to ease the lump in my throat. "I never…I don't know how…" My eyes sting and the action of my hands are becoming blurry. "I don't know how to love, Mom." My voice breaks on the last word and I begin to sob.

I don't hear her shift or see her move until I feel her arms wrapped around me. She holds me tight and rubs a hand down my back. When my cries become sobs and I can feel the tears soaking her shirt, she pulls me tighter.

"Piper," she whispers to me and it sounds so sad. "You do know how to love. You love so much that you're cautious on who you give your heart to. That's not a bad thing. You aren't broken, Piper. You are so brave."

I'm a sobbing mess in her arms. The last time I cried in my mother's embrace was when I was seven and stubbed my toe. Every time I cried after that, I hid myself in my room, far away from any prying ears. I hate crying in front of people. I hate being so vulnerable.

But right now, with my chest aching so much and head pounding like a hammer is beating against my skull, I realize how much I have deprived myself. How much I have longed for someone to take one look at me and know—I am broken and I'm *not* okay. How much I crave to have someone wrap me in their arms without a second of hesitation and tell me "I got you." I realize now how much I needed it from my mother.

Mom pulls away and rests her hands on my shoulders, leveling her gaze with mine as she bends. "Look at me, Piper. You. Are not. Broken. Do you understand me?"

I can't form words. All I can do is nod slightly as my lips tremble. She pulls me back to her and holds me tighter than before as though she's trying to squeeze all of the doubt, all of the sadness out of me.

"I'm scared, Mom."

"I know." She rubs a hand down my back. "I know, Piper. I've got you."

Chapter Thirty-Six

PIPER

TWO WEEKS LATER.

I swing the door to the bar open, welcoming the chaotic sounds that ooze around me like a smell clinging to my clothes. It's a Wednesday night so it's not as packed as I've witnessed it being before. There are a few full tables, but it's mostly individuals scattered around.

Taking a step inside and shutting the cold breeze out, I pull the scarf from around my neck and scan the room. Standing on my tiptoes, I see a mess of blonde hair behind the bar. I smile to myself, straighten, and head towards him.

When I slide onto the bar stool, he doesn't bother glancing up from his task. He's doing something with the limes. "What can I get you?" He asks politely and I realize just how much I missed his voice. I want to ask how he knew someone entered when I shift on the stool and hear the squeak below.

"A water would be perfection." *A water would be perfection?* That's what I went with? Really? Watching *Friends* in the days leading up to now may not have been the best decision.

His head jerks up instantly and when I finally get to see his handsome face, one of his brows is quirked. "What are you doing here?"

No "hi" or even a simple "Piper?", but I guess I deserve it.

"I came for a drink," I lie, although I do plan on taking a few sips of the water.

"I thought you don't drink."

"I don't. That's why I asked for water." God, I sound condescending. How is this already such a disaster?

He doesn't say anything else, just pours a glass of water and sets it in front of me. Without a word, he turns to stand at the other end of the bar. Probably to ask his colleague to take over this side for him. The side with me.

"Wait," I call out to him. He turns slightly but doesn't make a motion to move. "I may have come for more than just the drink."

After a moment of hesitation, he finally faces me again and stands tall with his arms crossed in front of him. The perfect bodyguard.

I run a finger along the rim of the glass, suddenly conscious of the situation.

I decided to start therapy a few weeks or so ago. I've only had a few sessions so far—decided to go daily— but it's helping to get things off my chest. To finally say the things I was too scared to. One of those things being how much I want Graham in my life. That, and I don't want to be alone anymore. I'm ready for more, but I want it with Graham. If he'll have me, that is.

So I made a plan with Hazel, put on the nicest outfit, and came straight here after work. I considered buying a gift on the way to give him, an apology of sorts, but I decided against it. I don't want to buy his forgiveness.

Now that I'm sitting in front of him and he's staring at me through boarded walls, my nerves are shot. A lick of sweat begins to coat my skin and I consider removing my coat.

"How are you?" is the only thing I manage to say.

"Fine." His response is quick. Short.

I need to find a way to get through to him. I hate how he's not smiling right now. Not telling jokes. But I know it's my fault. "Hazel told me you decided to go back to school." It sounds like I'm pulling at straws, but this one thing I'm genuinely interested in. He's so passionate about literature and helping others—something *I* was able to pick up on in the few weeks I knew him—that it only makes sense for him to further his talent.

He nods. Then, "Look, I have to get back to work."

I instinctively glance around the room, noticing no one waiting at the bar for a drink. My heart sinks a little. "Right. I just—" I take a deep breath and look him straight in the eyes. "I'm sorry."

He shifts a little as though he's uncomfortable.

"I was a jerk, and you didn't deserve that. You are such an amazing and nice guy and I—I went and ruined it all. I'm sorry. I'm not asking to go back to how we were or even for you to forgive me," despite how much I crave it. "All I'm asking is for you to give me another chance."

"A chance at what?"

"I want to try, Graham. I'm ready to be in a relationship."

"That's great, Piper. Really," He refuses to show any emotion on his face and in his voice and I hate it. I hate how polite his words are. I need a Graham smile. "But I'm not someone you can just pick up when you are ready to play with them."

A blow straight to the gut. I ignore the instinct to shrink back and walk away. "I know I was a jerk, Graham. I deserve every insult you have to throw at me, but this isn't me using you. I genuinely—"

"Like me?" The words are harsh on his lips, almost like he's insulted by the idea. He uncrosses his arms, shakes them, then crosses them again. "Do you remember when I told you about how I wooed other women?" I nod, hesitantly.

"Every one of them turned me down. Every one of them and everyone else in my life, including my own parents, told me that I go too overboard. That I am the reason no one wants me."

My heart breaks at his words. I never wanted him to feel that way. I wish I could walk around the bar and wrap him in my arms. Let him cry on my shoulder. Something tells me he doesn't get to do that often enough, if ever.

"I spent so many years of my life trying to find someone, anyone, that would love me in the same way I love them. When I met you—" he sighs. "I honestly thought we could be something, Piper. I thought you might be different. You *were* different, but then you went and left me hung to dry. I can't do that again."

"Graham." I don't know what to say. I want to erase every doubt in his mind. I want him to see just how much I care for him, but I don't know how to form the words.

"I can't, Piper. I'm finally getting myself in order and focusing on what I want."

There's a hesitant pause. Someone calls out to him, maybe for a drink or as a greeting, I'm not sure. I'm too entranced by the sincerity in his words. The tension between us vanishes in an instant.

"Listen, I really appreciate you taking the time to come and apologize. Really. And I promise there are no hard feelings between us," he says it like it's the truth, but it feels so much like a lie. "But I can't be in a relationship with someone who's not willing to go all in like I am."

I'm not sure when exactly he walks away. It's only when I hear someone burp obnoxiously that the empty space in front of me is visible.

Everything he said is true, but I *am* ready to go all in. Yes, I need to take it slow and be patient with myself, but I want Graham in my life. I want to be with him. If that means putting myself out there in the most terrifying way, then so be it.

CHAPTER THIRTY-SEVEN

GRAHAM

"Hey, what's the treat for today?" I ask Hazel as I pass her the bag of fresh pineapple in my hand.

Despite how things ended with Piper and my determination to stay away, I don't let it affect my relationship with Hazel. Hazel has nothing to do with us. Plus, I don't think I could ever live a life without her baked goods.

"Cinnamon cookies. Oh," she reaches into a large container and pulls out a pastry. "And cinnamon tarts. Trying something new."

I grab a paper bag and begin to fill it. She doesn't stop me or say anything, but I can feel her gaze boring into me.

"What is it?"

"What?" Her voice is full of feigned innocence.

"You're bouncing on your heels like you have something you want to say."

"I was wondering if you're free this afternoon. I thought about getting together and…hanging out?"

"Sure. What time?" I don't have anything to do today other than my shift at the bar and it doesn't start until this evening. Sebastian has someone else opening up.

This past week, I took some time to figure out my schedule. The school contacted me about starting classes in January, about a month from now, which gives plenty of time to get some more money saved up before I start. Then I will quit the construction job and only work at the bar— something Jeff couldn't have agreed with more.

"Wait. Really?"

Her surprise makes me smile through a bite of a cookie. The cinnamon is strong, but there's a hint of something sweet. It almost tastes like a cinnamon roll in cookie form. "Why are you so surprised? You're acting like there's going to be something that—" Then it hits me.

We haven't talked about her once in the time since Piper left me confused and devastated on the sidewalk. Then she visited me at the bar, and it took everything in me to stay strong and not cave in. I can't always be the one giving my all. I deserve someone who will show their affection just as much as I do. Even if that means giving up the one woman I think about constantly.

Sometimes, when the silence becomes too overbearing, I replay our messages just so I can hear her voice again. I say sometimes, but it's become a daily ritual. "Hazel, who's going to be there?"

She stares sheepishly at me, wringing her hands in front of her. "Just some friends. Nothing serious."

"Hazel."

A large sigh escapes her. "Fine, but I don't understand why you are avoiding her."

I want to argue, but avoiding is the only word that fits exactly what I've been doing.

"Yes, she ended things and then left you hanging for a week, but she apologized. And you two weren't technically together."

The words sting regardless of how true they are. We weren't technically together. We never put a label on it, but I didn't want to push her too far by doing that. Then again, I pushed her too far already by giving her these big romantic gestures when she told me she doesn't date.

"Look, you don't even have to stay the whole time. You can just show up, listen to what she has to say, and if you still feel the same, you can leave."

I stopped eating the cookie, analyzing it instead.

"Graham, she's different." I know that's true. She's different in every sense of the word. "She's never dated before. Never admitted her feelings to anyone before. She loves watching those romantic comedies and teasing me about guys I go out with and she never admits it, but I know that was part of the reason she was holding out for so long. She was waiting for the guy who would prove every notion she has wrong. She was waiting for *you,* Graham."

My head snaps up and I see the pleading in her eyes, hear the sincerity in her tone.

"It's up to you whether you want to believe me or not but just know that this is the first time she has ever told me about a guy. It's the first time she has ever gone on a date. It's the first time she has confessed her feelings."

There's a pause. She rips a paper towel off of a discarded roll on the ground by her foot, scribbles something on it, and passes it to me.

"This is where she'll be. Your choice."

"You're really not going to go." Jason states more than asks it.

He's standing beside our couch where I am sitting and staring at the TV. Not one scene on the screen has actually processed. My mind is playing its own movie in my head.

One in which Piper is in front of me at the bar again, except this time, I round the counter and wrap her in my arms. I whisper every word I have locked away in her ear because they—all of my words—are for her. She would giggle against my chest, and nothing would feel better than that moment.

The bar is five blocks away, though, and Piper is nowhere near ready for the storm of my emotions.

I don't know how Jason found out about this thing with Piper, but I bet it has something to do with Hazel. Unlike Hazel, though, Jason hasn't shut up about Piper since the day I came home and "looked like a lost puppy" as he claimed.

Surprisingly, he only accused me of being the problem once. Every other time, he didn't put blame on either of us.

"I don't get you, Graham."

"What's the big deal? So I don't want to waste my time on another girl that's just going to ditch me. Sounds like a smart move to me."

"No, it's an idiotic decision made by a coward."

I rub at my chest, trying to ignore the pain that statement caused. "Shoot a man while he's down, why don't you."

"Maybe it will finally knock some sense into you."

"Why are you so adamant about this, Jay?" I'm standing now, waving my hands in irritation. "Don't you always tell me how I need to stop going overboard? Now that I finally let it go, you can't seem to—"

"Do you love her?"

"What?"

"Do you love her?"

"What kind of question is—"

"It's a simple yes or no question, Graham. You either love her or you don't."

The memories of Piper and me are playing in my mind. I think of the way she says my name. The way her face changes at the words I say. The laugh she releases when I say something humorous. The fact that she *hears* me.

"It's not that simple." I say meekly because it's not. I thought I loved all of those other girls. Or at least, I thought I *could*.

"Do you love her?"

"Jay—"

"Do you love her?"

"Seri—"

"Do you love her?" His sentence is so loud it reverberates in my mind.

"Yes!" I'm out of breath and I don't even know why. The admission tore out of me. "Okay? Are you happy now? I can't get her voice out of my head. I love her and…" I can't have her.

He smiles, a rare sight. "Then why are you letting her get away?"

"Because she doesn't love me like I love her." No one ever does.

"Have you asked her?"

"What?"

"Did you ask if she loves you or did you just assume she doesn't?" His question makes me ponder Piper's visit to the bar. She admitted she wanted to date me, but—"Because if you had taken one look at her these past few weeks, you would have seen just how smitten she is with you. It's sickening really. She's almost as bad as you."

"What are you talking about?" None of this makes any sense. Jason and her were only together when we all had dinner and that lasted for maybe an hour and a half. Plus, Jason doesn't say these things. This isn't him. He's usually telling me right about now just how great it is that I chose to leave a woman in the past. So why…?

He stares at his hands, picking at specific spots. "Let's just say I hate roses."

I'm suddenly within inches of him, leveling him with my stare. "What are you talking about, Jay? Don't mess with me."

He points to the note I threw on the coffee table when I got back. The note without a single crease. "Ask her."

It's the cafe we first met in. The same one I saved her from a blind date and the same one she deserted me outside of. That's the address scribbled on the note. Right below the time of two o'clock.

When I left the apartment, it was already two fifteen. I ran from the second I made it out of the building to the moment I am now shoving the cafe door open.

Please still be here. Please still be here. Please still be here.

My heart is thumping frantically in my chest but it's not from my run.

I expect to have to push through a crowd of customers, but the room is empty. Not even Tia or Miguel is here.

"You came." It's a quiet sentence. So quiet I'm surprised I heard it.

When I turn my head in her direction, I find her seated at the same table she was at for the blind date. The same table I saved her from. But that's not what steals my attention. Instead, I see a banner hung behind her with the words "date me?" Typed on it. There are roses in her arms and a small smile on her lips. I hear a song playing from the speakers too. I can't quite make out the song title, but the lyrics strike me more.

I take a deep breath, try to control my beating heart, and slowly make my way to her. "What is all of this?"

"The grand gesture you deserve." She says it with so much pride and hope, my heart swells with warmth. If my face wasn't already red from running in the cold, it would be now.

Her smile falls when she takes in my appearance, her gaze stuck on my feet. "You're not wearing any shoes."

I look down, wiggle my socked feet, and laugh. "I didn't even notice."

"And your face is so red." She moves towards me, places a gentle hand on my cheek. "You're freezing." She grabs a mug off of the table and passes it to me. "Here. It's hot. It will help you warm up."

There's a white foam heart on top of the brown liquid.

"You did all of this?"

"What?"

I find her gaze and I can't stop the smile on my lips. "What does all of this mean, Piper?"

"I thought it was obvious," she avoids my gaze and picks at a rose from the bouquet in her hand.

"I need to hear it. Call me curious."

Swallowing a deep breath, she straightens. "I'm not good at this stuff. I've never done grand gestures before or any gesture for that matter and I don't know how to be in a relationship."

"I don't think this is coming off the way you are intending it to."

"My point is: this is all new to me. But I'm working on myself and—as long as you are willing to be patient with me—I want to do this thing with you."

"I hear what you are saying, but I need it clearer, Trumpet." I watch as the nickname makes her fight a smile.

"I can't say I love you." My heart sinks into my stomach, but she's quick to pick it back up. "I mean, I don't really know what love is yet and I only want to say it when I am one hundred percent sure. You deserve that. I don't know if what I feel for you is love, Graham, but I know that I hate life without you. We've only known each other for a little over a year and you have consumed every part of my life."

I feel so light, weightless, waiting for the drop. Waiting for the but, but it never comes.

"I've replayed your messages over and over again on repeat just to hear your voice again. I used to say that silence doesn't exist, but the second I hear your voice, the rest of the world falls silent. I don't know how to do any of this," she waves at the banner behind her, "but I want to learn if it means I can have you."

I take it all in, letting my heart process everything on her lips. Letting my mind replay all of our moments and imagine the ones to come. Everything seems to fall into place as I set the mug down, pull the roses out of her arms—which I notice have the thorns removed—and wrap my arms around her.

Softly in her ear, I whisper, "is this okay?" I don't want to push her even if she is willing to try.

I expect her to push me away, but she wraps her arms around my waist, hugging me tightly back, and says "it's perfect."

A grin fills my face. "I can't believe you did all of this."

"There were supposed to be hearts hanging from the ceiling and Hazel showed me how to make a heart shaped cake, but they both ended up in the trash. I may have dropped them on the way over."

I laugh into her hair. I love feeling her voice vibrate against my chest.

We stay like this for a while, both of us lost in the moment. I don't let go and neither does she. I want to pull back, but only so I can kiss her lips. So I can taste the surprise and feel the gasp on her tongue. But right now, this hug is enough. We have time and I'm okay with waiting as long I have her beautiful voice whispering in my ear.

"Graham," she whispers as she nuzzles her face into my chest.

"Hmm?" My eyes are closed, and I sway us a little to the music.

"I'm scared." I freeze. "But I think if you hold me like this and continue to whisper in my ear and tell me those awful jokes…I just might forget enough to fall in love with you."

Finally, I pull back a little and cup her face so I can see her gaze. I tuck her hair behind her ear and whisper so only she can hear, the rest of the universe doesn't get to have this, "Always, Trumpet."

EPILOGUE

PIPER

I shift the coffee from one hand to the other as I wiggle my legs. I tell myself its to warm up from the cold air, but I hope it will soothe the jitters in my stomach too.

It's been two months since Graham I officially started dating. Two months of me going to therapy and working on building the courage and confidence in myself to trust the people around me.

This entire time, Graham has been the most patient person I could have ever asked for. I am so unbelievably lucky to have him and I couldn't be more grateful that he decided to go to the cafe all those weeks ago.

I remember how short of time it took me to convince the owner to let me use the cafe for a minute to woo Graham. They were more than delighted to give Graham something special. I wish he knew just how important and valued he is, which is why I make it a point to remind him every day.

Today is the day of his first college exam. Even though he won't admit it, I know he's nervous.

I've been waiting outside of the library for the past ten minutes so we can go on a "you got this" date. Seeing him or the date aren't what's causing my nerves, though. He has never really made me anxious. What made me so anxious and feel those butterflies is the fear of a relationship. Of being let down. Graham has made the fear cower and disappear.

What is making me shake though is what I have planned for today. I'm going to kiss him. It won't be anything elaborate—probably just a quick peck—but it will be the first kiss of my life and it will be the first kiss I have given.

What if I do it wrong? Or what if our heads bump together?

Hazel attempted to give me pointers, but the second she went into too much detail, I launched a pillow at her. That didn't stop her from sending me "helpful" videos on how to do it. I considered blocking her.

"Hey," a familiar voice greets my ears as arms wrap around my waist. I can feel his warm breath fanning my neck. A smile instantly lights my lips. "Did you get me coffee?"

I turn in his embrace to pass him the cup. He takes a quick sip. "Figured you could use the caffeine."

"Yeah? What for?"

"Well, today is a big day." He raises a brow.

I wring my hands together as my gaze darts around.

"I mean, your exam and all."

"Are you okay? You're acting kind of funny."

"Yeah. I'm great." I try to say it with as much confidence as I can muster, but it sounds forced.

He scrunches his eyebrows in suspicion but doesn't say anything. Instead, he wraps one arm around my shoulders and guides us down the sidewalk. "So I was thinking we could go see a movie. I know it's not…"

He continues to talk, but every word is drowned out by the thoughts in my head.

I'm going to kiss him today. I need to time it just right. At the perfect moment. It's my first kiss. I have waited twenty-six years for this so it can't just be something sloppy.

Plus, Graham loves big gestures. Maybe I should have bought balloons. Do people buy balloons for kisses?

I've watched romance movies, but they all make it look so easy. So grand.

I don't realize I'm playing with the hem of my coat until I feel Graham's hand stop me and our feet stop moving. "I know you love the sound of my voice, but I didn't think you'd be that distracted to not hear the words I'm saying." It's a joke, but my brain is too stressed to process it.

Instead, I mumble a "huh?"

My eyes are trained on his lips. They are moving. Letting words pass to me. Words I should probably be focused on, but I'm too entranced by his lips.

Without a second thought, I stand on my tip toes, place my hands on his shoulders and kiss him. It's so quick that I'm standing back in front of him, watching him piece everything together, and wondering if it actually happened. He's frozen to the spot with his arms outstretched. Maybe

I didn't do it right. I should have taken Hazel's advice and shoved him against a wall or something, but that feels too violent for something that's supposed to be sweet.

"I'm sorry," I finally say. "I wanted to kiss you, but I've never kissed anyone before and I probably just—"

His lips are on mine in an instant. I'm frozen, my hands hovering over his arms. One of his hands is on the side of my face while the other is lightly gripping my side. His kiss is sweet, gentle, and when he finally pulls back, I'm left wanting more.

He leans his forehead against mine. "I'm sorry. I didn't mean to interrupt, but I—"

I don't let him finish before I grab onto his coat for stability and kiss him back. I think I'm getting the hang of this. At least, that's what the cozy feeling in my stomach is telling me. With the way his lips move against mine and the feel of his laugh against my mouth, I can see why people do this.

One of us breaks away. I'm not sure when or by who, but we are both breathing hard. He wraps his arms around my waist pulling me closer. There's a lazy smile on his lips.

"I only ever want to be interrupted if it's by your lips."

I giggle, grinning the widest grin. "You—" that's when it hits me. "Where's your coffee?"

"We'll have to get a new one. I may have dropped it on the ground."

"I didn't know my mouth was that powerful." I joke.

His words are barely above a whisper as he stares intently at my swollen lips. "Trumpet, silence cowers with just one word from your lips."

341

Sound Dates

A COLLECTION MADE BY PIPER & GRAHAM

- ✈ Midnight drives without music
- ✈ Midnight drives with music
- ✈ Read to one another
- ✈ Share truths
- ✈ Close your eyes and find the noise in the silence (play as a game of who can discover more sounds)
- ✈ A movie in a barn
- ✈ Make up stories from nearby conversations
- ✈ Game: try to recreate a noise
- ✈ ~~Dance at one of Jay's galas~~ *Jay said no*

PIPER & GRAHAM'S PLAYLIST

- *Never Been In Love* by Lauren Spencer Smith
- *Scared of the Fall* by Presence
- *Please Notice* by Christian Leave
- *In The Cards* by Jamie Miller
- *Slow it Down* by Benson Boone
- *Last Call* by Jamie Miller
- *Ilym* by John K
- *Hey Stupid, I love you* by JP Saxe
- *Bedroom Ceiling* by Sody
- *IDK You Yet* by Alexander 23
- *Someone to You* by BANNERS
- *Be the One* by James Arthur
- *Spiderman* by Em Beihold
- *I'll be Waiting* by Cain Ashcroft
- *I Guess I'm in Love* by Clinton Kane
- *Maybe Don't* by Maisie Peters, JP Saxe
- *Sandcastle* by Livingston
- *Holding Out* by Andy Grammer
- *Ily* by Lauren Spencer Smith
- *Bad Liar* by Selena Gomez

ACKNOWLEDGEMENTS

Before I dive into thanking all of the wonderful people who have helped in creating this book, I'd like to first acknowledge the wall of my college dorm. Without it, I wouldn't have all of the inspiration I do.

Falling For The Sound Of You is the first book in the Sense of Love series and is my first published novel. It took thousands of post it notes, five drafts, and lots of caffeine to make Piper and Graham's story come to life.

A special thank you to Summer for reading the earliest stages of this book—despite how much of a dumpster fire they were—and continuing to believe in what this work could become.

Thank you, Mckenna, for reading the work and leaving me little comments to analyze and cry and laugh about.

Thank you to everyone who has inspired the characters in this book, including the man who has no idea how crucial his random messages were in the making of this book.

I'd like to share my gratitude with Nadine. She has only known me for a few years but continues to be one of my biggest supporters. Thank you, Nadine, for being the amazing human you are!

Anna, thank you for your second set of eyes and the inspiration.

Lastly, to every reader that has opened this book and read. Whether you lasted the entire book or only made it a few words, I appreciate you giving it your consideration. Piper's story is close to my heart and I hope you will be able to find some comfort in this book.

Thank you!

ABOUT THE AUTHOR

Chloe Riggs is the author of *Soulmates are Overrated, Falling For The Sound Of You,* and many short stories. *Soulmates are Overrated* is her first published book, but she is prone to have a handful of drafts on her desk waiting for the finishing touch. She is known for writing fictional romance with gut-wrenching emotions.

She was born and raised in a small town of West Virginia. She worked in real estate and travel writing, observing all types of people and gaining lots of inspiration.

Chloe has been writing since she was younger. The love for putting her imagination into words on a page has always been a talent of hers. She hopes to be able to share these wild stories with a wide audience that is just looking for a great escape from the stresses of reality. You can find more of her works at blooming-narratives.com.

www.ingramcontent.com/pod-product-compliance
Lightning Source LLC
Chambersburg PA
CBHW030751310726
48969CB00005B/1364